WITCH TREE

WITCH TREE

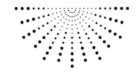

SUSAN BROWN   LINDA JORDAN   SUSAN OLD

3 WITCHES BOOKS

SUSAN BROWN LINDA JORDAN SUSAN OLD

WITCH FIRE

BOOK II

CONTENTS

POISON PLUM

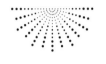

SUSAN BROWN

CHAPTER ONE

SUSAN BROWN

THE ROT, THE EVIL, WAS GETTING CLOSER.

To Meredith Kim, a witch with magically enhanced senses, the whole world had an unquiet feel as though a tide of wrongness rolled toward her and her precious holding, a great deconsecrated church in the heart of New York City, where she worked and practiced her green and healing arts.

"But why, Lola, does there have to be a threat when the weather is this dreary?" the witch murmured into the soft fur of her Pomeranian familiar snuggled in her arms. From the wide oaken doorway of the church, Meredith stared out at the unappealing February morning. The dog wriggled so that she could lick her mistress' chin.

Outside, sleet and rain poured down from gray city skies, pooling slushy wet across the wide gardens and old burial grounds. She knew she should have been out walking the land in her care hours earlier, but weather and exhaustion had lured her into lingering over her coffee.

"Maybe I should have gone to the climate change symposium, after all." Meredith put the dog down and pulled on her coat. "Picked up some tips, right? Almost everyone who's trying to fix the world is there – loads of politicians, members of the Select Council, some of my old friends…even my mentor, Rob Oakes, sent me an invitation to his workshop." She paused, memories of her time as Rob's student flooding over her. "He was the most amazing teacher, Lola. Absolutely inspiring. And Paul is a keynote speaker…" Her voice trailed off as she thought of her lover. "It could have been a lot of fun." Meredith tugged a knitted cap over her hair and sighed.

"Of course Celeste and Dad are there too. That would be much less fun…" Meredith winced, thinking of her overly demanding stepmother and father. Determinedly, she stepped outside into the cold. Lola whined, following with mincing steps. "Sorry baby. We have responsibilities right here."

The wind caught the witch's black hair and whipped it into her mouth. Meredith pulled her jacket tighter to keep the winter chill from seeping across her neck and body, then paused to tuck some errant strands back under her hat. "First the wards."

Instead of her usual barking or dashing about the churchyard, Lola sat on the path leading to the front entrance and looked pointedly from Meredith to the doors of the church and then back again. Two minutes and the black and white fluffball had had enough of the mid-winter cold and wet.

"Sorry, sweetie," Meredith said. "We both know something feels wrong. I have to figure it out."

Very wrong, she thought with tightened breath. It had started five nights ago with a rush of heart-pounding nightmares: *a clutch of venomous snakes hissing in the shadows; a harvest of withered figs dropping onto charred soil; the blooms of sacred plums rotting on leafless branches. And the good earth stinking with decay.*

After each dream, Meredith had woken up sweating, fist stuffed into her mouth and Lola crouched on the blankets beside her, shivering. The witch had pulled the little dog into her arms and buried her nose in Lola's soft fur.

"S'okay, sweetie. It'll be okay." The pup had shoved her muzzle under Meredith's chin and whimpered.

"Just a dream," Meredith soothed. But the dreams had returned the next night and each night after that, twisting darkness into her heart and mind.

More than just dreams...portents...

The thought was inescapable.

"I hate this," Meredith muttered. Lola whined, but, resolutely ignoring the dog, the green witch began her careful inspection of the land in her care. Above, a patch of blue sky suddenly opened, brilliant and brittle-looking, devoid of the usual New York City smog. Flapping crows gave a series of raucous cries. Behind that, the crashes of machinery clearing derelict housing in the block beyond the churchyard echoed on the wind.

"I hope they turn that land into a park," the green witch told her familiar. "You'd like that."

Meredith began her measured walkabout, Lola reluctantly following at her heels. "Maybe Celeste and Dad have headed to the Riviera instead of going to the conference..." As her sense of evil had grown, the witch had begun to reach outward, looking for confirmation of her premonitions. But her parents hadn't answered her voice messages. Her half-sister, Deirdre, had yet to reply to her texts. In desperation, Meredith had even tried to summon the Shadow Walker, Duncan Rhys, two nights ago.

No one responded.

Each evening, as soon as she drifted into uneasy sleep, the nightmares returned.

Each night, Meredith closely held a shivering Lola and stared around the dark silence of the church, wondering how malevolence could have breached its walls.

Each day, as soon as the sun rose, the witch lit white candles for purification, burned lavender to clear away evil, and walked her land – the wide churchyard and old burial grounds attached to the great remodeled church.

But she wished the creeping evil had chosen better weather to invade her life.

"It's got to be done," Meredith told Lola. The dog half-heartedly dug at the icy ground, then huffed and turned her back. "Guarding the Balance and making sure that damned portal stays closed."

Lola ignored her.

Her phone pinged and Meredith glanced at the new text. "Celeste and Dad. Finally. Streamed call tonight. Maybe they can actually help."

The phone pinged again. Deirdre.

"Something's up with Mom and Dad. Beware!" followed by a cross-eyed emoji.

"And maybe they won't help," Meredith muttered. "You'd think they messed me up enough by tricking me into being a guardian of a portal to the Shadowlands."

She glanced over at the apparently empty air between two gravestones. Six years ago when her prestige-conscious parents acquiesced to her passion for green arts and biochemistry by purchasing the deconsecrated church and its gardens for her, they didn't mention the portal. The gateway to the world of the dead lay hidden on her land, waiting for the souls who would ultimately pass through it.

Meredith shoved away the memories of the blood monster and the feuding ghosts who had also been attracted to the site.

Turning her back on the portal, she walked slowly, checking her wards, and reaching with her senses into the sleeping black earth. As a hedge witch, the winter hibernation of her garden was the hardest time. But there was plenty of work to be done, from spreading mulch to sprouting the plants that created the magical well-being Meredith sent drifting outwards into the throbbing life of the city.

Nurturing this land with its garden, flowers, and trees was Meredith's calling, her gift, and her passion.

Even now, she could feel the slow decay of leaves feeding the earth, the tiny budding roots, the silent language of the great trees bounding the sides of the old churchyard. But beneath this predictable passing of seasons, she knew something had twisted. Had coiled inward. Meredith could smell sour rot where there should be slumbering growth.

Something terrifying.

Something wicked.

Something that held death in its cupped hands.

But where? And what? Meredith forced herself to let out her pent-up breath. *How?*

"One more round," she told Lola. "Then we'll go in."

The dog whined her annoyance.

With a ghost of a smile, Meredith walked closely along the fence, pausing here and there to push against the magical wards. Typically, her protection spells were weakest along the tilting posts between the graveyard and the lane bounding her neighbor Barry Flynn's slummy apartment. His tenuous connection as a watcher for the Shadowlands somehow caused her wards to lose power. And the man used every chance he could to annoy her – from shrewd taunting to tossing garbage onto her land.

Meredith shrugged off her habitual irritation and moved on. Something worse than Barry's casual harassment was stirring.

In the northeast corner, she stopped for a moment. Once again a gust of chill wind swept around her. To her right and left, the trees lined the edges of her holding like giant sentinels, but this swath of land was unclaimed by either gardens or gravestones. Meredith wondered if church officials had held the ground in reserve in case the existing burial ground had filled. But there would be no more burials at this deconsecrated church.

"And as soon as I work out what's disturbing the Balance, Lola, we'll tackle this forgotten spot," she murmured. In apparent agreement, Lola trotted over and began digging vigorously. Meredith grinned. "That's the way. Maybe a few fruit trees. I've heard about new varieties of apples and plums being developed from grafts and clones. We'll turn this lovely land into something special – a very special pattern of plantings."

The witch gazed around at the waiting land. The hurricanes she and her sister, Deirdre, had narrowly averted last fall had come from the northeast. There was still an unquiet feel in this overly wide stretch of grass.

"Definitely needs healing." Meredith tried to shake it off, but the witch still felt the subtle distress in the land. When Lola yipped suggestively, looking toward the church entrance, the witch gave in and followed her familiar back to the warmth and solitude of her home.

Still mulling over how she could cure that stretch of land, she put the kettle on the stove. But before it had even begun to simmer, Meredith felt the warning tremor of someone trying to get past the wards on the churchyard's front gate. The spells held firm. A moment later the bell at the sidewalk entry buzzed and the intercom crackled to life.

"Package delivery," a bored voice announced. *"Need a signature."*

"Coming." Meredith switched off the com. "What package? Have you been ordering chew toys, Lola?"

Pulling on her coat once more, the witch hurried out into the chilly air. Lola stood at the open doorway and barked menacingly. Standing outside the gate, a uniformed delivery-man huddled against the cold. Beside him a long, thin cardboard box marked *Fragile* leaned against the wrought iron fence.

He glanced up when the witch pushed open the gate.

"Meredith Kim?" He held out a notepad. "Sign here."

Meredith scrawled her signature. Without even glancing at it, he climbed back in his truck, and pulled into the oncoming traffic. Horns blasted as the van sped away.

The witch shrugged and stared at the unwieldy box. It was almost as tall as she was but only a little more than a foot wide. The delivery address was clearly hers, but all the other printing was water blurred. Virtually unreadable.

Cautiously, she shifted the box, turning it to see if there were any clues to sender or contents. Nothing. But all across the cardboard, she could feel a sharp tingle of magic. More disquieting, she sensed a throb of ancient workings from deep inside the package.

Not Deirdre's…not her parent's…

Different…strange.

Maybe dangerous.

A few snowflakes swirled down, their patterns hypnotic.

Meredith sucked in her breath. What was going on? And who had sent her a box so thoroughly shrouded in magic?

The omens in her dreams, their unfocused danger, caused her to shiver. And now this weird delivery.

"Omens and portents and terrible dreams," she said quietly while studying the box for any kind of clue. "I have no idea what any of it means...except that it's bad. Very bad. And I think it has just begun."

CHAPTER TWO

SUSAN BROWN

Tentatively, Meredith reached out a finger to test the magical shields enveloping the box and then yanked back her hand. The carton had so many wards and spells on it that only the strongest magic would force it open.

Should she force it open? The nightmare-induced sense of catastrophe made her hesitate.

Pandora's box?

Maybe.

A neatly laid trap?

Perhaps.

But why her?

Who could have boxed up anything that radiated such formidable magic? And why?

For a long moment the witch considered what she should do. No return address. No way to find out who had sent it. No route to allow her post it back with a rude, *No Thank You!*

The sender clearly intended to remain anonymous. Clearly intended that Meredith would have to handle whatever was about to happen.

Despite possible danger, the witch knew she would have to open the box somehow. But not here. Not in the unprotected world. She couldn't release whatever magic the package contained here on the sidewalk...or cravenly leave it for some innocent passerby to get hexed.

Biting her lip, Meredith cautiously picked up the carton and balanced it against her shoulder. So far, so good. The protection spells enveloping the package seemed passive. The box was heavy, but not too heavy for her to carry.

Using only one hand, she managed to open the ironwork gate without jostling the carton. With the entryway closed and her wards again in place, Meredith hurried toward the church and then stopped abruptly. What was she thinking? No way she would bring such powerful unknown magic into her home.

Taking a sharp left turn, the green witch circled around to reach the stone shed where she worked so much of her plant magic. Inside, where seedlings grew in neat rows of small pots, healing herbs waited in glass jars, and magically enhanced tools hung on the walls, there was light and warmth.

And power. A lot of power. The power of growth and life.

Her power as a green witch.

Meredith propped the carton up against her potting bench and stepped back. The spells and wards on the box were practically throbbing in her senses, clearly responding to the magic in these surroundings.

Spells for good...or for evil?

In a much-used green porcelain bowl, the witch dropped four handfuls of herbs, rue, dill, sage, and rosemary, stirring them gently with her fingers while calling on her inner magic to enhance their properties. When they were blended to her satisfaction and their inherent goodness awakened, she dropped in a lit match. As the aromatic smoke rose and cleansed the air, she murmured spells for peace, health, and well-being.

By the time the herbs had been reduced to ashes, the air felt purified and the strange magic seemed to have calmed. Outside, the winter sun was slowly moving toward its early sunset. Her preparations had taken much longer than she had hoped and only a couple of hours remained before darkness would creep across the city. The clouded sun cast an uneven glow, making the trees that lined the boundary of her land appear solid and dark.

"Should I leave you be?" Meredith touched the carton again with one cautious finger. The magic blanketing the package was as strong as ever, but not, she sensed, seeping outward.

"Tomorrow," she told it. "In the day's first light, I'll find out what secrets you're hiding."

Leaving the building, the witch spent considerable time casting additional wards around the stone walls. Convinced that nothing could get in or out, Meredith looked up at the bank of great trees. She stood a moment, feeling their ancient, solid life.

"I'm counting on you," she murmured to them, "looking to you for strength."

A breeze ruffled their branches and a murmur swelled almost beneath her senses. Satisfied and grateful that she had been heard, the witch headed back toward the church. Just as she reached a side door, her phone pinged.

Deirdre, finally.

Home, Deirdre... she thought fiercely. *Something's happening. I need you to come home...*

Her sister's message was brief. *Caught a flight. Weird connections and weirder chatter. A day or two at most. Will try to call from the first layover.*

Meredith let out her pent-up breath. At least she wouldn't have to deal with whatever was in the package alone.

In the kitchen, Meredith ate a hasty meal of leftover lasagna, then put the kettle on to boil again, and then in readiness for her parent's call, opened her laptop on the counter. Willing herself to relax, to allow peace to seep into her mind, Meredith looked upwards at the church's coved ceilings. A beam of light from a street lamp shone through a stained glass window, painting a kaleidoscope of color across one wall. The history and stillness of the renovated building soothed her. After her parents called, she would light more purification candles and again burn herbs to sweep away evil.

The solstice had long since come and gone with its warm traditions of renewal and hope. Her sister, Deirdre, had trotted off to a Pacific Island to join a multi-national team of witches and shamans trying to maneuver climate-change gales away from endangered sea turtles. The storm witch, Sofia Moretti, had finally tired of New York and flown back to Italy. And even though Meredith's lover, Paul Kaufman, professor of microbiology at Columbia University, had gotten into the habit of spending more and more days and nights with her, the offer to be a keynote speaker at the prestigious scientific symposium in Zurich was too good to pass up.

Paul had asked her to go…but Meredith felt she had to be here guarding her holding – the church, its burial ground, the untouched land, and most of all, the hidden portal. An endless responsibility.

"I wonder how much Dad and Celeste actually knew about the portal when they set me up here," Meredith asked Lola as she poured boiling water over the herbs in her cup. "I mean, how could they have known this old church would attract so much really bad activity?"

Lola barked and looked suggestively at the bag of dog treats on the counter. The witch fished one out and dropped it in the floor in front of the pup. The familiar picked it up and happily crunched away.

"Even my status-seeking parents couldn't have guessed that much would happen." With Lola following, Meredith took her tea and went into the library. Her eyes strayed over the titles of rare magic books in the hand-hued cabinet. Some were written in Latin, some in early English, a precious few in old script inherited from her Korean ancestors. She touched each volume lovingly, but her mind was elsewhere.

Paul had flown out two nights ago, but not before trying to persuade her once more to go with him.

"Come on," he had urged. "I won't even be jealous of your old teacher." He smiled lovingly. "Unless of course this was part of his tutelage." He planted a series of very warm kisses on her chin and jawbone, finally pausing for a deep kiss on her mouth. "Don't witches get vacations?"

"Of course," Meredith had replied a little breathlessly. "But Paul…something bad is stirring."

He leaned back and frowned, eyes searching her face. "All the more reason to get away," he argued.

But she had shaken her head and, even though she was longing to go, Paul had left without her.

"Maybe I'm just imagining it," she told Lola as she sipped more of her tea. "What are the chances, right? How many evil magicky things can attack the Balance right here in my little corner of the world?" Meredith took another thoughtful sip. "I should have gone to the conference, Lola. Rob and his partner, Nina, are deep into magical research. He thinks I've spent too much energy on science. Maybe he's right. The green witch circles are always making new discoveries, creating new spells that might have made me stronger. Better equipped to maintain the Balance – and keep that damned portal to the Netherworld sealed. It shouldn't be this hard." She paused. "So why is it so hard?"

She wandered back to the kitchen just as the computer sounded an alert. Meredith put down her cup and accepted the call. Immediately her father's tired face filled the screen, with her step-mom's flaming red curls forming a halo behind his graying black hair. Celeste laid a hand on her husband's shoulder and leaned forward.

"Dad...Celeste...thanks for calling. How are you?" Meredith forced herself to smile.

"*Meredith, honey...*" Celeste answered.

Gregory Kim interrupted. "*Meredith, we need your help.*"

"*Greg,*" Celeste's voice warned. "*This isn't a secure link.*"

Meredith's dad's eyes darted around. "*Right. We're on our way for that visit we promised. We...we'll need your help scheduling a car at the airport. We'll let you know when we're going to arrive.*"

"Wait...Celeste...Dad!" Meredith cried.

But the call cut off.

"Well, damn." Meredith stared at the blank screen. She glanced down at Lola. "Deirdre was right. They're up to something. Or, hard as it is to believe, maybe they *are* in trouble."

The green witch frowned at the walls of the church while she tried to piece together what had just happened. "They globe trot and schmooze," Meredith mused. "What could they possibly do that could get them into danger? It sounded like danger, didn't it, baby?"

Lola lay down, clearly bored.

Impulsively, Meredith scrolled through her phone's text messages. The earlier note she'd had from Deirdre indicated nothing substantial. After a moment's hesitation, Meredith tapped in:

Celeste and Dad are all excited that they're coming for a visit. I'm so thrilled! Did they tell you about it? Can't wait to chat!!!!

Deirdre would get the subtext. She knew Meredith found spending time with their parents a trial – the elder Kims never concealed their disappointment that, despite her magical talent, Meredith had not taken her place in the powerful world councils they reveled in. Never fathomed her passion for the rigorous science of microbiology and the living magic of the natural world. Didn't understand her mind-numbing boredom with glitzy parties and sophisticated chatter.

Meredith went over to one of the church's huge leaded-glass windows and gazed out over her quiet holding. Her parent's world flashed excitement and power; her world exuded life and growth. This was where she belonged. Here. Only here.

"So how could any of their problems need my help, or intersect with my unimportant patch of the world?" she asked Lola.

Her eyes caught a sudden blaze of light in the graveyard.

"No...oh no!" Meredith exclaimed. Not bothering to pull on a coat, she tore from the kitchen, out the front door, and to the site of the portal. A gray mist oozed through the gathering night as the gateway to the Shadowlands gaped open and the discordant whispers of the Netherworld seeped into the surrounding air. The witch skidded to a halt a few feet from the portal, practically dancing with terror and anger.

"*No, no, no!*" she snarled. "Don't open, damn it!"

But she was too late. The door to the world of the dead had opened.

CHAPTER THREE

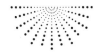

SUSAN BROWN

MEREDITH STARED HELPLESSLY AT THE GAPING PORTAL BEFORE her. As always, the two silent gravestones stood sentinel, flanking the hidden entrance. Sibilant whispers, falling below human understanding, and muted light pooled outward, making the hair on the back of her neck prickle. The witch scrubbed a frustrated hand across her forehead, her eyes darting around apprehensively for any intruders entering or leaving the forbidden door. Wondering how, as the portal's guardian, she was supposed to guard it.

A mocking voice spoke behind her. "What's wrong, my green witch? I thought you called me."

Meredith spun around. "Duncan Rhys, you rotten-hearted son of a…a…! Why's the portal open?"

Duncan's dark eyes flashed amusement. He stepped forward, touched her heated cheek with his warm fingers, and then waved a casual hand. As Meredith watched, the portal collapsed on itself. "I hurried to you, of course, and this was the closest door. Aren't you pleased to see me? Your message sounded so desperate."

Meredith glared, considered throwing a hex at him, and then thought better of it. She didn't actually know how much power the Shadow Walker wielded and she didn't want something nasty

17

bouncing back on her. Instead, she stalled for a bit of time to regroup.

"It's freezing out here," she said with as much as dignity as she could manage. "Would you like some tea?"

Duncan shrugged. "If you have nothing stronger."

Meredith lifted her chin. "I'm sure I can find something."

"It would be deeply appreciated," Duncan said. He gestured for her to go ahead and followed her into the church. Dropping heavily into a chair, he wearily rubbed his face. Lola leapt into his lap and quivered happily as he gently massaged her head.

"Do you really want something other than tea?" Meredith asked. With a surge of concern she noted the gray pallor underlying his dark skin. "I have herbal remedies that might be good right now."

Duncan nodded. "I would like one of your tisanes," he said, "providing you can also add a dollop of whiskey."

Meredith frowned and put on the kettle yet again. She occupied herself with taking a special mixture from the secret drawer of her tea box, all the while watching the Shadow Walker out of the corner of her eye. He was a tall, strongly muscled man, but other than his large hand stroking Lola's soft fur, he didn't move while she brewed the tea.

"Why did you call me?" he asked abruptly. "It sounded urgent."

Meredith felt heat rise in her cheeks as she splashed a generous portion of Scotch into his herbal tea before handing it to him. "I may have been over-reacting…"

"I doubt it," Duncan said as he sipped from the steaming mug.

"Portents," Meredith blurted out. "I've been having nightmares. They feel like omens of something bad. Something very wrong in the Balance. Here. In my holding. And I don't know how that can be."

Duncan's eyes met hers and he nodded. "You're a damned magnet for disaster," he said with only a little emotion in his voice. "I should have known that it would end up here."

"What will end up here?" Meredith demanded.

Duncan drained the mug, gently put Lola on the floor, and stood up. Meredith noted with mild satisfaction that her herbs were already working. The Shadow Walker's skin had lost its gray tone.

"What is *it*?" she repeated.

He sighed. "If I had any idea, my dear witch," he said, "I'd already have protections in place. I've been chasing wraiths...or whomever has loosed some evil over the world...for weeks. And finding nothing. Omens... premonitions...portents of death from both reliable and unreliable sources."

Meredith took a moment to try and process this. Then she fastened on the part that affected her.

"What am I then?" she demanded. "Reliable or unreliable?"

Duncan smiled wearily. "That, my hedge witch, remains to be seen."

With a shrug he turned and headed out the front door of the church. Meredith watched from the window as the portal opened, he stepped through, and the gateway closed again.

"Well, damn," she said to Lola. "This just gets better and better." Ignoring the sarcasm, Lola wagged her tail.

Her phone pinged – Deirdre.

Are you there? I magicked a window to stream a private video chat.

Meredith tapped a response. *Ready and waiting.*

A moment later, the alert sounded on her laptop. Meredith gratefully accepted the call.

"*What's going on?*" Deirdre demanded. Her red hair was more wildly spiked than usual and the skin on her nose had peeled with sunburn.

"You tell me," Meredith answered. "At least about Celeste and Dad. They're coming here. And it sounded like they were in trouble."

Deirdre ran a hand through her hair, adding to the disorder. "*I don't know. They were supposed to be in Zurich – climate change endangering species and all that – but they very quietly flew into and back out of Korea a few days ago. I only know about it because there's a Korean shaman on my team and she picked up the information from her contacts at home.*" Deirdre paused and then went on slowly. "*The parents have taken unauthorized trips to a few other out-of-the-way places as well. No one seems to know exactly what they're up to but there are important people having hissy fits about it. Some other less obviously important folks, too.*"

19

Meredith frowned. "Celeste and Dad don't ruffle feathers. They schmooze and throw persuasion spells to get things done."

"*Seems like they've escalated,*" Deirdre replied. "*Direct action has never been their style, at least not up until now.*" She paused. "*So what's going on in your little Garden of Eden that you were leaving me all those messages?*"

Meredith briefly told her sister about the portents and Duncan Rhys's cryptic comments. In a flash of caution, she chose not to mention the package awaiting her in the shed.

"*That guy's a pain in the backside,*" Deirdre commented. "*A very sexy pain in the backside. But something must be happening that's a big deal. He likes you too much to have ignored you otherwise.*"

Meredith felt her face get hot. "He likes fighting with me."

Deirdre grinned. "*Some of my best relationships started that way.*"

"Good thing I'm not you," Meredith snapped. "Paul has all my attention."

"*But Paul's in Switzerland.*"

Meredith couldn't help but laugh. "So…now that the turtles are safe, are you going to help me out here? I mean…you know what happens when it's just me and the parents…and besides, Deirdre…if there's something big brewing, I could use your help."

She was desperate to tell her sister about the package…but what if someone had broken in on their call? What if her parents' enemies were frantically searching for…what?

"*Turtles all the way down,*" Deirdre said thoughtfully. "*I'll be there as soon as I can. And I'll make a few calls as well. Catch you later.*" The connection cut off.

Meredith sat back. Improbable as it should be, an assortment of potential disasters were converging here. Her parents were jetting toward her bringing whatever problem they had found or created. Duncan Rhys had confirmed something vast was shifting the Balance. And those horrifying portents were crawling closer every night.

Most important was the package in the shed. The box wrapped in spells and oozing a magic so ancient she could barely comprehend it.

Meredith dropped her head on her hands. "Not again, damn it. Not again!"

Lola whined and once more looked at the bag of treats. Meredith sighed and got a tidbit for her pup.

Lola licked her lips and happily wagged her tail.

"I wish my problems were this easy to solve," the green witch muttered. Lola barked and gave her a doggy grin. Treats had been offered and so her life was good.

———

THAT NIGHT THE DREAMS RETURNED, BUT BELOW THE SOUNDS OF hissing snakes and the smell of polluted earth, Meredith heard a quiet dirge. The trees were mourning. They were holding onto their ancient strength but evil was pooling toward them like maggots wriggling in dead flesh.

Meredith woke up, her face wet with tears and Lola's kisses.

Whatever was happening she knew was getting worse.

Somehow she had become a focal point to disaster. But what disaster?

"Lola, sweetie, I know it's up to us," she murmured. Lying back on her pillow she stared at the soaring ceiling in her bedroom. "I just wish I knew what *it* is." She took a deep breath. "Tomorrow when we open the box, maybe we'll know."

And then she lay silently, staring into the darkness, wondering.

———

THE WITCH AWOKE TO EARLY MORNING SUNLIGHT PLAYING A kaleidoscope of colored beauty across the walls. Meredith sprang out of bed, nearly tripping on nightmare-tangled sheets. "First light," she murmured. "I want the first light of morning to open that package."

She grabbed her phone and groaned. A text from her parents. Even on the phone Meredith could tell the message was shrouded in misdirection spells.

Flight gets in at 10:57. Get a rental and meet us at Teterboro.

21

She swore softly and fluently. Lola watched, bright-eyed, from her nest on the bed. "I guess this means I don't open the box now," Meredith told her familiar. "The world might be falling apart, but I've got to get my parents. And a rental car." She began throwing on her clothes, not bothering to shower first. As she tugged on her jeans, Meredith ordered the assistant app on her phone to contact the closest car rental site. Within minutes she had reserved the kind of high-end vehicle her parents tended to expect. The agency was even willing to deliver it to her door.

Two hours later, Meredith waited in the luxuriously wood-accented lounge of Teterboro Airport and watched for her parent's private jet to land.

The green witch crossed her arms across her chest and wondered anxiously what her dad and Celeste had done to require such extremes of security. The historic facility with its extravagant amenities, outer security gates, and most importantly, proximity to Manhattan made it the favorite airport for people with a lot of money but very little time. As she waited, a couple of recognizable celebrities and a small gaggle of business people hurried to their waiting jets. A pilot walked wearily past her and disappeared into one of the lounges.

Meredith glanced at her phone and frowned. Thirty-five minutes past scheduled landing time.

After a few more moments of peering out at the skies, wondering if any of the landing aircraft carried her parents, she hesitantly approached one of the desks.

"Excuse me," she said to the man. "My parent's jet was supposed land almost an hour ago. Do you know if it's been delayed?"

She gave the meager arrival information they had sent her.

"Do you know what charter service they were using?" the attendant asked.

Meredith shook her head. "Just the arrival time. And that they were in Europe...I think..."

Had they left from Europe? She tried to remember if they had said, if there had been anything in the video chat that would indicate their location.

Nothing.

The attendant shrugged his shoulders and smiled deprecatingly. "I don't have any flights that match your information."

Alarm was building in Meredith's chest, banging in her ears. "Are there...are there any reports of flight problems?" *Or crashes,* she thought. *Please, no crashes...*

Again the attendant shook his head. "Sorry. Nothing. Maybe there was a mix-up in times or dates. If you can contact them, that might clear it up."

The witch nodded and numbly left the airport. Sitting in the rental car, she unlocked her phone and began sending a series of frantic texts...to her step-mom's number, her dad's number, Deirdre's number. And then she stopped. Who else might know? They had lots of friends, mostly members of the Select Council. Meredith sucked in her breath. Who could her parents afraid of? Power was the drug of choice for the Select. If her dad and stepmom were challenging the power of those witches...

Meredith stared out the windshield and tried to piece together what little information she had. Not much. A mysteriously magical package had been delivered to her. Deirdre had said their parents had secretly traveled to Korea and other remote locations. Important feathers had been ruffled. All while they were supposed to be at the same symposium as Paul.

Paul!

Meredith took a moment to text her lover. *Trying to get a call to my parents. Have they been having a good time at the conference?'*

It was late evening in Switzerland so, given the post-event meetings and parties, it might be awhile before Paul saw her text and responded.

But where were her parents?

"Not here," Meredith huffed. "Obviously, not here."

As she pulled away from the parking lot, the witch's frisson of anxiety grew steadily stronger. Her dad and step-mother rarely let anything bother them. But their very brief call yesterday indicated they were way beyond calm. Meredith checked the rearview mirror for suspicious cars. Nothing.

"You're getting paranoid," she muttered.

But, just the same, the witch began to chant concealment and misdirection spells that would cause an observer's eyes to slide away from the car and never realize it had been there. As she headed home, Meredith chose less obvious routes. Without slowing down, she passed the church, towering like a protective fortress over the city streets, and skirted the construction site where derelict buildings were being leveled. Only then did she circle around back and pull into the rutted laneway forming the boundary between her holding and Barry's slummy apartment building. Reaching out with her magic, Meredith searched for any unwelcome spells.

Okay for the moment.

As she switched off the engine, she spotted Barry watching uneasily from the shadows of the sparse trees that had taken root in the broken pavement. Meredith uncharacteristically waved at the watcher, relieved to see even his familiar face. Barry didn't respond but his watery eyes blinked in surprise as he strolled over.

"I wondered who was throwing magic all over the place," he said. "So what're you doing here?"

"Keeping a low profile." Meredith hesitated. "Seen any strangers around, Barry?"

"Nope. Place is dead." He jerked his head toward the graveyard and snickered.

"Right." Meredith checked her phone again. Still nothing.

Barry's expression melted back to its usual scowl but his eyes strayed over the top-of-the-line vehicle. "Want me to return this thing? Duncan told me something's going down and I got to help out. Like I'm your damned servant."

"Do you know how to drive?" Meredith demanded.

He snorted. "Yeah, I know how to drive."

Meredith hesitated. She needed to return the car but she also needed to be here in case her parents showed up. Reluctantly, the witch got out and tossed over the key fob.

With a smirk, Barry slid onto the leather seat and revved the engine. "Nice," he muttered. "Real nice. Got some power here."

"I don't want any attention drawn to a car I was driving," Meredith snapped.

"Don't you worry, Meredith. You just rely on your old pal, Barry."

The car shot forward, screeched to a stop, and then somehow flipped around in the impossibly narrow space.

"Careful!" she yelled.

He rolled down the window and grinned up at Meredith's furious expression.

"Like riding a bike..." he taunted.

As the car careened down the lane, Meredith shrieked after him. "Barry, do you have a license?"

One skinny arm waved out the window as the vehicle skidded around a corner. The roar of the straining engine reverberated back to Meredith's ears, and then the car and its echoes melted into the city's traffic.

"Well, damn," she snarled. "I just hope he's got enough magic in him to pull this one off."

With a snort of irritation, she stepped over the sagging fence, and with the ease of too much practice, propped it up again with wards and magic.

CHAPTER FOUR

SUSAN BROWN

Without much hope of success, Meredith opened her senses to feel for her parent's presence. If they had already landed in New York, and she had somehow missed them, there should be a tingle of their auras in her awareness.

Nothing.

At the door of the church, Lola greeted her by leaping up and down, running frenetic circles around her feet, and emitting yips of joy.

"I've only been gone a few hours, silly." The witch bent to ruffle her familiar's soft fur.

As she shed her coat and scarf, Meredith realized with an involuntary shiver that the afternoon sun was already slanting across the city. And the package still waited.

Should she risk trying to unlock those powerful spells without every possible advantage standing behind her? What if her own spells were too weak and the package erupted at sunset, the traditional time for evil to ascend.

"I'm turning into a complete scaredy-cat," she admitted to Lola. "But if my parents sent the box to me, and it seems like they might have, doesn't it make sense to find out what I can from them first?"

Lola barked.

"You're right. Better safe than sorry…I hope." The witch walked quickly to the kitchen and again checked her phone, scrolling through messages and alerts. "Maybe Celeste and Dad tried a chat or emailed me and I missed it." Lola barked sharply. "I know…that makes no sense at all."

Frustrated, Meredith stared at the contents of her inbox. Ads for things she would never need or want; requests for political contributions; a newsletter from the alumni association at Columbia…also asking for money; another from Rob Oakes' circle of green witches, *The Hedge Fund*, though not asking for a donation.

From her dad and step-mom…nothing.

She tapped in a quick message to her sister. *Seem to have mislaid the parents. Any ideas?*

Had whatever danger they had hinted at somehow overtaken them?

"I don't think a single witch among the Select is a match for Celeste and Dad," Meredith told Lola. "And none of those fossils would be dumb enough to gang up on my parents. Not that I'm trying to reassure myself."

In her hurry to get to the airport, coupled with the expectation that her parents would want to dine out, she'd skipped eating and now her stomach was fiercely complaining. Resigned, Meredith settled on a frozen pizza. As the microwave nuked her quick meal, she had ransacked her cabinet for any rare books that touched on ancient magic – the kind she had felt throbbing inside the package.

Hours later, all she had was an unhappy stomach and snippets of ideas.

Meredith huffed a breath of complete frustration. Maybe tomorrow when she opened the box, she would get some idea of what was going on.

As she was preparing for bed, a text came from Deirdre. *Noon at the latest. We got this, Sis.*

That night, the nightmares melted away to scenes like old movies. She watched in silence as Buddha received enlightenment beneath the Bodhi tree, heard the chants of ancient Celts worshipping under a vast oak, listened as Jesus taught his followers in the shade of a sycamore, saw Maori receiving life gifts from a kauri tree, felt the promised joy of the first frost-kissed blossoms of a plum tree. Time and individuals blended across her awareness as leaves swirled silently through the air, filling her with their sweet scents.

Green magic. Life magic.

When the first morning light filtered through the stained glass windows in her bedroom, Meredith stretched, peaceful and rested for the first time in days. It was as though the slow speech of the trees edging her holding had reached her. Her fingers smoothed Lola's fur as the pup yawned and snuggled against her blanket-covered legs.

Twenty minutes later when she was just stepping from the shower, Meredith heard her front door crash open. Cold wind whipped through the church.

For an instant she froze, then, wrapping a towel around herself, she dug into her magical core and readied herself to confront whatever magic had breached her defenses.

Lola began circling and yipping excitedly.

"Hush, you idiot," Meredith whispered.

Cautiously, with Lola prancing and bounding behind her, Meredith edged toward the front of the church. Pale daylight streamed through the open door, rain and sleet sheeting behind it.

Raging, she stopped. Duncan glared at her from the entryway.

"What have you done?" he demanded. "I should have known, witch, that the epicenter of the destruction of the Balance would be here. I should have known that if the world ends," he added bitterly, "it will be on your watch."

Aghast, water dripping from beneath her towel, Meredith glared at Duncan.

"How did you get past my wards?" she demanded. "And how dare you?"

He slammed the door shut behind him. The noise of the wind suddenly quieted.

"I dare because I must," he roared. "I have been travelling all over the worlds of the living and the dead, trying to find the source

29

of the rot. And of course, when I finally find a clear whisper, it's right here."

"Nonsense," Meredith snapped. She hitched the towel more tightly around herself, and then, furiously aware that it was too small for the job, turned and stamped back to the bathroom. By the time she had thrown on her clothes, Duncan was in her kitchen moodily staring at the coffee pot. The aroma of fresh brew filled the room.

"Please make yourself at home," Meredith snarled. "And maybe tell me what's going to warrant you breaking into my life."

Silence.

As she slammed mugs on the counter Meredith noticed that the gray pallor of exhaustion once again overlaid Duncan's dark skin. He rubbed a hand across his face and sank into a chair.

Quietly, she murmured a spell of well-being as she filled his cup – if she and Duncan were going to battle world-threatening evil or, better yet, have a really good quarrel, she wanted him at his best. She was certain that his best would be very good.

Pushing back that unruly thought, Meredith offered him the steaming mug. Duncan accepted it with a scant nod of thanks.

"I rang the doorbell," he said finally. "I can feel evil approaching and it didn't seem prudent to wait."

"And now it does?"

He shrugged. "I assumed the source was in here. Possibly attacking you."

"There is nothing attacking me here. I am safe in my home." She took her own mug and sat in the chair opposite his.

"It's approaching." Duncan stirred restlessly and took a gulp of coffee, wincing at the heat. "And you haven't been safe. Your dreams? Those portents you gabbled about?"

The witch scowled, really longing to toss a hex at the Shadow Walker. Something subtle, like toe fungus. And she really hated him for being right. At least this time.

Better safe than sorry, she thought with a flash of irritation.

Putting down her mug, she magically reached outward, carefully parting and examining each strand of magic woven through her land and church. Suddenly she sucked in her breath. Why hadn't she sensed it before? A pressure – something dark and rotting where there should be life. Just outside. Building like a debris-filled wave rolling against her protections. Her threads hadn't broken…not yet.

"No, no, no…" she whispered.

But how long before her magic was overwhelmed? Before the strength she'd rooted in the trees gave way? Barely aware of Duncan's hard hand touching her arm, feeding her strength, Meredith reached outward to the plant giants. Stress…danger… burrowed into them like voracious beetles. Thank the Balance she had sensed it before it was too late. She stood and stretched out her arms, fingers splayed, gathering power from all the corners of her land, winding the goodness around her body like fine yarn. When the green magic was woven, she sent it to mound like a healing blanket around the trees.

She felt their sigh of relief as they drew from her green magic, from the life of the entire land, to fight whatever was attacking them.

Finally she pulled back from the connections and shakily sat down. Duncan reached for her coffee and pressed the cup between her palms, as warm and comforting as the life magic within her holding.

Duncan sat back, frowning. The witch lifted her eyes to his.

"I spoke to the trees," she told him. "There is something about their strength, the way they are rooted in the earth and their great age that creates living magic."

"That is your strength, not mine," the Shadow Walker said. "This disaster doesn't have one location, but your holding is the only festering hole I've found."

"And now you think the source is here? Seriously?" Meredith rolled her eyes as anger shot through her. "First you can't bother listening to me and now I'm a hotbed of evil? You need your head examined."

Duncan smiled. "You have that effect on me, witch."

"As you can see, I'm fine. There is no evil here."

"Not yet." The Shadow Walker stood up, still swaying slightly from exhaustion. His usual scowl settled again and he looked around the room, as though sensing something. "What aren't you telling me?"

"Nothing," Meredith snapped. "Like you said, there's nothing happening here."

She tried not to think about the package in her potting shed. Her parents had said they needed her help. If they were in danger, if they were targets, she was determined not to be the weak link. As appealingly sexy as Duncan could be, she knew almost nothing about his powers, let alone his allegiances. He had battled evil at her side before, but what if his loyalties didn't align with her parent's decisions? She really knew so little about him. If he was arrayed against her parents, she wasn't going to give him any hints about their actions.

He started walking around the room, his head turning this way and that like a hound searching for a scent.

Meredith put down her cup and stood. "I'll let you know if I sense anything."

His eyes swept over her. "I expect nothing less, my dear witch." He sighed. "I have to report to the Council. It's not going to be pretty."

For a moment, Meredith almost felt sorry for him. Almost. She was fairly sure he could use his innate arrogance to carry off just about anything – even in the Shadowlands. Briefly, she wondered how much Barry knew about Duncan's mission.

"Be very careful, witch," the Shadow Walker warned. "I'll return later. I know that something is circling your holding." He strode toward her front door and stepped back into the wintery daylight.

A moment later, Meredith caught a reflected flash of light as the portal in the burial ground opened and then closed again. She slammed shut the church door. "Don't hurry back, Duncan Rhys."

She sighed and turned her attention to rebuilding and strengthening her wards around the door. To her magical eye, the old ones hung in tatters as though blown apart by strong winds.

"I wish I knew more about him," Meredith muttered. "And I especially wish I knew whose side he is on."

But the Shadowlands were off limits, not to be touched. As far as she knew, only the Shadow Walkers moved between the worlds of the living and the dead. And beings like Duncan didn't share their secrets.

"And neither do I," she told Lola. The dog looked at the closed door and whined.

Meredith shook her head. "Lola, you're a traitor."

CHAPTER FIVE

SUSAN BROWN

ONCE AGAIN, HER MORNING PLANS HAD BEEN DELAYED.

Meredith gulped down a hearty breakfast knowing she would need it to be ready for the work ahead. She checked her phone repeatedly for texts. From Deirdre and her parents, nothing. A brief reply from Paul read simply, *"Haven't seen your folks. The conference is amazing. Miss you."*

"Great," the witch muttered. "Looks like it's you and me, Lola. I can't put this off any longer."

While the dog ran back and forth to the front door of the church, Meredith pulled on her coat. Once outside, she surveyed the apparently quiet land. But acutely aware that the looming threat had almost evaded her protections, she realized she should recheck the wards around her property. After all, Duncan erupted into her sanctuary whenever he pleased.

Damn him.

She paused by the section of fence near Barry's apartment.

"I wonder," she muttered. On impulse, Meredith climbed over the fence and headed across the rutted lane and down the steps to the watcher's dingy apartment. On the church's side of the fence, Lola jumped up and down and yapped her disapproval.

"This will only take a minute," she reassured her familiar. "I hope."

The witch pounded on the door and waited. And waited.

"Barry, open up!" she yelled.

"*Go away!*" came the muffled reply.

Meredith grinned. "I've got a couple of good hexes with your name on them!" she called back.

A moment later the door opened a crack and Barry peered out at her. "Why?" he demanded. "Why are you persecuting me?"

"Because you have information I need. And you throw trash into my graveyard."

"Better than on your grave," he muttered.

Meredith pushed the door open and stepped inside. Just as she remembered, the apartment was a study in grime, garbage, and debris. "How can you live like this?" she asked stepping over a heap of coats and boots lying in front of the door.

"Don't see no white gloves on you," he retorted. "And why do you care?"

Meredith sighed. "I don't. It's just..." she looked around again and it struck her that the whole thing seemed kind of sad.

But, not her business. "Barry, what can you tell me about Duncan?"

"Nothing." The watcher crossed his arms across his chest.

"Nothing because you don't know anything, or nothing because it'll get you in trouble?"

He shrugged. "I don't know nothin'. The Shadowlands ain't a vacation destination and I wasn't on his hiring committee. Don't know where he's from and I don't care. He's my boss, not my buddy." The watcher leered at her. "He's a good-looking bastard though. What's he to you, Meredith?"

She scowled. "Not a thing, Barry. But something bad is happening and I don't know who I can trust."

He snorted. "And now you're going to take old Barry into your confidence? Gee, I'm touched."

Meredith huffed her annoyance. How did the creep get so smart?

"Don't you get it? Evil is happening, and I need to know if Duncan's a danger to me."

Barry shrugged. "Depends on if he's on your side, don't it?"

"How can I find out if you won't tell me anything?"

"Aw Meredith, I really don't care." Barry stepped around her and pulled his door open wider. "Cold air's getting in. If you leave, I can shut this."

Meredith turned on her heel and strode out. So much for good feelings about that derelict idiot. Maybe she should hex him just for the fun of it.

If she didn't have so much to do...

She checked her phone again. Still nothing. None of her texts to Deirdre or her parents had been opened. Deirdre was probably somewhere over the Pacific. But Celeste and her dad...? Meredith pushed back the shiver of anxiety.

No one she trusted was available and delaying any longer might be a really bad choice. For good or evil, she had to open that package.

THE SHED SEEMED UNUSUALLY DARK, DESPITE THE OPEN DOOR and unshuttered windows. The day had clouded over and a chill wind was skittering around the land. From several feet away, trying to glean some information without actually coming in contact, Meredith examined the carton leaning against her potting bench.

"What do you think, Lola?" The witch asked.

Her familiar was staring intently at the box, ears perked forward, her body almost quivering.

"I don't know either," Meredith said. "But I guess we'd better get started. Keep out of the way, sweetie."

Meredith had considered leaving Lola in the church, but over the months she had served as her familiar, the dog had started to gather power that seemed to subtly enhance that of her mistress. And today, the green witch knew might need that.

The spells wrapped around the box were complex. Created by

witches of considerable skill. Beyond that, Meredith could sense power throbbing from within the carton itself.

"If I'm supposed to open this, whoever put it together and sent it must have provided a key," she muttered. Gingerly she poked at the spells, looking for a weakness, or better still, a hint that would allow her to unwind the magic.

Drawing on her inner core, Meredith narrowed her eyes and looked at the package again, softly chanting a demand for revelation. To her inner eye, the spell shrouding the box shimmered and then clarified, showing itself as a hopeless tangle of ropes of varying thicknesses and colors. Blue, yellow, orange, red, green…green!

Gingerly, she magically tugged on a small green cord. For a moment, nothing happened. And then, as though the ropes were colored lines on a computer screen, they twisted and twirled in the air, slowly unraveling, falling into sparks and then vanishing. Only the green thread remained. Her hand wrapped in protections, Meredith reached out and carefully pulled. The cord unknotted like a loosely tied bow.

She sucked in her breath as the carton opened of its own accord.

Magic erupted outward. Strong magic. The strongest magic she had ever felt. It filled the shed and spread slowly across the land.

Green magic.

Her very life blood.

Inside the carton, roots wrapped in compost, lay five budding saplings.

Her soul was alight with joy as the hedge witch touched their bark, inhaled the fragrance of their growth, and felt the elemental life within the plantlets. The trees on her land sang out in welcome. Like small children coming out of a happy dream, the saplings seemed to stir into wakefulness.

Meredith lifted them from the box and cradled their thin trunks in her arms. As their life enveloped her, she laughed for the sheer joy of it.

"What are you?" she murmured. "Beautiful babies, I know you're all different, but what are you? And why are you here?"

As though she was waking from a dream herself, Meredith's

mind began to rev up. "Yes, why are you here?" she asked. "And what are you?" She glanced down at Lola who now sat, panting softly. "These aren't ordinary trees, are they?" She stroked the smooth bark of one. "But they still need a bit of care, especially after being shut up in a box."

Laying the saplings gently on her potting bench, the green witch partly filled five large pots with magically enhanced soil. With intense care, she set a sapling in each and then covered the roots with more soil. The trees were so strong and straight, she debated whether to add supports and then decided against it. Cautiously, she set each pot by a window, so that the saplings could soak up whatever winter sunlight shone through. Finally she watered them with her own fertilizer tea until the water ran into the saucers beneath the pots.

Her phone pinged. Meredith was barely aware of it.

Instead she turned her attention to drawing every scrap of magic from her core and from the land she nurtured. This she built into spell after spell of well-being, growth, and above all, protection… invisibility…sight turned aside.

Repelling any hint of rot or evil.

Then she roused more of her magic to weave a net of green vines throughout the entire building.

Outside, the witch added more spells, fostering the illusion of an ordinary winter shed – trays of seedlings just sprouting; scoured pots empty and ready for use; compost and soil waiting in bags and bins.

Not a hint of the saplings that had come into her care. Not a breath of that budding, ancient magic.

"And now I have to find out where you came from," she murmured. "Celeste and Dad probably…but why?"

She looked down at her familiar. "Lola, we need some answers. And fast."

The dog barked agreement.

"Very fast," Meredith murmured. She checked her phone again. Nothing from her parents, but a text had come from her sister.

"Late afternoon. I'm exhausted and I'll want food. A lot of food and booze."

Meredith laughed in spite of herself. "Deirdre to the rescue," she told Lola. "But in the meantime, we've got work to do."

Back in the church, Meredith headed straight for her library. "I wish the Internet actually had some of this information," she told Lola. Carrying a stack of leather-bound volumes, Meredith settled at her desk and began the slow process of searching for histories, spells, or mentions of the magic she felt was embodied in the saplings. She knew it was old, almost as old as the earth itself.

"Growth magic," she breathed. "Green life magic."

She stood slowly, looking upward at the patterns of light that danced across her walls as the sun poured through the stained glass windows.

With great care, Meredith rolled back her rug and moved the furniture to clear a large open area on the floor. With the ash of purification herbs, she drew a pentacle and circle. Around the perimeter she arranged candles of white, black, and purple, alternating with small bundles of the herbs. When the room was arranged to her satisfaction, she lit the candles and settled herself in the center of the figure.

Lola stretched out in the doorway, head resting on her paws, watching alertly.

Quietly, Meredith reached out, looking for answers, looking for a connection to the saplings hidden in her workspace. The trees bounding her land whispered on the surface of her mind, telling her something important.

And then the nightmare visions rolled over her. The witch felt her breath quicken, She fought down the impulse to shield her mind... the answers were hidden in these portents.

Her shadow self strolled over her land but beneath the verdant colors lay a different shadow — stinking rot...decay of living things folding in on themselves.

A sacred plum tree of her Korean ancestors had bloomed, the flowers frosted with the late winter chill. For an instant, Meredith's heart lifted. The plum was revered as the symbol of spring, renewal, and the Five Blessings: old age, wealth, health, virtue, and a natural death.

Dry wind rattled around her and a twig snapped, its pith desiccated and dead. Vibrations shuddered through the tree and, one by one, the petals browned and curled inward until the elegant form was blurred and lost.

Tears formed in Meredith's eyes and she stepped back, away from the veiled death. Her foot slipped and she looked down. Smoke rose from soil covered with blackened figs, their once lush fecundity withered.

In the background of her awareness, big machines rattled away in the distance. Crows rasped a warning, and then amid the rotting fruit she saw movement.

The plum had transformed into a giant ash tree. The trunk and leaves shone and danced upward through the clouds, drinking in the world's sunlight; the roots sank down lower and lower, through the earth, into the veiled regions of the Shadowlands, connecting every part of life. Meredith reached up to touch the glory of the World Tree.

Above her head and lifted arms, all seemed aquiver with the energy of creation. But then she caught a hissing sound.

Snakes...innumerable snakes...crawled from the belly of a giant serpent wrapped around the base of the tree. Small snakes wriggled upwards, twining around branches and twigs. They writhed downward between the roots of the World Tree, nibbling voraciously at the tendrils, slithering into the dark realms below.

The Shadowlands were forbidden...absolutely forbidden. This was the charge of the Shadow Walkers. Meredith knew she should turn her inner eyes elsewhere.

But she had to know.

The witch could see how every tiny bite spread poison into the tree... venomous brown threads of death creeping upward into the sunlit world and downward into the hidden world.

And now the insatiable serpents had become aware of her existence. Like a rolling wave they twisted toward her, prey ready for the tasting. At the last instant Meredith pulled away.

Her eyes flicked open and she shuddered with loathing.

As her breath hissed in and out of her lungs, she realized what she had seen. All the trees in her vision were once honored as sacred – holding in their great trunks and long lives the beliefs, hopes, and humanity of the people who revered them.

Meredith didn't know much about many of those other culture's traditions. But through the trees she was linked to the lives of all those who went before her, a link that should carry forward to the generations yet to come.

"To every person born and yet to be born," she whispered.

But the sacred trees were dying...one by one. Their unmarked deaths were killing the quiet soul of the world – the connections of all humanity.

Creeping disease had touched every corner of the world, possibly every living thing. Except the five saplings hidden in Meredith's shed.

CHAPTER SIX

SUSAN BROWN

Meredith wrapped her arms around her knees and wept. Finally she dragged her mind away from paralyzing despair and staggered out of the circle. In near panic, she erased the figure and then cleansed the room of evil using light, candles, and herbs. And then for good measure, she did it again. And a third time.

When she was sure she had cleared away any lingering traces of the disease, she returned her precious books of magic to their shelves and logged onto the Internet. The search was devastating. Hidden in not-much-interest news lay stories of a sacred tree cut down to make way for a highway, of groundwater pollution carrying death to ancient giants in all corners of the world, of commercial development eliminating habitat, of pathogens tracked in by tourists looking for photos to celebrate their adventures, of indifference by local populations as cultures changed and modern mores carried a message that what was once sacred no longer mattered.

One picture caught and held her. A huge old tree choked by plastic bags fluttering like malevolent ghosts in its dying branches. Throngs of people strolled, biked, and motored past without an upward glance.

The green witch sat back, aware of the solitude of her own home.

This beautiful church had once thrived with worshippers, but, as they became fewer and fewer, the diocese had made the difficult choice to deconsecrate the site and draw their followers to a more central and less expensive location.

It didn't matter the religion apparently; all over the world, that which had been sacred was slowly being forgotten.

Meredith held out her arms to her familiar. Lola leapt into her lap. "Maintaining the Balance will protect all of us, right?" the witch whispered. "But sweetie, I need some help."

Setting the dog back on the floor, she checked her phone yet again. No word from her parents. On an impulse, Meredith thumbed through her contacts and put in a call to Rob Oakes.

"*Hello...*" the bleariness of the voice let the witch know she really should have taken more account of time zones.

"Rob...I'm so sorry...it's Meredith."

"*Meredith...*" his voice brightened as he woke up.

In the background the witch heard a sharp voice. "*Who the hell is calling at this time of night?*"

She winced. *Nina*. She and Nina had never hit it off – something about which of them was Rob's favorite protégé. Nina had stayed at Rob's side and in his bed. Meredith had gone to New York and studied microbiology with Paul. Mentors and lovers all the way down. She flushed with quick heat at some of the better memories.

"*Shush, Nina!...Meredith! To what do I owe this pleasure?*"

Meredith could hear Nina grumbling in the background and that was enough for her to keep the secret of the saplings to herself. "I've been having dreams...portents..." she stumbled over the inadequacy of the explanation.

"*Go on,*" Rob urged.

"They're about death," the witch tried to explain. "Death of sacred trees...of the world tree."

"*Lovely as I find the idea, the world tree is a myth.*" Her old mentor's voice was dry. "*And life always requires change.*"

"I get it, Rob," she said impatiently, "but there's more to it than that. And you know more about plant magic than anyone I've ever met. I could use your advice."

44

"Still living in New York?"

"Yes…why?"

"As it happens, Nina and I are leaving in a few hours to meet with some UN officials. Give me a bit less than a day, and I will be there in person." Meredith could hear the well-remembered smile in his voice. *"You're a practical person, Meredith, so if you say something is wrong, I believe you. I'll help you get to the root of the problem."*

She could hear Nina swearing, ever so softly.

"Just like old times," Rob added.

Meredith felt a huge rush of relief. Someone she could count on. "Thank you. Thank you so much…There's one other thing…"

But the call had been cut off.

The witch sat back and looked at her phone, emotions thoroughly mixed. To be honest, she despised Nina. The woman was like an invasive vine, choking out everyone else to serve her own needs.

But when Meredith first came into her full powers and defied her parent's plans for her future, Rob had encouraged her to follow her dreams to be a green witch. He had felt like a wise old oak himself. Huge, sturdy, and strong, with dark eyes and a bushy beard that always reminded her of the nests of birds and mosses that thrived in ancient trees.

Impulsively she scrolled back through old photos to find an off-center one taken by Deirdre when Meredith had completed her studies with the Green Magic master. Rob had his arm draped around her shoulder. Nina glowered to one side and half of her father's back filled the other side. Her sister was a really terrible photographer.

Her phone pinged; she hurriedly answered and started talking. "Rob! Good! One more thing…"

"Who's Rob?" Paul's voice startled her.

"Rob Oakes…you remember, my green magic mentor," Meredith stuttered. "I didn't expect to hear from you, Paul."

There was a pause. *"Disappointed?"*

"Of course not. When are you coming home?"

"A couple of days. Three at the most. Will I get a warm welcome?"

Meredith laughed, her personal balance restored. "The warmest, I promise."

When the call ended, she sat back feeling a rush of relief at the prospect of the support of her mentor and the heat in Paul's voice. She could do this. She had to do this.

"*Yo! Meredith!*" a voice echoed loudly from the front door.

"Deirdre!" the witch shrieked. Forgetting everything else, Meredith pelted to church's entryway. Dropping an assortment of bags and cases, her sunburned and tousled sister leapt forward to give her a hug.

"I am so glad you're here!" Meredith exclaimed. "There is so much happening."

"So I gathered from all those hysterical texts," Deirdre retorted.

"Urgent. Never hysterical."

"Hysterical." Deirdre grinned at her, then wrinkled her peeling nose. "But couldn't you have an emergency in warm weather? I don't do snow and sleet."

Meredith laughed and helped her sister gather her belongings and cart them up to the usual guest room. "Hungry? Need tea...or something stronger?"

"Yes, hungry. Definitely something stronger."

For several minutes the sisters teased each other and got Deirdre settled in, while Lola leaped in and out of the open bags. Back in the kitchen, Meredith offered a glass of wine, a hastily constructed charcuterie board, and put a pre-made lasagna in the oven. Deirdre piled some salami and cheese on a cracker and munched down with a sigh of bliss.

"Okay...spill," she commanded. "What have you done with our parents and why is the world coming to an end?"

In spite of herself, Meredith giggled. "Of the parents, I have no idea. And the world is coming to an end..." She paused, trying to work out how to explain what she feared. "...not with a bang but a whimper..." she said finally.

Deirdre rolled her eyes. "If you're going literary on me, I may leave immediately."

Meredith smiled again, but this time it was forced. Briefly she told her sister about the dreams and the loss of so many sacred trees.

Deirdre slowly piled another cracker with meat and cheese. "So, not to be overly-dramatic, you're talking about the death of the soul of the world?"

Meredith slowly nodded. "The body may keep going for a while, but it's like a disease crawling across life itself. Weakening it bit by bit. When nothing is sacred, nothing matters, and death is inevitable."

Deirdre bit into her cracker and then took a healthy gulp of wine. "Why can't you have problems like aphids or a broken water pipe like everyone else?"

"Just lucky, I guess."

"I guess." Deirdre frowned. "So what has the oh-so-sexy Shadow Walker said about all this?"

"He says I'm the center of the rot."

"No question he's got a thing for you." Deirdre grinned.

"Please."

Her sister took another sip of wine. "What's his take on the saplings you've stashed in your shed?"

This time Meredith blushed. "He doesn't know about them...I'm not sure what his allegiance is and this is too important to risk."

"Not exactly being of this world, he probably does have a different world view," Deirdre agreed. "But I would think he has a stake in keeping the souls of everyone going strong. No souls, no need for the Shadowlands. And bang, he's out of a job." She paused. "Sister dear, I think you need to trust someone besides me. I do weather, remember."

Meredith nodded. "I know. Paul Oakes is coming here tomorrow."

"Him?" Deirdre rolled her eyes. "I didn't mean the hairy beast of your younger days."

Once again, Meredith felt her face heat up, this time with annoyance. "He is the foremost expert on biomes and green magic in the world," she retorted.

"Maybe, but he is too big and too hairy," Deirdre said. "Not my type at all."

"He doesn't have to be your type. He has to help save the world!"

"I reserve the right to insist that all men be my type." Deirdre grinned and gave her a gentle poke. "Relax. We will solve this. So do you want to show me these magical saplings of yours?"

Meredith knew her laugh was shaky but she stood up. With one last swallow of her wine, Deirdre followed her outside. Quietly, Meredith adjusted the wards draping the shed to allow her sister to enter unscathed.

Inside, the air was warm and humid, alight with magic.

"Wow," Deirdre whistled softly. "This has the feel of a jungle...or an Eden. I don't think I really understood what you told me until now." She walked over to the nearest sapling, now sprouting new leaves. "What kind of tree is this?"

Meredith joined her and gently caressed the bark. "Fig. That one over there is a kauri from New Zealand, I think. And there's a plum from Asia, a bodhi from India, and a sycamore probably from the Middle East. Each type of tree is important in both major and local religions."

"So why do these ones absolutely blast ancient magic? I mean, there have to be a lot of less formidable stands of these trees, right?"

"Well, yes, but..." Meredith froze as the importance of her sister's words washed over her. "These...these are *the* sacred trees," she said. "I can feel it."

"How?" Deirdre demanded. "They can't be there and here, too."

"Yes, but these must be clones. Identical to the first trees."

"You've lost me," Deirdre retorted.

Meredith frowned as she rapidly reviewed her range of knowledge in both science and green magic. "Botanical tissue culture," she murmured caressing the brilliant green new leaves. "With a hefty shot of magic thrown in."

When her sister cocked an eyebrow, Meredith took a deep breath and paused before attempting an explanation. "Gardeners have been grafting and cloning plants for decades. That way a perfect hybrid can be reproduced over and over without mutations or flaws."

"Okay, if you say so." Deirdre eyed the young trees. "But why are these particular saplings a big deal?"

"It wouldn't be if these were any old plants," Meredith explained. "But, Deirdre, these trees have been cloned from sacred trees – the first and greatest of the sacred trees."

"Meaning?"

"Meaning science and magic have worked together. These trees aren't just genetically identical, they're magically perfect – the sacred trees hold within them the template for all creation." She looked at her sister. "The start of a new Eden. A new Eden that's now in these trees." She sagged against the wall, the enormity of it weakening her knees. "And someone has entrusted this Eden to me."

"Well, hells bells," Deirdre murmured. "So now what, Eve?"

The green witch scrubbed her hand across her forehead. "Other than not taking a bite from a forbidden apple, I have no idea."

CHAPTER SEVEN

SUSAN BROWN

THE SISTERS SLOWLY WALKED BACK INTO THE CHURCH, BOTH uncharacteristically silent. Meredith tried to wrap her mind around the reality of the five saplings in her shed. She couldn't begin to guess what Deirdre was thinking.

A new Eden.

A new chance for the world.

But once again, a serpent was trying to destroy that future. Trying to rot away the hidden underside of the Balance. She was absolutely certain that's what her dreams warned of.

"What do you think the parents have to do with all this," she finally asked her sister.

Deirdre shrugged and pulled the overly-crisped lasagna from the oven. "They hear things most people don't know about."

"World tensions are fierce." Deirdre continued, sliding squares of pasta onto plates. "All we need is one power-hungry monster to set the end in motion. Maybe it's already started. Maybe the parents know it's started and this is their attempt to save us."

"But why me?" Meredith knew the answer before she asked it. She was a green witch, an extremely powerful green witch. If it was possible to save the first trees, she was one of the few people who could do it.

But it was too much responsibility.

"Rob Oakes knows more about biomes and green magic than I do."

"Does he?" Deirdre asked. "I never got your hero worship thing. And you have science as well as magic at your fingertips – even I can see that's a rare and potent combination." She stuck forks into the centers of the congealed pasta like mastheads. "And the parents know you, Mer. They've schmoozed too many people to be very trusting, but you've stood up to everyone to follow what you thought was right. How many people could say that?"

She passed over Meredith's plate and the two sat down and silently began to eat. Within minutes, as the witch felt sudden pressure against her wards, the intercom at her front gate crackled.

"*Package,*" the voice announced. "*For Meredith Kim.*"

Aghast, the sisters looked at each other and then together pelted for the door, with Lola bouncing and barking behind them. The same delivery man stood impatiently on the sidewalk, two tall cartons leaning against the fence.

"Sign," he commanded, holding out the notepad.

Meredith scrawled her name while Deirdre cautiously examined the boxes. Like before, the address was clear but no other information could be deciphered. The man got back in his truck and once again rammed it into traffic, oblivious to screeches and blasts of horns.

"That guy's got a death wish," Deirdre commented, as Meredith touched one of the boxes. The shrouding magic was palpable.

"The shed," Meredith said briefly.

Each sister took a box and headed to the stone building, trying to remain steady as the protection spells overlaying the ancient magic penetrated their senses.

"Okay here?" Deirdre laid her box against the potting bench. Speaking softly, she added her own wards to the ones cast earlier. "I can see some crazy tangle of spells. Same as before?"

Meredith nodded and spoke a revelation spell; again, when she found the green cord, the boxes opened at her magical tug. One box held four saplings; one held three.

"Twelve sacred trees," Meredith breathed.

"Damn," Deirdre whispered. "This *is* the start of a new Eden. Mer, what are you going to do with them? How can you hide them?"

Meredith shook her head, overwhelmed almost to the point of tears. "I don't know. I just don't know."

Deirdre threw an arm around her shoulders. "Don't worry. We'll figure this out." She paused. "We have got to find our parents. They've really done it this time."

"So what else is new?" Meredith snapped.

With only minimal conversation, they potted the saplings and then closed and warded the shed. Deirdre added her own protections to the ones Meredith had put in place. Back in the church's kitchen, they picked at the remainder of their now-cold dinner.

Deirdre pushed the last brittle shard of over-cooked pasta around and around her plate. "So, do you have anything personal of the parents that we can use for a search spell?"

Meredith thought about it. "Not much. They're way too careful. You?"

Her sister shook her head. "Nope, but we have to find them. Photos or anything?"

"No...wait. The photo you took of me with Rob when I finished my studies. I think the back of Dad's arm and shoulder are in it."

"It'll have to do."

Leaving their plates on the table, the sisters went into Meredith's study. The green witch found the photo on her phone and started it printing, then took a huge atlas from her shelves. "This could take a while," she said. "Because we barely know where to start."

"Korea?" Deirdre suggested. "Last known whereabouts."

While her sister set candles at the cardinal points around the atlas, Meredith cut out the blurry portion of her dad's body from the photo and hung it on a piece of silver chain. "Ready?"

Deirdre nodded and quietly chanted spells for locating and

53

revelation. Meredith held the chain over the map of Asia. They stared at the pendulum. It circled briefly, almost aimlessly, and then stopped moving.

"So not Asia," Deirdre said. "Europe?"

Again they dowsed for their father. Nothing.

Page by page, they searched for their parent, each time coming up empty. Finally, in exasperation, Meredith flipped to a page representing New York. The pendulum swung wildly and then hung at a slant, pointing to the city.

"I don't believe this," the witch muttered. "They're here. Somewhere. Why didn't I know?"

Deirdre slumped back, exhausted. "Because they're apparently in hiding and no one does concealment or persuasion spells like they do."

Quietly raging, Meredith held the photo of her father and enunciated a potent summoning spell.

Deirdre grinned. "You know they aren't going to like that."

"Too damn bad," Meredith snarled. "They aren't leaving me hanging with their version of how to save the world."

Deirdre laughed. "So maybe we'd better make sure they feel welcome."

Meredith glowered but didn't object when her sister searched her stash for a good bottle of wine and refreshed the tray of meats and cheeses.

They didn't have to wait long. Within an hour, Meredith felt her parents' furious passage through the front gate, the wards already bespelled to allow them entrance. The witch walked slowly to the front door, Lola uncharacteristically quiet as she trotted behind her. Deirdre loitered behind them both.

A gust of wind slammed the door open, and Celeste stormed in.

"Meredith, honey," she said, her voice brittle. "I think this time, you've actually gone too far."

"Really?" Meredith snapped. "*I've* gone too far?"

Behind his wife, Gregory Kim shrugged his wide shoulders. "This may be a good thing, Celeste." He dropped the bags he carried on the entryway floor, stretched and smiled at his daughters. "We'd thought we had more time, but we've been targeted by some rough magic. We have to talk. All of us."

Deirdre stepped forward and hugged her dad, then gave her mom a peck on the cheek. "Our thoughts exactly." She eyed Celeste and took the case she carried. "I'm just hoping we'll all have time to do some serious shopping this trip."

"This trip?" Meredith retorted. "I've been here six years and other than signing the original paperwork, this is exactly your second visit that has lasted for more time than it takes to drink a cup of coffee. Oh, and in case you forgot, the house warming present you sent me needs a few more instructions."

Deirdre's eyes danced and she took her dad's arm. "Meredith's a little stressed right now."

Her sister rolled her eyes and stepped back. She knew Deirdre was genius at handling their parents, and, right now, Meredith needed their explanations – not their exasperation. The green witch had never had any but the vaguest idea of what her parents' work was about, beyond the politics of avoiding climate change or patching up some looming ecological disaster. Once she'd moved to New York, their connection had been sporadic and superficial.

But as she welcomed them through the church doors, Meredith intentionally took a deep breath, savoring the blending of the inner warmth held in centuries of sacred stone and the outer cool breeze carrying the life of the world. It calmed her. It was all right. She was where she should be, regardless of her parent's machinations.

As the family settled in the kitchen, Deirdre continued to chatter soothingly, laying out the charcuterie board and plates. Her dad bypassed the wine and poured himself a tumbler of Scotch.

Meredith busied herself making a cup of tea, all the while eyeing her father's drooping frame and noting the dark circles under her stepmother's eyes. "So, what's going on," she said finally.

"Unfortunately," Celeste said, accepting a large glass of wine from Deirdre, "far too much."

A rueful smile passed over Gregory Kim's tired face. "We've

defied the Select Council and taken matters into our own hands. Made a few people mad at us."

Meredith stopped moving. "You did what?"

Her father's face hardened. "They've become immobilized... monolithic. Paralyzed by what the witch world has always done. Your mentor, Rob Oakes, has led the charge...or rather been the most vocal priest in the hardening of the ideologies."

"Rob?" Meredith demanded. "That's not possible. All he cares about is the botany of biomes."

Her father took a sip of Scotch and slowly rolled the glass between his palms. "How long since you've seen him?"

"Six, maybe seven years."

Greg nodded. "His views have changed. He thinks our species... every species...should evolve or go extinct."

Meredith felt dread freezing through her. "What does that mean, Dad?"

Greg sighed. "It means that even our short-sighted, greedy mistakes are a natural evolution and we have to live with them, evolve from them, or die."

Venomous snakes hissing in the shadows.

Withered figs dropping onto charred soil.

Sacred plum blossoms rotting on dry branches.

The earth bubbling with seeping decay.

"No! That's insane," Meredith protested. "What's he done? He can't..." She looked up in sudden panic. "I called him. When the saplings showed up. He's coming tomorrow."

"You did what?" Her father shot out of his chair.

"We thought we could trust you!" Celeste nearly shrieked.

"You didn't tell me anything," Meredith yelled back. "You dumped this on me without any warning. What did you expect?"

"She's right," Deirdre intervened. "Mer has enough power to sense the importance of what showed up. But you left her a little short on information."

Her father sagged back into the chair, his brown eyes somber. "It was all we could do to secure the trees. To smuggle them out safely."

Celeste snapped her wineglass back on the counter. "We didn't expect you to immediately broadcast their arrival."

Meredith glowered at them. "I didn't," she said tightly. "I haven't told anyone at all except Deirdre. But maybe she isn't to be trusted either."

"Really, Meredith," Celeste scolded. "You know that isn't what I meant."

Infuriated, the green witch turned to stare out her window, watching how the streetlights glimmered in a kaleidoscope of colors through the stained glass.

Her dad came to stand beside her, solid, comforting. She leaned her head on his shoulder.

"Meredith," he said heavily, "it's been a terrible and silent battle against unrelenting enemies. You are the one we've trusted."

She fought back tears and straightened. "But why this?"

"Celeste and I finally got tired of persuading and arguing and offering up facts. The witch world has always protected the planet but the Select Council has its collective head up its ass. Rob Oakes has convinced them that in order to evolve, the world and the sacred trees have to take their lumps from human stupidity. Some of that stupidity has even become a way to make some cash." His voice took on the tones of a huckster. "*Yes, you too can own a sprig of the divine – $29.95 for a sacred sapling…*"

"What?"

"We persuaded a few governments and a handful of witches and scientists to think the way we do. Buds were cut from the trees to be cloned. But then money got involved. Along with shoddy practices. Fungi and pathogens have inadvertently been cloned too – and they've mutated. The original trees are under attack by the plan that was supposed to save them."

He sat down at the table and dropped his head in his hands. "It's an unholy mess, Meredith."

"But what did you do?"

Her dad sat back and slowly smiled. "We stole the original clones. Every one."

"You did what?" Meredith's voice rose. "How? Why?"

"For you, Meredith. It's time for you to step up to your potential," Celeste told her. "Honey, the world is counting on you to cultivate and protect these saplings."

"But no pressure, honey-bunch," Deirdre murmured.

"But what about Rob?" Meredith said wildly. "The Select? What if they figure out what happened to the clones?"

Her father patted her hand. "If we have to fight them, we will. But I'm hoping that between the four of us, we can keep them from finding out. It doesn't matter the cost. We have to save those trees."

Meredith sat down hard. She knew both the power of the witches on the Select Council and the potency of Rob's circle of green witches. With a flash of awe, she considered the power and influence her parents had called on to find and hide their cache – until they could release the trees into their daughter's care.

But the responsibility of it.

The incredible joy to be the guardian of these trees.

The responsibility...

Meredith stared upward at the coved ceilings. "Biomes," she muttered. "Every sapling needs a particular type of biome. I can't just grow trees from all over the world without anyone noticing."

"Can't you?" Her father stood up. "You insisted on becoming a green witch despite our objections. Maybe you weren't wrong. But I never expected you to be too lazy or too afraid to follow the destiny you demanded."

Meredith stepped back, feeling as though her father had slapped her. "I don't know how to grow them and hide them at the same time."

Her father turned toward the staircase. "Your stepmother and I have done our part." His voice was heavy with exhaustion. "We risked everything. We're under interdiction from the Select Council. Now it's your task. No excuses. Just do what has to be done."

Meredith stared, aghast, as he walked heavily up the stairs. Celeste shot her an angry look and followed.

"I'll make sure they've got towels and such." Deirdre scurried after her parents, leaving Meredith alone in the kitchen. Lola whined and trotted over to lean against her mistress' legs. The witch sank onto a chair and absently stroked the small dog's fur.

"Got any ideas, sweetheart?" she murmured. "I think we need to come up with some...fast!" She paused, her hand in mid-air. "And Rob will be here tomorrow. Oh hell and damnation...what have I done?"

CHAPTER EIGHT

SUSAN BROWN

THAT NIGHT, MEREDITH BARELY SLEPT. THE NIGHTMARES returned, distorted from the original horrifying visions.

The snakes hissed and slithered over her body.

Her beloved garden smoldered with foul-smelling fire.

The sacred plum contorted into an agonizing tangle of dead branches and rotting blossoms.

Everything she touched withered and died.

At first light, head aching with anxiety and lack of sleep, Meredith slipped out of the church and went to the shed. Within the intensely warded stone building, her saplings had already shown growth. Buds had swelled and unfurled, branches had lengthened, the song of the trees existing below human hearing hummed in her enhanced senses.

Meredith gently touched each tree, felt the throb of its ancient power and drew strength from it.

"I'll protect you somehow," she whispered.

When she returned to the church, Deirdre was sleepily scrambling eggs and stacking enough toast for a banquet. "Always good to feed Dad well," she mumbled. "Got any fruit for Mom?"

"I think so." Meredith dug through her fridge and emerged with strawberries, grapes, and oranges.

Deirdre nodded approval. "That should mellow them out."

"Maybe," her sister muttered, "but who's going to mellow me out?"

Deirdre only grinned and laid plates out for the meal.

In Meredith's mind, this particular visit was not going to rank high on her list of good times. She received a text from Rob just as the coffee was being poured.

"Eleven o'clock," she told her family. "He's expecting to be here at eleven."

"Yay," Deirdre muttered.

Their father sat back. "I think Celeste and I had better leave. A confrontation with Oakes won't do us any good."

"But what about me?" Meredith's voice squeaked in anxiety. "I'm not sure I can confront him!"

"No reason why you should," her father said evenly. He wiped his mouth on a napkin and stood up. "He doesn't know about the trees. He thinks you called him about your dreams. Keep it on that level."

"Make yourself sound like a hysterical student." Deirdre grinned. "Let him be the big strong man who reassures little ol' you. Just like before."

Meredith made a face at her and raised a hand as if to throw a hex.

"None of that, girls," Celeste said briskly. "We trust you, Meredith."

"Do you?" her stepdaughter asked sharply.

Celeste's face softened into an affectionate smile. "You know we do. So, sweetheart, it's time to do what you do best."

"Lie through your teeth," Deirdre whispered. Meredith couldn't help but laugh.

Within twenty minutes her parents had gathered all evidence of their stay and left the church. The sisters smudged the rooms to ensure no lingering trace of their essence could be sensed and then sat down to wait for Meredith's old mentor.

THE GREEN WITCH FELT THE PRESSURE ON HER WARDS EVEN before the doorbell at the front gate clanged through the church.

"Show time," Deirdre said and gave her sister a thumbs up.

"Rob?" Meredith hoped her shrill voice over the intercom would be interpreted as happy excitement.

A crackly grunt, followed by a booming, *"Meredith! Your favorite teacher is here!"*

Deirdre rolled her eyes but Meredith felt a flash of warmth at the familiar greeting. There had to be some mistake...Rob had introduced her to so much that was good in her life.

"Opening the gate!" she called. She couldn't ignore the flush of pleasure she felt at the prospect of seeing him again. Maybe there was an explanation...

With Deirdre coming more slowly behind her, Meredith raced for the front of the church. Lola barked and yipped and ran in circles around her feet, until Deirdre scooped her up.

"I know," Deirdre murmured. "That bad old man wants to come in and you don't like him at all, do you sweetie pie? Clever little Lola."

Meredith shot her a fuming glance and then pulled open the door. Despite the wet snow of the morning, Rob stood massive and dry on the doorstep. His bag dropped as he held his arms out to his former student for a hug. The green witch couldn't help herself. She allowed herself to be folded into those huge, warm arms. His beard tickled her ear as he smacked a kiss on her cheek.

Behind him, Meredith was vaguely aware of Nina taking deep irritated breaths. She had a sudden vision that the tiny, dark-haired witch had somehow become Rob's familiar and was as anxious in her own way as Lola was in hers.

At the thought, Meredith pulled back and gestured for them to come in. "How was the trip?" *Inane.* "Nina, can I take your bag?"

"I'm just fine thank you!" Nina stepped across the threshold and looked around as though she had been invited into a barn – a manure-filled barn.

"I'm Deirdre, " Meredith's sister introduced herself. "We met once or twice several years ago."

Lola growled.

"I wouldn't keep a vicious dog," Nina sniffed.

"Really?" Deirdre cast a look at Rob. "People are different, I guess."

Feeling her face heat up, Meredith took Rob's arm to guide him toward her open kitchen. "It's great to see you after so long, Rob. And I can't believe you took the time to come just because of my stupid dreams."

Rob looked around cheerfully and rubbed his hands together. "Beautiful place, Meredith. Just beautiful. Mind if I sit?"

She pointed to a chair and he settled in apparent deep contentment. Nina perched on a stool. Deirdre, still holding Lola, took the one beside her.

"Now how about one of your tisanes?" Rob asked. "I want to see what you've done with my original recipes."

"I've made a few improvements."

"Like you could improve on anything Rob has created," Nina snapped.

The sense that a high wind was blowing her helter-skelter began to overtake Meredith. The green witch thoughtfully chose among the herbs in her secret drawer. A little something for relaxation and openness, she thought. She turned to smile at her former mentor. Something about his narrowed eyes caused her skin to prickle. As she brewed the tea, she quietly reached down into her own magic core.

Well, well, well. A very subtle spell drifted outwards from Rob, a bit like an exquisite perfume…one that also encouraged openness, trust, and a damping down of inhibitions. Was this something new, or had she not had the sophistication to see it before?

Her teacher was so big and open…was that a camouflage for secrets?

The witch shivered slightly at the thought. Softly, Meredith chanted a counter spell so subtle she was sure her old mentor would not sense it. A glance at her sister showed that Deirdre was also whispering a spell into Lola's soft fur. And Nina was shifting uncomfortably on her chair as though long-tight muscles were protesting.

As her spell took effect, Meredith's long affection for Rob seemed to seep away. Had it ever been real? Her hands shook as she poured the boiling water over the cup. Deirdre put Lola on the floor and smoothly piled a stack of store-bought cookies onto a plate. She placed it on the table beside the man.

"So Meredith," Rob said. "Tell me again about those portents you've seen?"

Meredith hesitated, reviewing them in her mind. They were completely clear to her now and it was not in her personality to lie or mislead. But the thought of the saplings and their fate pushed her to dissemble just a little.

And the trust she once had in Rob Oakes was gone.

"I dreamt about snakes devouring every living thing, of figs withered on smoking ground, of plum blossoms rotting on dead branches," she said bluntly.

"Sounds terribly biblical," Nina snickered.

Meredith took a deep breath and smiled blandly at the other witch.

"Sounds like the end of the world to me," Deirdre snarled. "Or isn't that a big deal to you?"

"Of course." Nina rolled her eyes. "But only idiots can't see the world needs to evolve. Idiots who use science to destroy the natural order." She glared at Meredith.

"And sometimes use science to fix things," Meredith shot back.

"That's like using black magic and saying it's for the good," Nina snapped.

"You're so lucky," Deirdre murmured, "that you have crystal-clear vision of what's good and what isn't. No shades of gray."

Nina shrugged. "I know evil when I see it."

"Girls, girls," Rob intervened. "We all have one objective. The welfare of our world."

"Don't you just love a good sound bite," Deirdre purred. "How is this welfare going to be achieved?"

"We nurture that which is natural," Nina shot out. "And let the unnatural, the weak, simply die out."

Meredith glanced sideways at Rob. He sat quietly, as usual, his eyes gleaming approval at Nina. The little witch flushed with pleasure.

"Seems a bit too simplistic for me," Meredith said. "Victims deserve to die? Let the invasive species over run the native ones because there are no inherent predators? Come on, Nina...Rob... you know life demands a little more reflection and action."

"You just don't get it," Nina spat out. "You wrapped yourself in science instead of keeping with the purity of the natural world. You are the kind of person who should be contained..."

Deirdre had risen to her feet, her hands splayed to cast a spell. Her cheerful face had hardened. "Enough of this gibberish," she snarled. "You've outstayed your welcome."

"Nonsense," Rob said easily. Meredith could feel his charm spell strengthening. She pulled from her own protective magic to defend herself.

"So Meredith," he went on, "I hear your parents have been pretty active lately. Left the party line. What've they said to you about it?"

His eyes were earnest and beneath his soft beard his lips curved into a friendly smile.

Meredith shrugged. "Oh my parents and I don't talk a lot. We have such different interests."

"I suppose," Rob agreed. "But I heard they've started dabbling in our specialty, green magic."

"Really?" Meredith felt her face heat up. "I wouldn't know."

Rob stood and stared at her. "You are a terrible liar, Meredith. Even when you tried to convince me you were not interested in science, I knew all about it. I truly regretted when you left the purity of our magic behind."

"He didn't need you, because he had me," Nina bragged.

"I grew up," Meredith said coldly. "I had to make my own decisions and choose my own path."

"Even when that meant defying your parents, ignoring the directions of the Select Council...and abandoning me?" He reached out to touch her. "Meredith, my little hedge witch, isn't it time for you to stop this science nonsense and return to the green path?" His voice hardened subtly. "Now Meredith, tell me...where are those trees?"

The spell that had held the green witch for so long intensified and wrapped around her again. She longed to do what he wanted... he understood green magic. *He understood her.*

Meredith took a step forward.

Without warning, Lola's teeth fastened on her ankle.

"*Yeow!*" Pain shot through her leg. Meredith looked down at her familiar in disbelief.

CHAPTER NINE

SUSAN BROWN

THE PAIN IN HER LEG SNAPPED MEREDITH AWAKE. SHE LOOKED down as Lola howled her distress. And then the witch's eyes swept to Rob's face.

His expression had contorted in anger. Lola gyrated in uneven circles, whimpering. Meredith reached down and scooped up her pup. "What have you done to her?" She demanded. She could hear the hysteria building in her own voice.

Once again, Rob's face smoothed into planes of concern. "Well that was a surprise. Is your dog okay? How can I help?" He reached out again to the witch.

Orange flame, swirling like the eye of a hurricane, rocketed through the air, pulsing between Rob and Meredith. "Don't you dare touch her," Deirdre snarled. "Don't you ever touch her, you sick bastard!"

"Meredith has strayed too far from the green path." His rich voice was sorrowful.

Lola slipped down from her mistress' arms and dashed forward, too fast to see. With a rising growl, she bounced around Rob's legs doing her best to fasten her teeth into his leg.

"What the...!" Rob roared. "Enough!"

He raised his huge arms and the spells Meredith had previously only sensed flared into roaring existence. "Nina!" he commanded.

The small witch threw her own powers into the brown light shooting outwards from the man.

"*Mer!*" Deirdre screamed.

Meredith's hands went up, but a fraction too late. She felt her former mentor's magic singe her cheek.

"I'll kill you!" Deirdre screamed. Her magic burst outward like a lightening ball, pushing back Rob and flattening Nina. The small witch sagged and slowly crumpled to the floor, unconscious.

"Out, Rob!" Meredith commanded. "Leave my house!"

Her green power surged outward, abetted by the centuries of sacred power embedded in the stones of the church. She and Deirdre forced Rob back, step by step until he had gone out the great doors and stood in the sleeting day.

"You'll regret this," he said, his voice full of warm sorrow. Meredith felt the old ties tugging on her. It would be so easy to be the witch he had loved...

Her hands dropped. She stared down at the dead grass. In that instant, as Deirdre turned to her in concern, Rob summoned his powers, and unhampered by the church's wards, sent a shattering blow at Deirdre.

With a soft moan, Deirdre fell onto the icy turf.

"*No!*" Meredith screamed.

Rob raised a wall of magic, encasing her, holding Meredith unmoving on her own land.

"Where are those trees?" he ground out.

Desperate to free herself, Meredith tried to call on the magic lying within her holding. But so much had gone to give strength to the trees, to support the growing saplings. She fought wildly, feeling the blood in her veins congealing with rot.

"Hey buddy," a whiny voice pierced her senses.

Barry.

"Yo, bro," Barry said loudly. "You're making way too much noise for this dead neighborhood." He jerked a thumb at the graveyard and snickered at his own terrible joke.

Momentarily distracted, Rob turned his head.

Meredith wrenched herself loose and ran...ran for the only bolt-hole she knew of. "Open, open *open*," she pleaded. Whether the Shadow Walker somehow heard her, whether her own magic triumphed, or whether Barry somehow greased her passage, the portal to Netherworld unfolded. Meredith threw herself inside.

The sibilant whispers, the oozing mist made her nauseous. Her body felt loose, like clothes that were three sizes too big.

A myriad of lights, like dancing lightning, filled whatever this space was. Behind her the portal still gaped, the gray world of the churchyard behind it.

"*Noooo*," she breathed. The word was discordant, like another language.

For a second she saw Rob framed in the entry of the portal. Then he plunged in, shouting her name. She felt the pull of his magic but fought against it. Not here. He had no power here.

Neither did she.

"Duncan Rhys," she tried to summon the Shadow Walker but her voice had no strength. Mustering the little energy left in her, Meredith ran, but her body was dissipating, flowing into nothingness.

Behind her she could feel Rob reaching for her, trying to grasp her soul. That was what he'd always wanted...what she had escaped from...

His magic had turned to rot. A desire to control, not nurture – no matter how he wrapped his needs in fine words. A serpent of venomous intent. The downfall of Paradise.

His last shreds of his power still reached for her...*such a familiar blanket.*

The witch knew she was dying and in death she would be trapped within the Shadowlands. A trespasser, not supposed to be here.

But she would not give in...

With her last gasp of power, Meredith turned on Rob and shoved back his energy. Broke the connection he had spent so many years creating.

71

I might be dying, she thought, *but I'll be free...*

As she saw the being that had been Rob writhe into a brown ball of energy and flicker out, a tall blue flame soared into her awareness. She looked at her hands, still miraculously shaped like her body. They glowed green.

But as she watched, the green fire in her pulsed and weakened.

Now...she would die now.

The blue flame beside her became a man's shape and a hand held hers.

"Duncan," she whispered.

"Come, my witch. It's not yet time for you to be here."

Her own power rose into her like spring sap in her beloved trees. Fully trusting, Meredith followed the Shadow Walker across the uneven landscape of the world of the dead. When she stumbled and fell, he lifted her up and carried her forward. Only vaguely was she aware of his body solidifying, of her own green magic growing and restoring her.

Duncan carried Meredith through the portal into her own world, past her worried sister, hysterical Nina, and yapping Lola. Effortlessly, he mounted the stairs up to her bedroom.

Tenderly he laid her down.

"Wait," Meredith reached out and caught his hand. "Don't leave me," she whispered. "Not yet."

"I won't," his voice was soft. He leaned over and kissed her, his lips soft and warm. "I won't ever abandon you, my witch."

Meredith, sighed, closed her eyes and reached her arms up around his neck. "Good," she murmured. "So good..."

WHEN MEREDITH WOKE UP HOURS LATER, THE SHADOW WALKER was gone. She stretched languorously, remembering every moment since Duncan brought her home.

On the floor below, she could hear the muffled movements of Deirdre and the voices of her parents. At that, Meredith considered yanking the blankets over her head.

Her phone pinged. A text from Paul.

Been delayed for a day. Some exciting developments here. I'll tell you all about it when I get back. Love you!

Meredith let out a long breath. Paul. The man she loved.

Duncan Rhys was a…what was he? How could she…?

"Seriously, Meredith," she muttered.

Propelled by a complete refusal to try and sort this out, the witch got out of bed and luxuriated in the shower until the hot water ran out. Finally, she pulled on her clothes and went downstairs.

In the kitchen, her father was absently creating and dismantling glowing tendrils of spells, Celeste was tossing a salad, and Deirdre was pushing another tissue on the sobbing Nina.

"But did he love me?" Nina wailed.

Deirdre's bored expression indicated that this had been a lengthy and repeated refrain. Meredith stepped in.

"Of course he did," she soothed the small witch. "But Rob's ideals kept him from showing his real affection for people…for you."

"Seriously, you think so?" Nina looked up hopefully.

"Seriously?" Deirdre muttered. Meredith shot her an exasperated look.

Nina got to her feet slowly and sniffed one more time. "It's up to me, now," she said. "It's up to me to keep his mission strong."

"Right," Meredith said.

"You do that," Deirdre began maneuvering Nina toward the entryway while muttering a spell to fog the witch's memory of the last hour's events.

It was a relief when the outer door closed and Deirdre returned. "Even without my spell, I don't think that little idiot had any idea what that man was doing or that Mom and Dad were fighting him."

Meredith grinned. "Rob wasn't big on sharing information." Her smile faded. "Will the Select Council figure out what happened?"

Her father snapped his fingers over a complex whispering spell and shrugged. "Without Rob charming the fools into his way of thinking, they'll forget it soon enough. Who'd have guessed the man could weave such subtle persuasion spells." He shook his head.

Celeste put the salad bowl on the table. "There is one thing,

Meredith." She hesitated. "The Select will know you went into the Shadowlands. There will be consequences. We'll do what we can…"

"She was fighting for her life," Deirdre protested.

"It doesn't matter," their father said. "The Shadowlands are absolutely forbidden."

And what about a Shadow Walker? Meredith wondered. *What about Duncan Rhys?*

She looked out at the snowflakes, colored by the stained glass and streetlights. "I'm going to check on my trees," she murmured.

In the shed, she drifted from one tree to another, marveling at their unfurling leaves and satiny bark. Whispered to them like dearly loved children.

A moment later, she was aware of Deirdre and Lola entering the shed behind her.

"So Mer, I've been thinking about how to solve this little problem of growing a virtual forest of magical trees and not have anyone notice."

"I'm listening."

Lola gave a sharp bark of encouragement.

"There's that block behind the churchyard where they've taken out all the buildings."

Meredith nodded glumly. "Concrete, rubble, and soil that's been smothered for decades, if not a century or two."

"Then it's time to rescue it," her sister said. "Can you bring that patch of ground back to life?"

Meredith paused, head cocked to one side. She reached out cautiously, trying to find the heart of the strangled land. It was there, parched and empty, crying for life to come back to it. She let out a long breath.

"I can."

Deirdre grinned. "I knew it. And when the land is ready, I'll create the weather each tree needs. This Eden will be a heaven of plants in their own biomes. And of course, the parents will conceal it from everyone who might threaten it. Think the birds will come back?"

Meredith laughed. "I know it. Eden will live again, right here in New York City."

"That's a scary thought." Deirdre grinned.

Lola barked and Meredith scooped her up. "Nope, it's a good one. A very good one."

She walked to the doorway of the shed and looked out. From this angle she could barely make out the empty air between two gravestones, the portal to the land of the dead. In the distance, she could hear the roar of machinery as the last of the old buildings crashed down. The site where the lost Garden of Eden would be reborn.

The responsibility. The appalling responsibility was now hers.

Meredith sighed and buried her face in Lola's fur. "It's going to be okay, sweetie," she murmured. "It will all be okay. I promise."

COVEN'S RISING

LINDA JORDAN

CHAPTER 1

LINDA JORDAN

PEARL SAT CROSS-LEGGED ON THE OVAL RAG RUG GRANDMA MADE before she died so many years ago. Beatrice, the Himalayan-tabby mix lay cat, curled up behind her.

As she blew out her meditation candle and watched smoke spiral upwards, Pearl shifted her stiff body. The rug sat on the hardwood floor and was still in good condition. Despite nearly thirty years of use. Lucille, their house, took good care of things.

Pearl didn't feel so sure about her own body. She was second from the youngest of her sisters, but at thirty-two, aches had begun creeping in where they hadn't existed before. She needed to start doing yoga or stretching again. Motivation always waned in winter, despite the new year.

But today she felt bloated and clumsy. Maybe her period was coming. It was always irregular, so she never knew for sure when it would show up.

Her fingers splayed out over the cloth taken from muted rose-colored dresses, peach blouses and a pale-yellow apron, all of which had been woven together into the rug. Grandma, a gifted seer, must have known who Pearl would be in order to use her favorite colors.

Had she also anticipated the mess they were all in now?

There were twenty-eight people sheltering within Lucille's walls. Hiding from the demon Caorthannach and the sisters' distant cousin, Ryan McMahon. They'd won the first battle at Samhain. Routing him from his hiding place. Maybe they'd even kept him from summoning more demons. They did rid the world of two demons but the strongest one, the fiery demon Caorthannach, had come back several times to attack them. The demon killed one of the demonologists, which had been a terrible loss.

The demon's most recent attack came just before Winter Solstice. They'd barely fought her off. Ryan McMahon wasn't anywhere to be found. Perhaps he too was in hiding, like Pearl and all her friends.

The fire demon was still loose in the world. Or perhaps in her own world, making babies. She *was* called the Mother of Demons. Problem was, no one knew what she was up to. Or more specifically, what she and Ryan were working on. Whatever it was, their plans didn't bode well for humanity.

It meant control, carnage and death for humans.

The household of witches, shamans and demonologists were at a loss about what to do. The wheel had turned, the new year rolled around. It was just past mid-January. All the lights and holiday decorations had been put away and the dark-gray days grew slightly longer.

The morning looked crisp, maybe even clear, after weeks of dark rainy days. The cold downpours had kept people and most of the animals inside. Getting on each others' nerves.

All of them stuck in the house. Plotting, planning and arguing endlessly about what step to take next. And getting nowhere.

They just didn't have enough information.

Beatrice got up and stretched, walking around Pearl to plop down in her lap. Pearl stroked the long cream-colored fur. The cat had dark points at her ears, nose, feet and tail, with light striping on her back and upper body that hinted at her mixed parentage. Her eyes, a blue like the clearest summer sky, gazed up at Pearl.

"You know, if you're on my lap, I can't open the door for you to go downstairs and eat."

Beatrice mrrowed at Pearl and didn't move.

"Okay, let's go."

She unfolded her legs and the cat scampered across the floor to the door. Pearl stretched and rose in one motion — at least she was still able to do that — even if it was clumsy. Tugging her long sleeved t-shirt into place, she walked to the door and opened it. Beatrice slid through and raced down the stairs.

Pearl looked around at her room. Bed made, curtains open, closet closed. Everything in place, just the way she liked it. The room looked peaceful in the dim pre-dawn light.

Pearl loved the tranquility of this time of year. Clouds muting the sun's intensity. The fog which sometimes appeared.

It also quieted the noisiness of neighbors and the normally busy life of the house. With four sisters there was a lot of energy to dim. All of them were powerful women and at times their power was just too intrusive.

But now, with all their friends taking shelter here, the energy felt overwhelming. Pearl had asked Lucille to add padding to her walls so she could focus and find some solitude and tranquility. That peace was crucial for her to reenergize. Without that, she couldn't do any bodywork on anyone, let alone any energy work. Although there wasn't a lot of call to do energy and protection these days. People were hesitant to ask, she knew. And that felt just fine.

She felt sort of lost and very, very grumpy.

Pearl sighed and closed her door. She hoped no one else was around yet. Walking down the stairs, her bare feet cold from the wood stairs. The kitchen sat empty.

She was the first one up. Many of the witches, shamans and demonologists living here stayed up very late. Those who were scheduled to be on watch, starting at dusk, were up all night.

The cat door flapped twice and the black cat streamed in, closely followed by a tortoiseshell. The big yellow guy wandered in from the living room and a fluffy white cat pranced down the stairs.

"Only five for breakfast?" asked Pearl. She opened a large can and a gray tabby, then a yellow and white cat joined the throng. "I'll open another can, shall I?"

More cats would appear with time. Most of the people staying here had cats, dogs or other pets.

Pearl set ten bowls of wet food on the floor and refilled the three dry kibble bowls. Then put the kettle on and perused the tea selection, choosing a black and lavender tea for her first cup.

While waiting for the water to boil, Pearl took the hair tie off her long hair which was always escaping confinement. Bending over, she smoothed the hair into another pony-tail, wrapped it around in a loose bun and secured the mass with the last twist of the hair tie. It would hold for a few hours.

She poured boiling water over the teabag in her cup and the rest into a teapot with looseleaf Irish breakfast tea in it. Then plopped a tea cozy over the pot. Sapphire always got up early and needed caffeine. Her sister was trying to quit a coffee habit, substituting tea. So far, so good.

A couple more cats came in and then Beatrice showed up so Pearl opened another can and set more bowls down. She took the teabag out of her mug, then poured in some cream.

There was a tug on the bottom of her yoga pants and she looked down to see the solid-gray kitten sitting on its haunches, front paws on her leg.

"You want up, huh little one?"

Pearl picked the kitten up. It was about three months old. Born late in the season to a stray, their vet hadn't been able to find a home for it. She'd come for a house call last week to see one of Beryl's many cats and brought the kitten, probably hoping Beryl would adopt it. Which she did. He was adorable with orange-gold eyes and they'd named him Hema for short, Hematite officially.

She carried the kitten and her mug over to the table and sat down. Hema cuddled up to her neck, purring loudly.

Outside the garden was becoming visible as the sun moved up from the horizon. Pearl could feel the earth's energy even inside the house. She was still sleeping. Winter held her in its cold grasp.

But beneath the surface, roots were growing and taking up nutrients. Buds were forming, even if they were still tightly held by the plants. Spring would arrive in a month but winter wasn't ready to leave yet.

Beryl had a good crop of onions and garlic going. There were also a lot of salad greens in the unheated greenhouse. Luxuries like tomatoes, basil and eggplant grew in the heated greenhouse. Many plants still producing from last summer. Some of the herbs were growing out in fully-exposed beds. Rosemary stood tall against the light frost on the ground.

Off near the far fence, Pearl spotted Tau and his black lab, Coal, making their rounds. They often took the night watch. Tau was tall and muscular, a big formidable looking guy with the darkest skin she'd ever seen. She felt her cheeks heat up just thinking about how he looked at her.

She had mixed feelings about whether a relationship with him was a good idea. With all of them trapped here in the house. If a relationship went south, things could get ugly.

Still Jet and Bera were making one work.

At least Tau was taking his time. Maybe he wasn't sure either. There had just been a few exchanged looks, nothing spoken about it. Maybe he was waiting for her to make the first move. But she had a lot on her plate.

The stairs creaked and Beryl entered the kitchen, her wavy long hair mostly tied back with a green ribbon. She wrapped a brown cardigan around herself and smiled at Pearl.

Beryl poured a cup from the teapot, added cream and glanced at the cat bowls. Probably satisfied there was still food. She petted a black cat stretched out on the windowsill above a radiator, then sat down at the table.

"Good morning," said Pearl.

"Morning. How is it that you're always up first?"

"I don't spend all night researching down in the library."

"There is that," said Beryl, sipping her tea.

They sat in silence. Hema jumped down from Pearl's lap and raced off. Following the big yellow guy, who half-heartedly swatted at the kitten on his return to a prime sleeping spot in the living room. The kitten was trying hard to make friends. Too hard.

Sapphire came downstairs, got her tea and sat at the table, saying nothing. Pearl could feel the anger and frustration leaking from her.

After draining her mug, Sapphire asked, "Where's Jet?"

"Sleeping probably," said Beryl. "She never gets up this early."

"But we're supposed to meet in ten minutes," said Sapphire.

"Who's we?" asked Pearl.

"The five of us," said Sapphire.

"No one told me," said Pearl.

"I knew," said Beryl.

"Well, you better get Ruby up. She's never up this early either," said Pearl to Sapphire.

Sapphire got up, poured another cup of tea, set it on the table and went upstairs.

"Why are we meeting?" asked Pearl.

"Dunno," said Beryl. "But I think Sapphire's annoyed at the lack of progress we're making."

"Aren't we all? The entire household is on edge."

Beryl stood and got out two mixing bowls, flour, butter and assorted things Pearl couldn't identify. Then began mixing things in the bowl.

Lucille, their beloved house, switched the oven on to heat it. Beryl rolled some dough out and began cutting it into triangles. She set them on a baking sheet and put the first one in the oven.

By then, Sapphire was back at the table with a notepad and pen. She scribbled down paragraph after paragraph and kept glancing at the stairs in irritation.

Marcea and Ginny, two shamans, came downstairs at the same time. They both poured mugs of tea for themselves and set to making breakfast without speaking.

Ginny began making another batch of dough with Beryl's instruction. Marcea rolled out and cut the last of the dough Beryl had made.

By the time Jet and Ruby came downstairs, the first batch of scones was out of the oven.

Pearl put two on a plate, split them, added butter and slathered each half with rose petal jam Beryl had made last summer. Then she poured herself a cup of the Irish breakfast tea with cream.

Nadya, a witch, and Anya, a witch and demonologist, entered the kitchen. Anya began making coffee. Nadya did some dishes while waiting for coffee.

"Let's go meet in the small dining room," said Sapphire. "That way people can eat in peace."

This was apparently a private meeting.

Pearl followed Sapphire and Beryl. Jet and Ruby were still filling their plates.

The small dining room held a table with five chairs. It looked out onto the back garden and was painted a spring-green color, both of which made it feel full of life. On the wall opposite a window hung a painting of a glowing path through the forest. As a child, Pearl had always wanted to go down that path.

Ruby and Jet came in and closed the door. After they sat down, Pearl bit into her scone. It had tiny lavender flowers and tart lemon zest. The rose petal jam added just the perfect amount of sweetness. A breath of summer vitality in the middle of winter.

Beryl always knew exactly what the household needed.

"Why are we meeting again?" asked Ruby.

"Can't you feel it?" asked Beryl. "The tension in the house is at a bursting point."

"And we're making no progress," said Sapphire. "It's been over two months and we still don't know where Ryan is. Or what he's up to. And Caorthannach probably hasn't been idle. You know she's called the mother of demons. She'd probably been birthing them nonstop."

"We've been trying to track down Ryan. But he's gone silent. No one knows where he is. He's left assistants fully in charge of all his businesses and completely vanished. There's only so much I can do trapped here," said Ruby.

"No one's blaming you," said Sapphire.

"But you are," said Ruby. She glared at Sapphire.

"She's blaming herself," said Beryl.

Ruby looked at Beryl, her face scrunched up in a question.

85

"Sapphire blames herself for not being able to subdue Caorthannach on Samhain. I thought you all knew that," said Beryl.

Jet nearly spat out her tea.

Ruby leaned back in her chair, as if considering that thought. "That's ridiculous. You know that, don't you? Kweera-what's-her-face was beyond all our understanding. I still can't pronounce her damn name."

"Queer-a-nock," repeated Beryl. "It's important to use her name correctly. If we don't respect her power, we can't deal with her properly."

Pearl had guessed that Sapphire blamed herself. It looked like Jet and Ruby hadn't.

"It's true," said Sapphire. "If Caorthannach was gone, everything would be different now."

"You don't know that," said Jet.

"Think about it. We'd only have Ryan to worry about. We wouldn't have a gazillion people living here. I might even still be at the firm."

Sapphire had taken leave from the legal firm that she loved and lived for. It hadn't been safe to be there anymore. Not with Caorthannach having destroyed Pearl and Willow's office where they did massage and bodywork and having burned Bera's van. Some of the other witches had been targeted as well.

Sapphire felt she was putting everyone else who worked at the legal firm at risk.

"Is that what this is about?" asked Jet. "Is this about your work?"

"No. It's about the quagmire we're in here. We're all stuck in our beloved house, trying to be safe. While our enemies are out there, preparing for battle and we have no idea where they are or what exactly they're up to. And we can't see where they'll move first," said Sapphire.

Just like Pearl had realized earlier that morning. They needed more information.

"All of us being trapped here is keeping us stuck. We need information that can't be gained through the internet or over the phone," said Pearl. "I can't believe I'm saying this, but someone needs to go back out in the world. Several someones. Aren't a couple of the demonologists trackers?"

There was silence. No one wanted to say it.

Finally, Jet said, "Bera is."

Bera was Jet's sweetheart. The two women had met just before Samhain and become friends, then lovers.

"We have to ask for volunteers," said Beryl. "No one can be forced to do this. And we'll also need to get people get inside his management team or whatever they call it. We know he's hands on with all his tech investments and that he oversees everything. We need someone close enough to him that we can find out his whereabouts."

"We tried that a couple of months ago," said Ruby. "Only one person in the inner circle of assistants knows where he is or when he'll check in next. And that guy, James Erickson, is unreachable. My team had a connection and got a friend of a friend, who wanted to help, hired on as an assistant to Erickson. The man's completely close-mouthed. Doesn't open up to anyone. Never has. He lives for his work and is absolutely loyal to Ryan."

"Do we know any hackers?" asked Sapphire. "Ryan seems like the kind of person to put everything on his phone. Or laptop, maybe. At least his schedule."

Ruby leaned back, obviously considering the idea.

Pearl sipped her strong tea, wishing she'd added more cream. The bitterness of a pot-too-long-brewed came through.

"I might," said Ruby. "Why haven't we thought of that before? He must be trackable online. By someone good enough. I'll ask around and get back to you on that."

Sapphire said, "If we're asking for volunteers to go back out in the world, we need to be clear on what they're doing and why. Ideas?"

"We need to track Ryan, in person," said Ruby.

"To locate Caorthannach and find out if her attacks are random or if there's a pattern. And if they can, find out what she's up to. Is she birthing more demons?" said Jet.

"Find out what Ryan's plans are," said Beryl. "Not his little plans, his ultimate plan."

"I'm not sure we'll find that out unless we've got him cornered and helpless. Maybe not even then," said Ruby. "But I will wipe his demented brain."

There was a strange thudding at the door.

Jet got up and opened it.

Pearl didn't see anyone there and then she saw the gray kitten race out from under the table on the far side and get stuck in the corner of the room. The big yellow guy growling at him. The kitten was hissing and spitting.

"Oliver, you've made your point. Thank you, now go back out and find a place to nap," said Beryl. "I'll deal with Hema."

Pearl wouldn't have wanted to be on the end of that glare Beryl gave the kitten.

Oliver looked at Beryl, then back at the kitten. Taking a half-hearted swipe at him, Oliver turned and stalked out of the room. His tail held high and twitching.

Jet closed the door leaving Hema in the corner. He began to bathe as if nothing was amiss.

She sat back down, looking unsettled.

Pearl knew Jet didn't want Bera to go back out in the world and put herself at risk. And Bera would volunteer. She wasn't doing too well cooped up. To deal with her restlessness, the demonologist had demanded to take a watch shift every single night with no days off.

"Anything else we want them to find out?" asked Sapphire. "We should call a meeting this afternoon."

"How are these people supposed to go about finding Caorthannach's whereabouts?" asked Pearl. "My understanding is that she's elsewhere and then blips into our reality when she attacks. Then poof, she's gone again."

"That's exactly what she does. But Anya says she's been able to sense the demon now that she's aware of her. The demonologists think it's possible to make a more concerted effort, perhaps with a few of the shamans, and find out what she's up to," said Sapphire.

Anya, a witch and demonologist, was one of Sapphire's closest friends.

"Is that safe?" asked Beryl.

"Maybe, maybe not. That's why she hasn't done it. But Anya and I have been talking and we both feel we need to get past being safe. It's not helping us find them. We can't prepare or act. We're just waiting for them to attack," said Sapphire.

"Let me do a reading this morning," said Beryl. "I want to mull this over before you begin asking for volunteers."

Sapphire said, "So how about we all go off and do what we need to. Ruby, you contact your hacker friends. Beryl will do a reading or talk to the spirits. Jet needs to talk to Bera. Pearl, you might want to go talk to the shamans and find out what happens if they get into trouble. How can we help them return from dangerous territory and recover? I'll spend some time talking with the demonologists. Then we'll have lunch together and meet with everyone after lunch."

"It's a plan," said Ruby.

Beryl picked up the kitten and said, "We're going to have a chat, my friend." Hema was squirming, trying to escape.

Pearl took Beryl's and her own dishes to the kitchen. There were about ten people in the room, which was a flurry of movement. Some putting scones on plates, others getting tea. Ginny was doing dishes and took the handful Pearl held, adding them to the pile.

"Thanks," said Pearl.

The large dining room was full of people. Pearl considered who to start with. There were six strong shamans in the house. Others were studying with them. She'd talk to those most likely to have pushed the boundaries. That meant Kasya, Anya and Tau. Anya was also a demonologist, so she was first.

Pearl wandered through the house but didn't see her. Finally, she climbed to the third floor where Anya's room was and knocked on the door. Hoping she wasn't too early.

Anya opened the door, her long brown and silver dreadlocks looking more askew than usual, although she was dressed.

"Did I wake you?" asked Pearl.

"No, I just haven't gotten fully presentable yet."

"I need to talk to you."

"Sure, come on in."

Lucille, their house, had managed to create a room that was larger on the inside than looked likely. It had space for ten of Anya's floor to ceiling bookcases, her double bed, a rust-colored couch, a matching overstuffed chair and a rather large table containing an altar.

Two throws sat on top of the upright couch cushions. Upon which lay a long-haired, black cat with lime-green eyes and a white cat with blue eyes. They glanced at Pearl and went back to sleep.

"Have a seat," said Anya, gesturing to the chair. "Carbon and Cream are perfectly contented staying in my room. They venture downstairs to eat but don't like it. Too many dogs and other cats. And that kitten.... No matter how often Beryl tells them they're safe, they feel better in here. Among all their things and with that kitten on the other side of the door."

Pearl sat down in the chair, which felt more comfortable than it looked. Anya sat on the couch between her cats.

"We're talking about changing some things. About asking some people to go out in the world so we can get more information. I know Sapphire and you have talked about it."

Anya nodded.

"I'm trying to talk to those of you who might have wandered closer to the darkness while in other realities. So I can begin to create a plan to help you with returning or support you when you get back. Since I've never done this, I need input. I'm assuming you're one of those shamans. And if you know of anyone else, let me know so I can talk to them too."

"I understand. Well first, no one should go off searching for demons without a lot of solid experience behind them. I do the same things to return as I normally would. I intend to return to my body. No matter how distracted I am, there's that intent. And when I'm back, I ground myself in the physical. If I'm drumming, I stop. Or turn it off, if it's a recording. I drink water. Stretch my body and do whatever it takes to feel fully present again. But I'm older. I've been doing this for decades. If I've gone to a really dark and disturbing place, I try to go outside. Smell the fresh air or feel the rain. I do what's necessary to distance myself from the evil I might have encountered. You know, really, this should be a discussion. Can we find Tau and Kasya? And Raven Blue? I think you'd learn more from all of us talking. I might remember something I've forgotten."

"That works," said Pearl.

"Let's find them and go talk," said Anya. She stood and grabbed a scarf off her dresser, tying the dreadlocks into a bundle.

They went out the door and across the hallway to Kasya's room. Anya knocked.

Kasya answered and Anya explained.

"Okay, let's go to Raven Blue's room. They've got a large enough space for all of us. I'll go hunt down Tau," said Kasya, shrugging on a flannel shirt over her green t-shirt and jeans.

"Yeah, like that'll be a challenge," said Anya. She turned to Pearl. "If Tau's not on watch or sleeping, he can be found in the kitchen or dining room—eating. For both him and Coal, the way to their hearts is through their stomachs."

Anya and Pearl walked down the hallway to Raven Blue's room. They answered the door and Anya explained.

"Great, come on in," they said.

The room was decorated in elaborate large batik banners. The colors were bright in the crisp sunlight that streamed in through large windows. Raven Blue's dog, Jennet, a tan Rhodesian Ridgeback, lay curled up on a pillow but wagged its tail at them. Pearl remembered the dog was now a senior.

Pearl went over to Jennet and let the dog smell her hand. The tail continued wagging and she petted the dog.

They all sat down on folding chairs Raven Blue pulled out of the closet. Jennet finally got up and went to sit by Raven Blue, who fondled the dog's ears.

It wasn't long before Kasya, Tau and Coal joined them. Coal went around the circle and nuzzled everyone, along with Jennet, who seemed fully revived by his presence.

The two dogs, who'd become fast friends since everyone moved into the house, curled up together in a patch of sunlight and went to sleep. Tau sat holding a plate and eating a scone. His fourth, he said.

"I'm relieved we're finally going to do something," said Raven Blue.

"It's time," said Kasya.

"We've only got an hour," said Anya. "Let's go around the circle and tell Pearl what we do to return and afterwards, when we've encountered something disturbing in a journey. Who wants to begin?"

"I'll go," said Kasya. "I don't intentionally seek out disturbing beings when I journey. But one time, I was helping a friend of a friend. He was besieged by nightmares and waking visions. Really dark stuff. I didn't know if I could help him but I did a journey, with him present. I had all my guides and protectors with me. We removed something really dark and ugly from his energy field. My guides destroyed it. I did some healing on him afterward—filling that hole in his field with light and love. Afterwards, I had a hard time. I came back to myself like normal but felt really drained. As if I'd been training for a marathon or something. It took me a couple of weeks of strong self-care to get to feeling normal again. I didn't journey for months after that. I know now that I was psychically drained but I was younger back then. New at journeying. I should have asked for more help for my guides. Should have journeyed for myself that evening. For my own healing."

"So how could the Healing Team support you if you did such a thing again?" asked Pearl.

"I'm guessing, the sort of thing you all were doing at Samhain and at the move-in here. You cleaned our energy fields. Made sure nothing attached to any of us. Filled us with peace and light and love. You guys are amazing."

"Thank you," said Pearl.

Raven Blue spoke next. She crossed her leg, foot on knee and retied a running shoe.

"I've done a few healing journeys for people. Many of them into dark places. I've dealt with demons before although not any as powerful as Caorthannach. But ones as strong as the two we dispatched at Samhain. Like Kasya, I didn't really have trouble coming back. It was the aftermath that totaled me. I didn't have the energy to journey for myself, even though I knew that would be the best thing for me to do. And I didn't know any healers like you, Pearl. I didn't even know any other shamans. I thought what I did was unique."

Raven Blue laughed and Jennet looked up at her and then went back to sleep.

"I think what I'd need most would be healing. I've always been strong enough to come back on my own. Anyway, I'm done."

Anya said, "I already told Pearl my issues, before we decided to have a discussion about it. Pretty much what you two said. So you're next Tau."

Tau had finished eating but still held the empty plate.

"I've dealt with some really evil stuff. A lot of guys feel comfortable coming to me as clients. Guys who've been to dark places people shouldn't go. I've had to peel off some really ugly entities from them. I've also had trouble coming back after some of those journeys. Coal helps if he's around, which he nearly always is. He'll lick my face if I can call his name. Once he was at the vet for surgery though. It was a real struggle to return. The demon who had hold of me wouldn't let go. I panicked. When I finally had the wherewithal to ask one of my guides for help, he took care of the demon for me. Was just waiting for me to ask. A painful lesson there."

The big man shuddered and said, "And like all of you, once I get back from a journey like that, I really need to ground. Coal helps with that too. And eating helps. There's always eating." He grinned. "I also had to take some time off from journeying until I felt renewed. Once I was going out with another shaman and she helped me a lot after a really dark journey. But the relationship didn't last. Mostly, I just depend on my guides and Coal."

Upon hearing his name, Coal rolled over and groaned.

"Go back to sleep, buddy," said Tau.

"So all of you need support afterwards but not so much with returning. Although we should keep that in mind in case someone gets in trouble. Because we're stalking a very powerful demon. Have I got that right?" asked Pearl.

They nodded.

"Okay, I'll relay this to my sisters and the Healing Team."

"So are we really going after the demon?" asked Tau.

"We need to find out what she's up to," said Pearl. "We're not entirely sure yet though. We'll be meeting for lunch. Which is soon. But if we do, it will be volunteers only. No one will be forced into doing this. And we'll probably have a meeting this afternoon."

"I might be sleeping by then, but I volunteer in advance," said Tau.

"Okay, got it."

"Me too," said Kasya.

"Same," said Raven Blue.

"You know I'm in. I've been thinking a lot about this," said Anya.

"All right. I'll let my sisters know what we talked about. I'd better get going. And thank you, all of you. If you think of anything else, let me know."

CHAPTER 2

LINDA JORDAN

PEARL SAT AT THE FAR END THE LARGE DINING ROOM, AWAY FROM the door. The walls had turned an unpleasant burnt-orange color since breakfast. It felt heavy and dark. Foreboding.

Lucille didn't normally make this sort of direct statement but the house was responding to Beryl. Who sat on one side of Pearl. Knitting manically.

Pearl knew her sister was trying to keep it together. The click, click, click of the knitting needles made a staccato sound which unnerved Pearl even more.

The furious energy roiling around Beryl mingled with that of the rest of the room. Fear. Dread. Fury.

Pearl closed her eyes and breathed deeply. Pulling up energy from the earth below. Grounding herself.

Finally, she got up, went into the kitchen, took a candle off the windowsill and grabbed some matches. Ruby would be able to light it without them. But this was Pearl's offering to the meeting. She grabbed a smudge stick and plate as an afterthought.

She returned to the dining room and set the candle in the center. She lit it with a match and then dipped the stick of sage into the flame until it began to smoke. Pearl walked around the room, which had fallen quiet. Even Beryl's needles stopped.

Pearl called the directions in her head, since this wasn't a ritual. Just an informal meeting. She banished the fury and fear as much as possible. By the time she ground out the sage onto the plate and sat down, the room felt more calm.

Beryl touched her arm and said, "Thank you."

Pearl smiled.

Sapphire sat scribbling on a notepad. Jet's face looked closed. She wasn't letting any emotion show, although her body looked rigid. Determined. Bera was absent, probably sleeping in preparation for watch tonight.

Everyone who was awake had crowded in, maybe nineteen humans. Anxiety and excitement still filled the air. Some people were eating lunch, a few had breakfast on their plates.

The room felt stuffy and closed. Too many people. Pearl wanted to get out the door and go be alone.

The room was almost silent. No one spoke. Not even in hushed tones. They were all sensitive enough to catch the vibe. The only sound was Beryl's click, clack.

The smell of the people's chili nauseated her. Even though she'd had it for lunch. Pearl's stomach still felt twisted in knots of dread and fear. She couldn't even breathe her way through it. But kept trying. One slow long breath after each exhale. Her eyes closed. Waiting.

Ruby sat on the other side of Pearl and tapped her long fingernails on the table. Anxious and full of righteous fury. Her sister was a fireball, ready to explode.

Pearl felt unsettled from the divisive lunchtime discussion with her sisters. Unable to pull herself together. Vulnerable.

They'd argued for about half an hour, which hadn't helped her digestion. She should have made some mint tea to drink at this meeting.

Ruby's hacker friend knew someone who could probably get into Ryan's phone. For a price. Ruby had given the okay and was sending the money.

Jet had talked to Bera and although Jet wasn't happy about it, had conceded that they needed to do something. She voted for moving forward.

Sapphire outlined a strategy and a plan to track Caorthannach. To find out where she went and make sure she wasn't birthing baby demons. Although what they could do about it if she was, Pearl had no idea.

The three of them were solidly in the taking-action camp.

Beryl wasn't.

Her reading had been disturbing. Defeat and struggles would come out of the plans as they were now.

Pearl knew better than to go against Beryl's intuition. They didn't have the right plan yet. Acting now would just muck things up.

But the vote had been three against two.

Sapphire glanced at her watch and said, "Let's begin. I don't want to waste anyone's time. We've been holed up here since the beginning of November. Two and a half months. Just waiting for another attack. And we've had no solid plan other than staying safe."

She continued, "In the meantime, Ryan is growing stronger and probably working on his next move—whatever that will be. We have no idea what the demon is doing. All we can do is react. We need to take action. Control this story and the outcome. Here's what's going to happen.

"This is volunteer only. Several demonologists and shamans are going to track the demon. I'll post a schedule so they aren't interrupted, once we've decided where they'll be. Pearl's Team will stand by in case anyone needs help upon returning from their journey. We also believe we've found a hacker who can crack Ryan's cell and laptop, although we don't know what kind of information that will give us. Once we have a location of either the demon or Ryan, we may be sending people out into the physical world. Again, this will be volunteers. Jet will be rearranging the staffing for watches as needed. I know we'll need more people on nights as some of those folks have already volunteered. They'll be spending their time either journeying or going out in the world. Does anyone have any questions?"

Willow held up her hand. She was one of Pearl's dearest friends. They'd met way back in massage school and been fast friends ever since, despite their age difference. They'd shared the same bodywork office before the demon had set it afire. Willow was in her sixties, one of their elders.

Willow said, "I understand you're all restless. But we used so much time and effort to get us all here to safety, are you really sure there's no other way to do this than to go back out? Have we exhausted all other options? Life is short, let's not spend any of it thoughtlessly."

There was a rush of people talking all at once.

Sapphire held up her hand. "One at a time, please."

"I'm ready to fight them," said Jamilla, who was a Capoeira teacher on Ruby's team.

"I would like to volunteer for tracking down the demon," said Karl. He was a witch and shaman on Sapphire's team.

"I agree with Willow," said Maria.

She and Gabe, her partner were also elders. Pearl nodded in agreement with her.

"We're open to other plans," said Sapphire. "But we've been here for months and haven't found another one. Regardless of what we come up with, we're going forward with the journeying and the hacking plan. After that we'll see. We might find a way out of this without leaving Lucille but right now, it doesn't look likely."

Beryl continued to knit. She made eye contact with no one.`

"So you're pulling rank on us," Willow said to Sapphire.

"Yes. But only because all of us have been arguing back and forth for months and getting nowhere. If we continue to sit and react, we give away our power," said Sapphire. "Somebody had to make a decision, so I chose the five of us to vote."

Jet said, "Somebody had to do it. Sapphire's right. We can no longer sit and wait."

"There are some of us who would have simply gone out on our own," said Ruby. "I can't sit still any longer. I need to go out and find that bastard before he does more harm to the world."

Willow gave a deep sigh.

"I still think it's not the best course of action but you're right. We don't have another plan. Since the five of you, who've so graciously opened your home and your lives to us and supported us in so many ways, have voted to do this, I'll go along with it. I agree—it's better to take conscious action than to react. I'll help in whatever way I can. And I'll continue to ponder other plans."

"As we all should," said Gabe.

Most of the people around the table nodded.

Sapphire said, "I'll pass around a sheet of paper. There are tasks to volunteer for. Some are support and involve helping those going out—either shamanically or physically—but you would not be leaving the property. If you don't want to volunteer, that's fine. There will be plenty to do around here. Watch shifts to be filled. Assisting in the kitchen or garden. Thank you."

Pearl felt a small relief that something had been settled. All she could do now was help.

The uncertainty in the room had shifted as the meeting had progressed. Lucille's walls had faded somewhat and although they weren't back to the normal light peach tone, they weren't as burnt as before.

Beryl had stopped knitting and was talking to Willow. Pearl glanced down the table. June and Mariah, two other healers on her team, were looking at her. Asking silently for some sort of guidance.

She smiled at them. Then mouthed a silent, "We'll meet later."

They nodded in reply. She'd talk to Ben, Johann and Sarah as well. Set up a meeting on how they could best assist those journeying. Right now, she just didn't have the mental energy.

It was going to take a good long while to unwind from that ugly lunch.

Willow smiled at her, probably understanding Pearl needed some time before talking about things. Pearl stood and went over to the candle, blowing it out.

People began to filter out of the room, taking their dishes and belongings. Tau stood up as Pearl went past him.

"How are you doing?" he asked.

"Good, I'm good. I thought you'd be sleeping."

"Couldn't sleep. But no, I mean really, how are you doing? You take care of everyone else. Who takes care of you?"

He patted the empty chair beside him, inviting her to sit.

She sighed.

"I do have friends. And sisters, who take care of me."

"But you're not happy at all about this. Why?"

"I don't think it's safe. I agree with Willow. We spent so much time and energy just trying to get everyone here...."

"But journeying isn't strictly leaving."

"No, but Bera and the others going out and hunting demons is."

"That's stage two. It may not even come to that if journeying gives us the information we need. And if the hacking works."

"You're right. It might not. But I'm worried about the journeying. Who knows what that will stir up?"

"I don't know. But I've made hundreds of journeys. I'm not afraid to try this. In hopes we gain enough information to make a difference," he said, touching her hand.

She felt his skin on hers and fought not to pull away. It was so intimate. And there was no time for that right now.

She should be doing...something. Frustration rose up inside her.

That was it, really.

Sapphire was running meetings and planning. Jet was patrolling the boundaries and organizing the security team. Ruby was gathering information and plotting. Beryl was running the household and keeping everything and everyone stable. And Pearl had been left with precious little to do once everyone was moved in. She'd just been pitching in to help wherever needed. Without a plan.

And she needed to be working. Her practice had closed right after the fire. She'd been doing some bodywork on a couple of people who were having health problems. Mostly people didn't ask and she didn't volunteer. Her energy felt stuck, despite all the time spent in meditation and yoga.

She said, "Okay. I'm relieved that you're not afraid. My issues are about my own shit. I need to figure it out by myself."

Tau hesitated, then said, "I get that. But please let me know if I can help in any way. You would do the same for me or anyone else here."

Pearl nodded.

CHAPTER 3

LINDA JORDAN

AFTER THE MEETING FINALLY BROKE UP, PEARL RETREATED TO HER room to meditate. Everything still felt wrong.

Even Lucille felt off. The day continued on with things going awry.

The water heater quit working. Their regular plumber was called. He dropped by, checked things out and promised to bring a new water heater the next day.

Then the dryer wouldn't start so the two people on laundry duty strung up rope, crisscrossing the basement room. Then draped clothes over it because the clothespins couldn't be located. Folks would just have to wait to get more laundry done until the first load was dried.

When the stove wouldn't heat up, Pearl came upon Beryl. Her sister stood in the corner of the deserted kitchen, weeping.

"Okay, this isn't going to work," said Pearl. "What's going on?"

"I have such a feeling of dread," said Beryl, wiping her face with the back of her hand. "I've tried to release it, let it go. But the sense of it is overpowering. It keeps flooding back in."

"Let's get our coats and go outside." She needed to move Beryl out of the house and into the fresh air.

"I need to get this in the oven. But it's not working." She gestured to the waiting rounds of bread dough, laid out on baking sheets.

"Let's just leave it to Lucille, shall we? Put the bread in the oven. Then we can go out. You need a break and to talk."

Beryl took a deep breath and nodded.

They got their coats and on the way out the back door, Pearl said, "Lucille will you please sort this all out. We need you to function and the oven to work. I'll take care of Beryl."

Lucille didn't reply.

Outside, the light was dimming in the overcast sky. It would be dark in an hour or two. At least the days were getting longer, even if the progression seemed glacial.

The cold air bit into any exposed skin while they walked past the mostly dormant vegetable beds. A couple rows of garlic still grew in one bed. Mustard greens, kale and chard took up the end of another.

Pearl sank her power into the earth, drawing up some extra energy. Feeling it flow through her body. Making her feel fully alive again.

"This is better," said Beryl. "I wish it wasn't so cold out but that's winter for you. I'm ready for spring. All of us crammed into Lucille. I can barely breathe sometimes."

"I feel the same way. Jet must be feeling it too. Maybe that's why she takes the night shift so often. Or maybe that's how she spends time with Bera. It feels like there's less energy around at night. It's overwhelming and I know Lucille masks it for us."

"Sometimes I feel like my whole world is about to explode," said Beryl.

"You're more sensitive than the rest of us," said Pearl.

"That makes no sense. You're the healer."

"But you're our seer. You're more sensitive to the unseen than I am. I'm in communication with what I touch. I sense energy from the person I'm working on. The one I'm focusing my attention on. You pick up energy wafting through the aether and everywhere else."

"I guess I do," said Beryl. "But I know you do too."

She stopped to pick off some dead leaves still clinging to a thornless blackberry cane, letting the cold breeze take them away.

"But what if I'm right?" asked Beryl. "What if we fail?"

"Well, what's the worst that can happen? Ryan succeeds in whatever his plans are. He uses demons to take over the world. Or at least this part of the world. Or they use him. I can't see Caorthannach being under his control. Can you?"

"No. She's too powerful."

"So they'll fight. He'll be destroyed or thwarted somehow. We'll need to stay out of the crossfire.

"But what if we can't?" asked Beryl, her face wrinkled with worry.

"Well, the worst that could happen, that I can think of, is that we all die. In the pursuit of doing the right thing. Doing the thing that many people can't. We won't care, we'll be gone."

"It would be worse if some of us died, leaving the others to grieve," said Beryl, quietly.

Yes, that would be worse. So we need to be the ones to win, don't we?" asked Pearl. "We'll need to incapacitate the demon and Ryan. Plus any other demons they've brought into our world. There's no other way."

"I guess you're right. But something's wrong. Inside Lucille, I just don't have any clarity. I can't seem to figure things out. It's like brain fog but on a psychic level."

"I've felt it too," said Pearl. "I think it's time to begin working on the spring garden, don't you? Isn't there some pruning to be done? Or turning the compost or something outside?"

"I guess I should be spending more time outside. Maybe it would help me get clear on what the problem is. Thank you. I'll ask some of the others to take over cooking for a couple of weeks."

The last meeting of the day passed in a flash. Pearl sat with the other healers, Willow, June and her golden retriever, Maybelle. Mariah, Ben, Johanna and Sarah were there too. They sat in the large meditation room, on pillows in a circle. The pale-peach colored room felt comforting, even if there was a chill in the air and the hardwood floor felt cool beneath Pearl's feet.

They discussed ways to help the shamans. Both Mariah and

Johanna had done shamanic journeying and had helpful things to add.

They all seemed uneasy with what the shamans were intending to do.

"I don't think there's any way around it," said Willow. "They're clear that they think it's the next step. We've voiced our objections. All we can do now is support them as best we can."

After the meeting, Pearl decided to go for another walk in the garden. This time it was raining.

She found a secluded section behind the evergreens and stood in the cold pouring wetness, letting it wash her face. Feeling like it cleansed away her frustration and dread, Pearl breathed deeply and on her exhale released as much negativity as possible. After several minutes of doing it, she felt clearer.

It was moving towards dusk. Dinner would follow shortly after, provided the stove was working. As she walked, Pearl stopped at the orange-flowered witch hazel and sniffed. Between the rain and the cold, the fading blooms had no scent left. It had been flowering since November.

The yellow-flowered one was about to burst into bloom. Something to look forward to.

THE NEXT MORNING, PEARL DRAGGED HERSELF OUT OF BED AND looked out the window. More rain. Another dark day. Maybe she needed to get out into the garden too. It was lighter outside. Even with the extra vitamin D, the lack of sun was getting to her. She normally woke full of excitement for the day ahead. Not this winter.

She quickly dressed in gray leggings, a long-sleeved spring-green t-shirt and thick wool socks, then went downstairs, skipping her usual morning meditation.

Lucille felt unsettled. Doors banging and windows rattling. Something was wrong and Pearl needed to see what it was.

The kitchen was empty. Was no one else up?

The wrongness came from beneath her. The basement. Either the laundry, storage or the library.

Pearl grabbed the poker from the living room fireplace and went down the stairs. An enormous amount of power was leaking from the small storage room. She doubted the poker would help but gripped it anyway.

Whatever it was, she couldn't let it escape. Pearl grounded herself and pulled in all her energy, forming an aura of immense power to surround herself.

Footsteps coming down the stairs startled her.

Jet. Equally as protected.

"On three," said Pearl. "We can't let it out."

She gripped the doorknob.

"One...two...three," said Jet, quietly.

Pearl flung open the door. They were in. Lucille slammed the door behind them, locking them inside. The room had no windows, no other way out.

In the middle of the room stood Beryl. Glaring at Hema who sat on an old table. He returned Beryl's withering stare, his tail lashing.

"What's going on?" asked Pearl.

"Look at him. He's not normal," said Beryl, not taking her eyes off the kitten. A slash across her cheek dripped blood.

"He's just a kitten," said Jet.

Beryl would never hurt a kitten. But she had murder in her eyes. What was going on?

Pearl lay the poker on a shelf. Then loosened her boundaries somewhat and let her energy move out towards the kitten. She felt wild kitten energy but there was something else. Something darker.

Trying to isolate it, only made the power squirm away. It dove deeper into the kitten's energy. Trying to hide.

Pearl followed it and grabbed hold. It felt slimy and gruesome. She kept hold of that ugliness, slowly reeling it out of the kitten. A huge amount of power had been cloaked in that tiny body. She felt Jet and Beryl containing what she extracted.

Pearl kept pulling. The thing was snakelike—long and skinny. It had sunk its fangs into the kitten and wouldn't let go. Hema mewed in distress and lay panting on the table.

Beryl used her power and whomped on a section of the thing that she and Jet held. It gasped. Its teeth released their hold on the kitten.

Pearl yanked the rest of it out of Hema. Beryl and Jet had rolled the energy into a ball. Then tied it with their energy.

The kitten collapsed onto the table. Panting. Pearl went to him. Stroking the silvery-gray fur gently to reassure him. He felt clear of that evil thing but nearly drained.

There was pounding at the door.

Ruby yelled, "What's going on?"

Pearl felt Sapphire's energy outside the door, too.

"Have you got this?" asked Pearl, glancing at Jet.

"Yes."

Lucille opened the door.

Her sisters would destroy whatever the hell that was.

Pearl picked up Hema and cradled him. He didn't struggle but he shivered uncontrollably. She went out the door into the main laundry room.

Grabbing a dry towel off a pile of folded laundry, Pearl wrapped him in it and then went into the warm library, closing the door behind her.

"Lucille, fire in the fireplace please."

Lucille lit a blazing fire which warmed the room even more.

Sitting in a leather chair in front of the fire, with Hema on her lap, Pearl grounded herself deeply and pulled up power from the earth. Then drew light down from the sky. She melded them together and filled the kitten with that energy. Poor thing had plenty of empty holes to fill. Holes that creature had used to hide.

After a time, Hema began to quietly purr, then curled up and went to sleep. Pearl continued to work on him for another half hour. Until she felt satisfied he was stable and full of healing energy.

She sat and gazed at the books surrounding her. Old and new. The library smelled good. Lucille kept it warm, clean and just the right humidity for the books to be perfectly happy.

The library felt safe. A safe enough place to contemplate what that thing had been.

Was it a demon? Not a fire demon but something else. And where had it come from?

Eventually, her sisters came in. Worry filled their faces. They pulled up leather chairs to form a circle.

"What was that?" asked Pearl.

"A demon," said Sapphire.

"Is it gone?"

"We destroyed it. With Lucille's help," said Jet.

"But how did it get in?"

"I think it came in with Hema," said Beryl. "He's been troublesome since the start. Whenever I talked to him, things felt off. I couldn't figure out why. Then this morning, I was in the kitchen and he wouldn't stop fighting with Anya's cats. They hate other cats but we've had conversations and the two of them would never retaliate against a kitten. Hema wouldn't leave them alone. Had them backed into a corner. So, I picked him up by the scruff of his neck and brought him down here. To have one final chat before I tossed him to an animal shelter. And he attacked me. That's when you came in."

"I felt the darkness inside him," said Pearl. "But none of us felt it in him when he came."

"Did anyone examine him? The way we've done with every single delivery or repair person who's come in? Or the vet?" asked Sapphire.

"I didn't," said Jet.

Ruby shook her head.

"I didn't. I had a talk with him about behavior. Knowing I'd need to have it more than once because he's a kitten," said Beryl.

"I didn't either," said Pearl. "He was a kitten. I never thought...."

"From now on, any living being that passes our borders, human, mammal, bird, fish or insect gets examined. Got that Lucille?" said Jet.

Air moved through the library, pushed by the fan switching onto high. Then off again. Lucille understood.

"Will he be okay?" asked Beryl.

"I think so. He'll be depleted for a while. That demon stole a lot of energy from him. I've done what I can for now. He needs to sleep peacefully. I'll take him up to my room."

They left the library and went upstairs. Pearl carried Hema up to her room. Setting him on the bed in a valley between two pillows. He stretched slightly but didn't wake.

Beatrice got up from the windowsill and jumped on the bed. Pearl petted the long-haired cat who walked back and forth beneath her hand. Then Beatrice went over to Hema, sniffed the kitten and began bathing him. Finally, she curled up next to him. Obviously satisfied with her work. Pearl pulled a blanket over the top of them to add a little heat.

Then closed her door and went downstairs to the kitchen. Lucille would open it if they needed out.

Pearl felt wide-awake but poured a cup of tea out of habit. Several people were in the kitchen making breakfast.

Beryl sat at the table drinking her own tea.

"I feel clearer now," she said. "I think it was the demon, clouding my brain. But I will go out and spend some time in the garden today. Get started on pruning the fruit trees and vines."

"Good," said Pearl, sitting down.

Breakfast smelled good. Maria had made quiche of some sort and the scent of it cooking made Pearl's mouth water.

"What are you doing today?"

"After breakfast, I'm going to sit in on Tau's journeying. Willow and I are his support team. And Coal, of course."

Beryl gave a deep sigh.

"I sure hope this works. I hope something works."

"Me too."

Ruby came in from the living room, sliding a phone into the back pocket of her jeans.

"Okay, I just talked to Connor, the hacker. He's sure he can get us the info we're looking for and is excited to do the job. I sent him a down payment. He expects the rest on delivery of the info."

"Wonderful," said Sapphire, who'd followed her in. "This is going to get things rolling."

Ruby headed towards the plates. The first quiches had just been pulled from the oven.

"I'm starving," said Pearl. "Shall we?"

Beryl said, "Yes, it's been an eventful morning."

They took their food into the large meeting room. Others were coming down the stairs, awakened by the smell of cooking food.

It wasn't long before the table was filled with people. The only sound was the clanking of silver against china. The wrongness Pearl had felt earlier that morning was completely gone. Instead, she felt contentment and harmony.

Everything was working the way it should. The oven, the water heater, the plumbing. Lucille was happy. Her residents moving about their day in peace. None of the humans or animals seemed to be having problems with each other.

How long had it been since things had run this smoothly? Maybe since Solstice. Certainly before Hema's arrival, with the demon.

Of course, the peace was just momentary. They were about to start rocking the boat by journeying to find Caorthannach. And hacking into Ryan's tech. Who knows what all that would uncover?

Tau came into the room and took the last chair, at the far end of the table. He only had one piece of quiche on his plate but ate it quickly. Instead of coffee or tea, he had a glass of water. Pearl grinned at him. He grinned and then set into devouring the mushroom cheddar quiche.

Willow was nowhere to be seen. She often spent mornings in meditation, Pearl knew. She kept an electric kettle and a large assortment of teas in her room and rarely bothered with eating breakfast. She'd meet them when it was time.

Pearl drained the last of her black tea. It felt cold now.

She glanced at the clock on the wall. Nearly time.

Standing, she picked up her dishes and took them to the kitchen. Marcea, the shaman, took them from her and added them to the pile to be washed. Then continued making another pot of tea.

"Thanks," said Pearl.

"You're welcome. The energy in the house has shifted hasn't it? It feels positive. Like we're actually doing something."

"Yes."

Pearl realized they needed to make an announcement to everyone about the demon they'd dealt with. People needed to know what to watch out for. Later. She'd make sure Sapphire added it to the list of things for the next meeting.

She climbed the stairs and went to her room. Opened the door to peace. Beatrice and Hema were still curled up sleeping. She petted both of them and went over to the Meditation Room, where most of the journeys would be happening.

Sapphire had posted a schedule on the outside of the door for everyone to see, so people would know to be quiet in the center hallway. Even though many shamans journeyed to drumming, which would drown out any ambient noise.

Pearl went inside and stood looking out the window. Rain poured down, only adding to the grayness. She could barely make out Puget Sound and the Olympic Mountains were hidden completely. Winter, ugh.

She sighed and began feeling her way into the rain. Feeling its moisture water the soil and hydrate the plants. She felt the evergreen leaves and needles sleeting the sprinkles towards the roots, so it could be taken up and used. She breathed in the moist air which surrounded her.

"Goddess thank you for the rain that nourishes all of us."

Pearl began doing some stretching exercises to warm up some. Bending to touch her toes, holding the stretch. Then stretching to the side and holding it. Breathing deeply. Coming fully into her body.

The door opened and Willow came inside.

"Oh, good morning. I thought I'd be the first to get here."

Outside, Pearl heard the clicking of dog toenails and thudding toes on the stairs, as a canine raced up them. The door opened again and Tau stuck his head in.

"You're here. I just need to get a couple things and I'll be ready."

Coal pushed past him and came in to say hello to them.

"No hurry. There's time," said Willow.

A few minutes later, he returned with a blanket and a drum.

"Shall we begin?" said Willow.

CHAPTER 4

LINDA JORDAN

PEARL SAT CROSS-LEGGED ON A LARGE PILLOW STREWN ON THE hardwood floor. The slick wood felt cool to her bare feet.

Willow sat on the floor, her long legs stretched out in front. She reached down, grabbed her ankles and held the position. Pearl hoped to be half as limber when she made it to her sixties.

Tau spread out a plaid wool blanket, then handed Pearl his drum and the drumstick. He lay down on the blanket and Coal took his place beside the tall man.

"Do you need us to light a candle, close the curtains, anything?" asked Willow.

"Nope. I smudged myself and I'm ready. Just drumming, a slow methodical heartbeat, is all I need. It's a blessing to have someone drum for me. Usually it's either me drumming and journeying, or I use a recording. If I have problems coming back then drum a little faster. Maybe some energy work. Whatever your gut tells you to do. Coal will know if I'm having problems. It's really rare though."

"How long?" asked Willow.

"No idea. Ten minutes. Maybe twenty. Maybe half an hour. When Coal gets restless, it's time to drum faster. It might take me just a few minutes after that. I'll move my hand if I need more time but you can stop drumming."

Pearl held the handmade drum by the sinew on the backside, resting the wood circle on her thigh. She began to hit the drum with the wood-handled beater, matching the rhythm of a heartbeat.

"Louder would be good," said Tau. "Drown out the sounds of traffic and planes."

Pearl hit the drum harder, watching him.

Tau's eyes were closed and his breathing rhythmical. Matching the drumbeat. He really was a gorgeous guy with those prominent cheekbones and sensual lips.

Pearl shook her head to clear it. She needed to focus on holding space.

Coal lay with his head on outstretched paws. Watching Tau. And waiting.

Pearl lost herself in the rolling sound of the drum. She could feel Willow doing energy work, although wasn't exactly sure what the purpose was. Protection for the room maybe. Whatever it was, Willow was running a lot of power.

Tau lay completely still. No movement other than the breathing. His face blank. His energy felt—gone. Possibly so deep inside as to be unreachable. Or perhaps he really had left his body and the room entirely.

Five minutes passed on the small clock on the corner table. Then ten. Pearl's arm felt tired. Rubbery. She kept on drumming. Keeping the beat steady.

Coal just watched Tau intently.

The drumming made Pearl even warmer. No shoes and socks had been a good idea. She shifted position and put her feet flat on the cool wood floor, resting the drum on the pillow beneath her. Never missing a beat. Another ten minutes passed.

Coal raised his head but stayed motionless, his eyes intent on Tau. Was that a signal?

Pearl kept drumming. Her right arm felt completely exhausted. She straightened her legs and shifted the drum back to her thigh.

Coal stood up and went to sit at Tau's head.

Pearl switched the drum and the beater between hands and began drumming faster. A signal to return. She felt Willow's energy shift as well. It felt stronger.

Tau's breathing became more rapid. As if he were running.

Pearl caught a whiff of smoke but kept pounding on the drum, feeling the echo in her bones.

Coal stood beside Tau's head now. Anxiously waiting.

Five minutes of fast drumming went by.

Coal began licking Tau's face. And alternately whining and barking. Tau's hand twitched.

Pearl stopped drumming and set it down on the floor, laying the beater on top. She closed her eyes, dropped her arms to her sides to let them relax. Then tried to sense Tau's energy. It felt nearby but unreachable.

The room had fallen silent except for the traffic in the street below. Coal was still licking Tau's face.

The energy felt off. Pearl could feel Willow and a very worried Coal, but not Tau.

Then, there was something else. Powerful and huge. Pearl threw up a shield and that power battered against it.

She felt Lucille add her energy to the shield. And Anya, then Jet, followed by several others in the household.

Through it all, she sensed Willow dragging Tau back to his body. He sat up, gasping.

At that moment, Anya slammed an energetic door closed and the world felt almost normal again. Pearl let her senses wander. Seeking any leaks.

Finding none, she opened her eyes. Tau sat spread-legged, his arms wrapped around Coal, face buried in the dog's short coat. Willow was on her feet, her hands on his shoulders. Helping him ground.

Pearl stood up and looked out the window. Trying to calm herself. Everything looked normal. It was raining and cold. And getting dark, although it had looked dark all day.

"How are you feeling?" asked Willow.

"That was one helluva journey," said Tau.

There were steps on the stairs and a knock at the door.

"Can we come in?" asked Anya.

Tau nodded.

"Come in," said Pearl.

The door opened to admit Anya, Jet and Sapphire.

"What happened?" said Anya, handing Tau a glass of water and a plate with three chocolate chip cookies.

Tau gave a deep sigh. He drank most of the water, then set the glass and plate on a nearby table. And ate half a cookie in one bite.

"Okay, well, I asked my guides to take me to where Caorthannach lives. Or hides. It was deep inside a mountain. A volcano, not currently active. I hid and asked them to tell me about her. What was she doing there? Is that where she stays all the time?"

He ate the other half of the cookie. Coal, who'd been looking longingly at it, lay down in resignation. His head on Tau's knee.

"They said she moves around a lot but this was her...most treasured place. Her real home. She had given birth to her babies there. Other demons. She was safe there. And gestating. Ready to give birth to more."

"Crap," said Jet.

"I asked if there was a way to destroy her. Before she gave birth. Or to make it so she couldn't leave that place ever again. And then she must have sensed me, before I could get an answer. I fled and she wrapped tentacles of fire around my legs, trying to hold me. I could feel Willow and Coal pulling me back. And my guides pulling me. Then I felt Pearl throw up a massive shield and I knew what side of it I needed to be on. I bit those fiery tentacles and sliced them off. Then came back as fast as I could."

"Wow," said Anya. "I did a journey this morning. My guides couldn't find her. Knew nothing about any fire demons."

"It was terrifying to be in her presence," said Tau, quietly. He closed his eyes and took a deep breath. Then opened them and reached for another cookie.

Pearl said, "I smelled smoke near the end of your journey. But we lit no candles."

"I'm going to gather a couple of others and have a look around. Just to make sure," said Jet. She left the room.

"What are we going to do?" asked Sapphire, standing just inside the door. "We can't let her birth more demons."

"No, we can't," said Anya, standing next to Sapphire, arms folded across her chest.

"Tomorrow, I'll do another journey. This time to just talk with my guides. Find out anything I can. I'll ask if there's a way to stop her," said Tau.

Pearl had no answers. She wouldn't have been able to stop the fire demon if Lucille, Anya, Jet and the others hadn't helped. She whispered a thank you to her guides and to Lucille.

Lucille brightened the room momentarily in response.

Even after chamomile and lavender tea, Pearl found it difficult to calm down. She did a full set of difficult yoga poses to wear herself out. After smudging with sage smoke, she meditated for half an hour. Finally, falling into bed at midnight.

THE NEXT MORNING, PEARL WOKE AFTER FITFUL DREAMS OF BEING chased. Running down the streets of downtown Everett and crossing the five-lane road just before Port Gardener Bay. And running straight into the Sound to get away from the fire demon.

She felt as exhausted as the night before. Despite blinding sunlight streaming in through her window. Pearl dragged herself out of bed and looked outside.

On the other side of the garage, Ruby had spread a large tarp. She made multiple trips to the shed, pulling out paint cans and brushes.

Ruby was never up this early. Or maybe she hadn't gone to bed yet. That was possible. But it looked like she had a big project going. One that wouldn't be finished in a couple of hours.

Pearl did her morning meditation. Dressing in purple yoga pants and a blue long-sleeved t-shirt. She tied her long hair back and went through a short series of poses, stretching her body into awakening. Then went downstairs for breakfast.

The kitchen was already bustling. She must have slept late. Beryl was making hazelnut-apple muffins from the oven. Two teapots were set up on table. Pearl poured herself some caffeine tea, which smelled like bergamot. And splashed cream into it. She got a plate with a muffin on it and went into the large dining room.

There were at least four separate conversations going on. Two about demons, one about defenses and another about Ryan McMahon. Anya and Raven Blue were talking about ways to deal with Caorthannach. None of her sisters was in the room.

Nor was Tau. He hadn't been on watch last night. Might still be sleeping.

Hema jumped up on her lap, licked a front paw nonchalantly and curled up. He'd been clingy ever since they'd removed the demon from him. Most of the other cats still avoided him out of habit.

"Hiya buddy," she said, petting his smooth fur.

She could feel his purring against her legs.

The muffin was delicious. Moist from the apple, crunchy from the hazelnuts. It was just the right amount of food, along with the tea.

When she'd finished, Pearl said to the kitten, "Hey buddy, let's go outside for a walk. Find out what Ruby's up to."

She picked him up, slinging him gently over her shoulder, his feet resting on her arm. Then carried the mug on top of her plate with the other hand, depositing them in a bin someone had thoughtfully put near the kitchen sink, which was already full of dirty dishes.

In the hall closet, she got her outdoor boots, sliding bare feet into them. Then squirmed into a green puffy coat, one arm at a time, the other holding the kitten. She snapped the coat up with Hema inside. He purred all the while and hung on, happy to be near her.

At least it wasn't ugly-cold outside. Hopefully, they were moving past that weather but it was still January so anything could happen.

Which meant Imbolc was on its way. And Ruby's birthday. She should ask Beryl if anyone was planning a ritual. And a party.

Outside the air felt almost warm. Pearl sensed the energy the earth was radiating, bringing the plants back to life. It was the beginning of the end of winter. The first hint that spring rebirth was coming.

The witch hazels were blooming in colors of orange, yellow and red now. And the Hellebores were in full flush, along with snowdrops. Winter moving into spring. Beryl hadn't finished pruning the fruit trees yet but piles of branches lay beneath the ones she'd done. It looked like all the berries were complete. They looked trimmed and the remaining raspberry and blackberry canes were all tidy and tied up.

The breeze blew past and a Stellar's Jay squawked at her as she walked past. As Pearl looked up, the bird flew higher into a fir. The wind was coming off Puget Sound this morning. Bringing with it scents of salt, kelp and fish.

Ruby worked over near the south fence, just past the garage. She'd put down a base coat of blue-green on one section of the solid wood fence.

"Whatcha doin?" asked Pearl.

"Witchery. Why?"

"Just curious. Isn't it too cold for the paint to dry?"

"Nope. Gonna hit the 50's this afternoon. It'll dry slow, but it'll dry. And I think we need it."

"A blue fence?"

"No. Are you even awake?" Ruby glared at her.

Then she dipped a smaller brush in dark blue and began to paint a convoluted design on the lighter color.

Then Pearl sensed it. Ruby was moving power with each stroke of the brush. It was incredible magic. With each stroke, her sister reinforced the boundary of the fence. There were waves and sigils and symbols. Pearl had nearly forgotten her sister used art as magic. That was her strongest gift.

"Oh."

Ruby grinned and beneath the waves painted whales and octopi, hydra and selkies. Pearl stood there long enough to see others come out of the house. Drawn to Ruby's work. Asha and Jamilla put base coats down on other sections so Ruby could continue working her magic down the fence line.

Beryl brought Ruby out a thermos of coffee and a muffin.

Pearl watched for an hour, entranced, while Hema napped inside her coat. Then he woke up and wanted out to go stalk around the garden.

Sapphire and Jet came and went. Both of them smiling at Ruby's magic.

Others picked up brushes and began painting more of the base coat farther down the fence. At the rate they were going, the entire fence would be covered by midday. Just waiting for Ruby to finish things off.

Pearl kept watching.

The flow of her sister's energy felt inspiring. Ruby didn't always have it together but when she was on, it was breathtaking to behold.

Pearl felt a presence beside her and looked up to see Tau, holding a sandwich. Coal stood beside him, his body wagged by its tail as Maybelle, a golden retriever, approached.

"What's Ruby doing?" Tau asked.

"She's warding the property."

"Wow. I've never seen it done before. Is that what warding usually looks like?"

"No. Ruby's got her own unique style of doing everything," Pearl said, laughing. "Normally, warding is invisible to most people."

"If it's visible, doesn't it give things away? Like how to unravel it?"

"Not really. What she's doing is so complex and with so many different symbols, some of which I'm sure Ruby has made up, that I don't think anyone else could unravel it. And she's also putting her power into it. Her energy and the energy of the land. Of our ancestors."

"I could feel the power from inside the kitchen. It's immense. I never knew she had that much."

"Most people don't. Ruby keeps in reined in. Unless she needs it."

Coal was jumping up and down, bouncing against Tau's leg.

"Just go play, Buddy," said Tau, waving his arm.

Coal and Maybelle raced off across the yard, weaving around humans. Biting and leaping at each other.

"He's been still too long," said Tau. "Needs to get some yayas out."

"Haven't we all," said Pearl. "I almost wish I was a runner and could go for a long, long run. Meditating and yoga aren't helping me deal with all the stress."

"You could dance it out," said Tau. "We all could."

"That's an idea."

"After dinner, warn the household that it'll be loud for a couple of hours. Let's crank up the music on the main floor and us humans can shake it all out."

"That's a really good idea. Although Ruby will be sad to miss it. Once she finishes here, she's gonna drop into a coma."

"We'll have another one. Just for her. Another evening. Because the stress has been way too much lately. For everybody."

"You're right. Lucille has been trying to muffle it but I can feel it building. Right. I'm off to find Beryl and Sapphire and demand we have a dance party tonight."

"Great. I'm feeling wiped out from yesterday. And sleeping badly. I'm gonna have more to eat and nap."

"Are you going to journey to your guides?"

"I will if I think I can stay awake. Maybe after the nap."

They returned to the house and Pearl kicked her outdoor boots off into the hall closet and hung up her coat. Her bare feet felt cold but they'd warm up now that she was back inside.

She poured another cup of tea and went off in search of her sisters. To arrange the dancing and more.

CHAPTER 5

LINDA JORDAN

THE ENTIRE HOUSEHOLD HAD BEEN EXCITED ABOUT A DANCE party. Jet, Bera and several others had even thrown together costumes. Beryl and Willow broke out several bottles of wine.

Even Ruby made an appearance after washing some of the paint off. She danced a couple of dances but mostly just watched and sipped a glass of wine.

Anya, Tau and Gabe took turns playing songs from everyone's CD collections. And between the CDs, several people drummed on the seemingly vast number of drums in the household.

Pearl danced until sweat ran down her sides. And danced some more.

She was determined to release all the stress. Her legs already felt rubbery. She went to the kitchen and drank a full glass of cold water. Then went back and danced longer.

The drums pulsing through her body as she moved to the beat, made Pearl feel ecstatic. Becoming one with the music. She wasn't dancing with anyone in particular, just the music. Most people were dancing in a group, without partners. Those who had partners, like Jet and Bera, Gabe and Maria, were still dancing with the group.

Pearl took a deep breath and smelled the fresh cool air Lucille vented into the large living room. Wearing a tank top and yoga pants, her hair tied back in a braid, feet bare, she still felt overheated.

Breathing heavily, she decided to take a break. Pearl wiped her forehead with the back of an arm and stepped off to the side, close to the vent where the cool air came from.

Ruby came over and said, "This is wonderful. We should do this more often."

"We should, shouldn't we? Life has been pretty grim lately."

"Today was a good day."

"What prompted the wards?"

"Tau's journey," said Ruby. "I feel we're too exposed. And all I can do is sit and wait for the hacker to do their job."

Pearl said, "Waiting is difficult."

"Especially for me. I just want to do…something. Anything."

"Well, I think it's a good thing. How far did you get?"

"Halfway. I'll do the other half tomorrow. It's supposed to be warm again."

"If you can call fifty degrees warm," said Pearl.

"Yeah. So what's up with you and Tau?"

"Nothing."

Ruby rolled her eyes.

"What?" asked Pearl.

"He follows you around like a lost dog looking for a new home," said Ruby.

"No he doesn't. We're friends."

"I don't think that's all he has in mind."

"Maybe not, but this isn't the time or place to…."

"It might be the only time we have if Caorthannach comes and fries all our asses."

"That's not going to happen," said Pearl, realizing her fists were clenched. She took a deep breath and released them.

"Listen, little sister, if he was looking at me the way he's looking at you, I'd drag him upstairs and jump his bones," said Ruby.

"I hate casual sex. Been there, done that. Not doing it again."

"I don't think anything about him is casual. And I don't get that's what he wants either."

Pearl took another deep breath and let it out slowly. She avoided looking at Tau because Ruby was staring at him.

Ruby said, "Don't let him slip away. I love you and I hate watching you put your needs behind everyone else's. Stop doing that and let yourself have some fun. And some love." She drained her glass and said, "I'm going up to bed. Gotta get up at dawn to paint again or I'll never rest. Goodnight."

"Goodnight," said Pearl.

Ruby was infuriating.

Pearl had already figured this all out. Ruby's observations made it necessary to rethink everything. And she didn't want to.

But her sister had a point, which made it all the more irritating.

Pearl returned to the dance floor, her body moving to the beat with a frenzy. Trying to dance out all her warring emotions.

Not long afterwards Tau came out onto the floor near her. Dancing at half the speed of the beat, his tall body slowly rolling to the rhythm. He grinned at her and closed his eyes as if reveling in the drumbeat of the music. This one was by a band that sounded like a fusion of Caribbean and Japanese music. Very strange but incredibly danceable.

The evening seemed to go on forever, but at one point, Pearl noticed the crowd in the room had thinned to four people. She and Tau were the only ones on the dance floor. Gabe and Willow sat on pillows near the stereo, shuffling through CDs and discussing the merits of each one.

Pearl glanced at the wall clock. It was 11:30. Long past her bedtime. The dance had only supposed to be until ten. So everyone could sleep.

"It's 11:30," she said. "I had no idea it was so late. I've got to get to bed."

"Do you turn into a pumpkin?" Tau asked.

"Probably a potato."

"Mmm. I like potatoes. But you're right. It's late. And I've got things to do in the morning. We should let the household sleep."

"We should."

They walked to where Gabe and Willow sat.

"We should all go to bed and let people sleep. I didn't mean to dance so long," said Pearl.

"You needed it. We all did," said Willow. "We've been carrying everyone's stuff. But it's time."

The older woman stood in one smooth graceful motion, which Pearl still couldn't do. Then picked up several mugs and glasses to take into the kitchen. Gabe began to shut everything down.

Pearl and Tau headed up the stairs. She felt him following closely behind. On the second floor landing, Tau took her hand and spun her towards him.

"I don't know how to do this. To say this. Is there any chance you could be attracted to me?"

Pearl's mouth dropped open but no words came out. She just stood—frozen. Feeling like an awkward teenager.

"I'd say that's a no then," he said, sadly.

"No, I mean yes. I am attracted to you. I just don't know if this is the right time...," she said.

"There is no right time."

He pulled her to him and gently, but firmly, kissed her lips. She felt electricity roll up and down her spine.

It was a luscious kiss, which would have gone further if Gabe and Willow hadn't started up the steps.

Tau pulled away and said, "I'm going to be dreaming about that all night long. I'll see you in the morning and maybe we can find a quiet time to talk."

Pearl had no words. She simply smiled. And floated off towards her room.

He grinned back at her before going into his room and closing the door. She opened her door and saw Hema and Beatrice curled up on the bed together in the dim light.

She undressed, deciding against a shower. Tomorrow. Then pulled on some fuzzy pjs and crawled into bed. She fell asleep still feeling that kiss.

The next morning, sunlight streaming into her room woke Pearl. It was early still and she lay there just basking in the warmth. The days were growing slowly longer. This gorgeous sun break would shift into cold cloudy weather again soon.

She remembered the wards her sister, Ruby, had painted yesterday. Was she already at it today? When Ruby was on a roll, she slept very little.

Pearl's window faced the side street, not the far back of the garden where Ruby had ended her painting last night. So Pearl would have to go downstairs to see.

She should get up, shower and go help with something downstairs. Feeding cats or breakfast. And at ten, she was going to be with Raven Blue while they journeyed. Just to make sure there were no problems.

Pearl got out of bed and let Beatrice and Hema out of her room. She stretched. Her muscles stiff from dancing. She quickly showered and dressed in yoga pants, a thick loose turtleneck and wool socks, knowing she'd be outside a lot today. Watching Ruby do her work was a blessing that didn't happen often.

She pulled a brush through her long hair and wrapped a hair tie around it several times, rolling it into a knot on top of her head.

Then she sat on the yoga mat to meditate. But her focus was all off. She kept thinking about that kiss last night. She *had* dreamt about it all night long.

Tau often showed up in her dreams, but last night he'd been there in every single one that she remembered. And they were all about making love. She really didn't have time to a romantic relationship right now. Not when people's lives were in danger.

Pearl needed to focus. On doing what she could to keep everyone safe. And to keep the collective running strong.

Finally, she gave up trying to meditate. She made her bed, tidied her room and went down the stairs.

No one else was in the kitchen. The oven was on and the kitchen was filled with the scent of butter and cinnamon from the cinnamon rolls Beryl had left baking.

Cats swarmed beneath her feet.

"Okay kids, I'll feed you," she said, to a chorus of meows and yowls.

She filled eight bowls with wet cat food and two with dry. Then washed the water bowls and refilled them.

After that, Pearl made a pot of black and another of herb tea. While they steeped, she glanced out the window.

Ruby was working on the fence at the far corner. Where she'd left off last night. A bit more than halfway around the fence line. Pearl could barely see her through the trees but that glowing red hair popped through the bare branches.

Pearl poured a mug of the black tea with rose petals, adding cream to it. She sat down at the kitchen table and gazed out into the bare garden. The mug warming her cold hands. This was how she used to spend her mornings. Alone.

It was strange to have twenty-three extra people living here now. And all the extra dogs and cats. Solitude could rarely be found.

The stairs creaked and she turned to see Marcea.

"Good morning," said Pearl.

"Hullo. Oh good, there's tea."

Marcea poured a large mug of the black tea and checked the oven timer.

"Ten minutes till cinnamon rolls. I can't wait. It almost makes getting up this early worth it."

"Not a morning person?" asked Pearl.

Marcea was a friend of Jet's and a shaman on her team. But Pearl barely knew her, although she quite liked the woman.

Marcea laughed. "Before all this happened, I used to spend my evenings acting in local theatre. And then going out with the cast to wind down at some bar or another. I'm used to going to bed at three and getting up around eleven or noon. But living here has me completely turned around."

"I think it's turned all of us around," said Pearl.

"Yes, it must be a shock for you and your sisters. To have your house invaded."

"We have good friends who are wonderful guests. It's like an ongoing sleepover, I think."

Marcea laughed.

They were joined by Maria and Ginny, who immediately made coffee, put on aprons and began fussing around the kitchen.

The two of them were having an ongoing conversation about who would be best suited to go out into the world. Searching for Caorthannach and Ryan McMahon.

Pearl said nothing. She didn't want to even contemplate leaving the safety of Lucille.

Beryl reappeared just as the timer went off and removed two pans of perfectly baked cinnamon rolls from the oven. She immediately began chopping onions to put into scrambled eggs.

Pearl plated up a hot cinnamon roll, refilled her tea and went into the large dining room, so as to create space in the kitchen for those working or dishing up.

She sat near the door for a quick escape. It was already eight, so she'd eat and go outside for a couple of hours before returning to help Raven Blue.

But before she could finish her cinnamon roll, Tau came in the door and sat in the empty chair beside her. His plate laden with eggs, red peppers and fresh basil from the heated greenhouse. And another plate with two cinnamon rolls on it. Willow came in carrying two mugs of tea, one of which she set in front of him.

"Eat up. You'll need your strength today," said Willow, winking at him and going to the far end of the table to talk to Sarah, one of the healers.

"Why do you need your strength?" asked Pearl, sipping her tea and loving the combination of roses and cream.

"I'm going to help Beryl do some pruning this afternoon."

"You're a busy man," said Pearl.

"I am. But that doesn't mean I've forgotten we need to have a talk." He grinned at her.

"Maybe this afternoon sometime. This morning I'm helping Raven Blue. And I think you have a journey too, don't you?"

"I do. Not like the other day. Don't want to alert the demon. Just talking to my guides. To get more information. And Willow and Anya will be there. In case I run into trouble again."

"Good," said Pearl. She at the last bite of cinnamony-buttery dough. It was bliss on a fork.

"Have you talked to Ruby yet?" he asked.

"No, why?"

"I overheard her tell Jet this morning that the hacker's having some luck getting into Ryan's phone and grabbing info. It was all pretty vague. They're going to announce any findings at a meeting. Tonight or tomorrow. Not sure Ruby will be able to talk tonight considering how intensely she's working out there."

"She does get into her work. I hope the news is good and they find something useful."

"Me too. We need a break. Several breaks."

She looked into his warm eyes, then away. Draining her mug, Pearl rose.

"I better get going."

"All right," he said, touching her hand. Creating tendrils of energy that went up her arm. "I'll see you at lunch. Or maybe after."

Pearl turned away, her face flushing. She felt awkward.

Carrying her dirty dishes into the kitchen, she left them in the bin near the sink. Then went to the hall closet to get her outdoor boots and a warm coat.

She asked Beryl, "Has anyone taken a cinnamon roll to Ruby yet?"

"No. Would you?"

"I'd be happy to."

Pearl put one on a plate and Beryl handed her a thermos of hot tea to take out, then opened and closed the door behind her.

It was still cold out this morning, maybe still in the 30s. Maybe the low 40s. The wind was whipping off the Sound. If her hair hadn't been tied up, she would have had trouble keeping it away from the cinnamon roll.

She reveled in the change brought by the wind. It felt as if her cobwebs were being blown out. That the long dark winter was ending.

The sense of it was everywhere. In the trills of the varied thrushes as they flipped over rotting leaves, searching for insects. It was in the whirr of the Anna's hummingbirds' wings. She felt it in the energy the earth gave off as it grew closer to spring.

Pearl stood near the fence and waited for about five minutes before Ruby even saw her.

"Oh, is that a cinnamon roll? For me?"

"Yep."

"Thank you, thank you, thank you," said Ruby, putting the brush down. She picked up the pastry with her purple-painted fingers and ate it quickly. Licking her fingers when done.

Pearl handed Ruby the thermos. Ruby poured a cup and sipped the hot tea. Fire was her element and she loved heat.

"How's it going?"

"Excellent. It's coming out just great. I've got a lot to do but I can finish this today. The energy's flowing even stronger than yesterday. Lucille's boosting me, too."

Ruby finished the cup of tea, put it near the thermos and went back to painting.

Pearl sat on a large boulder their great grandfather had uncovered and dug up, decades ago. The ground nearby rustled with movement from varied thrushes. Their orange, white and brown feathers moving quickly as they flipped over and dug through rotting leaves in search of insects.

An Anna's hummingbird zipped past going between the yellow-flowered shrubs that she always forgot the name of. All Pearl remembered was that they had prickly leaves but edible tart berries.

She sat for a long while, basking in the sun and the heat of Ruby's energy. Others came out to watch as well.

Eventually, she looked at her watch. 9:30. She should go in and warm up. And get ready to help Raven Blue.

Pearl stretched, her muscles still sore from dancing last night. Picking up Ruby's empty plate, she made her way back to the house. Everyone's energy seemed lighter.

They should make dancing a regular thing. Maybe every other week. She should get Willow to teach a yoga class. And maybe Asha and Jamilla could teach Capoeira to those interested. Everyone needed to be more active to deal with the massive amount of stress they were all under.

Why hadn't she thought of it before? It shouldn't have taken so long. But she was so close to things there was no seeing the forest for the trees.

Inside the house, the kitchen was bustling with those making lunch. Beryl stood in the center of it, like a conductor.

Pearl put the plate in the bin by the sink and went to the hallway. She kicked off her boots and hung up the coat.

Upstairs in her room, she sat down on her mat and meditated for ten minutes. Then stood and went to the room Raven Blue would use for her journey.

Pearl got out floor pillows for Marcea, Bera and herself. She lit a candle sitting on the windowsill and another on a small table. Then lit a small cedar bough to smudge the room and herself. Marcea came in and she waved the still-smoking branch in circles around her.

Raven Blue came in with a large wool blanket which they spread on the floor along with a small rug. Their dog, Jennet, followed, said hello to the two of them and lay down on the rug. Marcea closed the door and Pearl smudged Raven Blue. Who then sat down on the blanket.

Bera was the last to arrive. The tall woman had a water bottle with her. Pearl smudged her and Bera sat down on the pillow. She rubbed her eyes as if sleepy.

"Were you on watch last night?" asked Pearl.

"No, I took a night off so I could be here. Sapphire decided there should be a demonologist at each journey. Just in case."

"Well, I'm relieved you're here," said Marcea. "I've only dealt with a demon alone once on a journey. After that I called on Jet. I knew I was in over my head. Today, I'm here mostly as a shaman."

"I'm relieved too," said Pearl. "Thank you all for being here."

"I'm almost embarrassed. I don't usually need anything when I journey," said Raven Blue. "No drumming or music. I've never had any problem returning. Jennet will let you know if something's wrong. Although I appreciate your presence and energy. I could maybe use some energy work when I return. Demons are gross."

"Okay, so we'll simply hold space for you," said Pearl.

She sat down. Raven Blue lay down on half the blanket. Marcea crossed her legs and Pearl felt her grounding. Bera just sat quietly, staring into space. Pearl could feel the woman reaching out, searching for anything amiss. Jennet just lay stretched out, eyes open and calmly waiting.

Pearl sat and breathed. She monitored the energy within the room. Raven Blue felt empty. Just like Tau had. Pearl had never been around when others journeyed before. So perhaps that was absolutely normal.

It felt eerie. As if their body was lifeless. Which it wasn't. Raven Blue's body lay still, the only movement the rising and falling of their breathing chest.

This journey seemed longer than Tau's. There was no drumbeat with which to measure time. Just the outdoor noises of cars and humans. A party of crows passed through the back garden.

Pearl sensed Marcia's energy shifting. As if she was journeying along with Raven Blue. Or perhaps on her own journey. Bera's energy stayed the same. Endlessly searching.

Pearl closed here eyes and drifted. She sensed the cold depths of Puget Sound below her. And on the shore, there was a battle. Her sisters were there, except for Beryl. Pearl sensed her energy pouring down from her garden on the bluff above. Pearl felt surprised to see herself there too.

Ryan, Caorthannach and several other demons were fighting the entire household. Other humans were behind Ryan, amplifying his power.

But the witches, shamans and demonologists were pulling in energy from the earth, sea and wind. They were also sucking up the fire from Caorthannach and turning it back towards Ryan. Most of the household's power was coming from the earth.

And they were winning. Caorthannach's fire was put out... drained. The other demons were conquered. Ryan's power burnt out, he was tied up and Ruby went to work on wiping his mind. His followers had all been killed by Caorthannach's fury.

And then, Pearl just peacefully floated on the Sound. The battle was over. She was in her element, water. But felt more connected to the earth than every before. And to the entire household.

Finally, Raven Blue's energy bounded back into the room. Jennet's head came up. Then Raven Blue opened their eyes, sat up and looked around.

"You're back," said Bera.

Marcea also looked present and alert.

"I am," said Raven Blue. "Wow, that was a strange journey. I wasn't myself, I was all of us."

"All of who?" asked Marcea.

"All of us shamans and witches and demonologists. This entire collective. We were fighting Caorthannach and Ryan again. Near the water somewhere. We were…together. It was like we were one being, all of us melded together. And our energy was immense. We felt connected to each of the elements but somehow earth was especially strong. Somehow we used the earth to conquer both of them. And even after the battle, after we won, we stayed together. We all loved each other so much and felt such…connection that we couldn't part."

"Wow," said Marcea.

"Exactly," said Raven Blue.

"Have you had predictive journeys before?" asked Marcea.

"Never. And this one might not be a prediction. Might just be a wish."

"Might be," said Bera. "Might not. I think you should spend some time talking to Anya. See if she knows anything about earth connections and using them. Maybe that's a piece we're missing."

Pearl said, "Also tell Beryl about your journey. She's our seer. And she's also got a powerful connection with the earth."

Raven Blue nodded.

"How are you feeling physically?" asked Pearl.

She stood and walked over to Raven Blue, searching their field for anything out of place. They glowed with energy. But it was all positive and joyous. Nothing that felt wrong.

"I feel wonderful. Like I can do anything. But not alone. I've never felt this connected to anyone," they said, wiping tears away.

Pearl grinned.

"It does feel good, doesn't it," said Bera. "The people in this household are amazing. Sometimes annoying but I've never worked with anyone like them. I sure hope your journey is a prediction and we destroy the demon and Ryan."

"Me too," said Raven Blue.

Pearl blew out the candle. Raven Blue collected her belongings and she and Jennet went off to find Beryl. Marcea walked to the basement to work on laundry and Bera to the kitchen in search of food.

Pearl just sat looking out the window. She felt hopeful after hearing about the journey. But she knew that even if it was true, they were a long ways from that endpoint. They had a lot to do to get there.

And she didn't know what her part in it was. She couldn't fight. Her entire life had been about learning how to heal people. How to keep them safe and their energy fields clean.

Not about causing destruction. No matter how much that being or person might deserve it. Yet, she had protected Hema. Removed the demon from him. Knowing it would be destroyed. And she had removed other entities from people.

It wasn't that she couldn't do it, couldn't protect those she loved. It was that she was ill-equipped for this war. And they were at war.

Pearl stood up. She could see that Ruby had passed the far corner and was now painting the sections of the fence leading back to the house. She'd probably finish about dinnertime.

It was time for lunch. And after that to talk to Tau. She had no idea how to tell him no. That this couldn't happen right now.

Because deep down, she didn't really believe it.

CHAPTER 6

LINDA JORDAN

RUBY FINISHED PAINTING JUST BEFORE DINNER. AFTER DINNER Beryl made everyone who was awake go outside to the back garden.

Pearl followed along, wondering what was happening.

They stood among the mostly bare beds of the vegetable garden looking at Ruby's gorgeous fence. Pearl could feel the wards, fully active.

Then she felt something else. Turning slowly to look at the house, she saw more paintings begin to appear on the outside.

Ruby stood beside her. Staring at the house, Ruby sucked in her breath.

Lucille was painting wards on the back of the house.

Pearl ran inside and out the front door, looking back at the house. Wards were being painted there as well, although they faded from sight as fast as they appeared. But they were still there, pulsing strongly. And on the front of the garage as well. In the dim light, she could just see them forming and disappearing on the outside of the fence, running in both directions at once.

Pearl returned to the back garden. Everyone was still standing there.

"Wait for it," said Beryl.

The full moon had risen high in the winter sky. It was a clear, crisp night. It would probably freeze.

Pearl felt the exact moment when the wards met on the outside of the fence at the far end of the garden. It gave a ping of rightness, like a lock snicking into place.

Then the energy rose up over the fence. It continued upwards, meeting from all sides over the tops of the trees and forming a seal of sort. There was a deeper ping as the energy met below them, deep in the earth.

Those in the garden gave a collective sigh. It was a moment of beauty and rightness. A breath before the storm.

Pearl and the others stood there for a good long while. Then they went inside to get warm. In the kitchen, Ruby grinned and poured herself a whiskey. Which she downed in one gulp and afterwards, went up to bed.

Pearl made herself a cup of lemon verbena and mint tea. She sat at the kitchen table. Lucille had cranked up the heat and Pearl sat near the vent, absorbing as much warmth as possible. Anya, Sapphire, Willow and Beryl were also there.

No one spoke for a long while. They were simply basking in the afterglow of Ruby's magic and Raven Blue's journey, which held so much promise. The gist of it had already made the rounds of the household.

"When are we meeting next?" asked Beryl, finally.

"Tomorrow. Sometime after Ruby gets up and has a chance to recover. Since she'll be talking about what the hacker's found out," said Sapphire.

"So after lunch," said Beryl.

"Probably. Ruby'll need a lot of extra sleep tonight," said Sapphire.

"Do you want me to talk about what we've learned from everyone's journeys so far?" asked Anya.

"Yes please. We have decisions to make."

"About what? What have you learned?" asked Beryl.

"Can we just wait until tomorrow?" asked Sapphire. "I want to just soak in Ruby's magic for a while longer. And not have to think and explain everything again and again."

Sapphire never asked to have time for herself. She was usually the first to leap into over-analyzing things.

Pearl sipped her tea and watched Beryl nod in resignation and sigh deeply. Beryl was afraid and trying to prepare any way she could for whatever was going to come up at the meeting.

Wrapping her fingers around the large mug was getting her fingers warmed up. She was drinking tea mostly for that. Pearl still felt tired from last night. And there was a nagging dread about talking with Tau.

She hadn't seen him since morning, so they hadn't spoken yet. And what was she going to tell him?

Hema came over and stood on his hind legs, front paws on her thigh and eyes pleading.

"Okay buddy, you can come up for a while," she said, lifting him onto her lap. He walked in a small circle, kneaded and curled up. Purring loudly.

"There's nothing quite like cats purring, is there?" asked Willow. "He's doing much better at fitting in."

"Yes, he is," said Pearl.

They didn't mention the demon Pearl had pulled out of him, although everyone in the household knew. He was a completely changed little being since then. He still liked to play a lot, like any kitten, but he didn't harass the other cats. Instead, he waited for them to come to him.

Just then the back door opened and in burst Coal, followed by Tau.

"Settle down," said Tau, to the dog, who was almost dancing in circles. "He's excited, just saw a rabbit and chased it out of the vegetable garden."

Coal stood in the middle of the kitchen, panting and his tail wagging his body.

Jet came down the stairs and Tau gave her his report from coming off watch. She went back upstairs. He peeled off his warm coat and took a couple of cookies off the plate on the counter.

"Is this a private party or can I join in?" he asked.

"We're not really having a party," said Beryl. "But you're welcome to join. We're just basking in Ruby's amazing magic."

Tau pulled up a chair and Coal lay down at his feet, groaning.

"That was something else," said Tau. "I was out at the far fence line when all the wards began to light up and connect. And then that energy coming over the top of the fence. I was stunned. I sensed it was Ruby and someone else. It sure was wonderful."

"It was Lucille," said Pearl. "Ruby and Lucille."

"Wow. Lucille sure is one powerful being. I wouldn't want to cross her," said Tau. He ate one of the cookies.

"How can you eat so much and never gain weight?" asked Anya.

"I've always been like this. My mama used to complain that I was going to eat her out of house and home. Just before she laughed and pushed seconds at me."

The conversation turned to other things and Pearl lost the thread of it. She kept trying to figure out what to tell Tau. Finally, she had a short speech. She rehearsed it in her head over and over.

Willow stood up and said, "Well, I'm up early, so it's time for bed."

Beryl followed and said, "I've got research to do," and headed downstairs to the basement.

Sapphire and Anya got up and went up the stairs to their own rooms.

So it was just her and Tau. And Hema and Coal, both asleep.

"Is it time for that talk now?" asked Tau, moving his chair closer to hers.

"I suppose so. I just need to say that, yes, I find you very attractive. You're gorgeous and kind and smart and gentle. If things were normal, I would already have asked you out. But this isn't normal. And we're all working together so closely, if things should go wrong between us...if you decided I'm too annoying or I decided I don't want to do this, well, it would make the entire household uncomfortable. And I don't want that. And I need to focus on my work. It might save someone's life. And me not being focused has the potential to cause any number of screwups. I don't think I can do this. Not right now," said Pearl.

"Whoa, deep breath now. Slow down. You've already gotten us sick and tired of each other and we've only had one short kiss."

Pearl opened and closed her mouth. She didn't know what to say.

"You have some good points there. I can't deny that there's a risk. But I think, if we take things slow and calmly, we can make this work without it turning into a disaster. Let's just become good friends first. With the idea that one of these days, weeks, months, years, we'll become lovers. When the time is right. It might not be until after this whole thing is over and the bad guys lose. Or it might be right in the middle of everything. I don't know. But I do know, that I can't take my eyes off you. I long to be near you all the time. And I'm tired of making excuses about why I can't do that. I want to know who you are. What you most want out of life. Where you want to be in ten years. So I can see how I fit into your life," said Tau.

Pearl listened to his words and felt the rigidity leave her body. They didn't have to figure this all out right now. It could wait.

"All I'm asking for is baby steps," he said, looking into her eyes.

"Baby steps I can do. Or at least try."

"Good. We'll take it from there."

All of a sudden, the weariness from the long day hit her.

"I'm exhausted," she said.

"Well, let's get you upstairs then."

Tau took her empty mug and put the dirty dishes in the bin. Pearl lifted Hema off her lap and put him over one shoulder. Then climbed the stairs, feeling like her legs were lead.

At the top of the stairs, Tau asked, "I don't suppose I could have another one of those blissful kisses, could I?"

Pearl moved closer and kissed him. He returned the kiss and it made her feel all soft and squishy.

As they parted, he said, "I hope I never get used to that. Wow. I'm gonna have great dreams again tonight."

They headed off to their separate rooms, Tau followed by Coal.

The next afternoon after lunch, everyone not on watch crowded into the large dining room. This time the walls were a normal peach color, although Pearl felt an aura of tension from most people.

She sat near the doorway. Ruby, Sapphire and Anya sat at the far end of the table. Beryl and Jet were on opposite sides of the table. Beryl fiddled with a deck of tarot cards. Shuffling and reshuffling them, pulling a card and then putting it back in the deck. Unobtrusively and silently.

"Let's get started," said Sapphire. She turned to look at Ruby and waited.

Ruby said, "Okay, so the hacker has been able to get into Ryan's email and calendar. It turns out he does have everything online, although it's encrypted. His calendar seems divided into two parts— his current project time and workout time—he takes kickboxing lessons at his home. The current project is called Forest Fire and he's scheduled himself to work on it for the majority of his waking hours. Almost all the meetings about it are virtual except for one. Every Wednesday evening, he meets someone called Max at a bar in Lynnwood. Next Wednesday, we'll be sending two people to the bar. We already have many volunteers, so no more please. We're just going to see what's happening. And our hacker's trying to get into Max's phone and find out more about him. That's the info we've gotten in less than 24 hours. I'm expecting a lot more will come in. And the hacker assures me that he'll be able to get video of the online meetings. Apparently Ryan's phone and laptop are severely lacking in security."

Sapphire turned to Anya.

"We're on our fourth day of the shamans' journeys. There have been fourteen separate journeys done in this time by several people. We've had mixed results, but there are some things we're certain of. We have found where Caorthannach is spending most of her time. It's not in our reality and it's in a semi-active volcano. And she is pregnant with a demon or demons. We have no idea how this happened, if we can do anything about it, or when she'll give birth. We must expect there will be more demons next time we meet and they may very well be born fully-formed and ready to attack. Our guides have told us to stay away for right now because she's at her most dangerous. A fierce mother demon. That will change once her "children" are born and out on their own. But our guides have a different sense of time than we do and can't provide us with a reliable timeline for that. But she is busy and probably, so they say, won't attack us again until after she gives birth. Which doesn't mean there aren't other demons who Ryan has control of. Like the one that came in on the kitten."

"So where does that leave us?" asked Sapphire.

"In the same place we were before," said Anya. "Except for Raven Blue's journey. Which feels like divination. Even Beryl says so."

Beryl shuffled her cards.

"So, it seems like the key is our connection to each other and that earth energy," said Anya.

"Beryl, do you have anything to add?"

"I do," said Beryl. "I've been doing reading after reading all day long. And it comes down to those two things. Our connected community here in this house and juicy earthy energy. We'll need to tap into that power more deeply. Lunar Imbolc is just over three weeks away. The darkness of the new moon gives us all an opportunity to go deeper into our work with the earth. We need to do some intense ritual work that night."

"I'm always up for an intense ritual," said Ruby.

"Good," said Sapphire. "Beryl will be in charge of planning the ritual. Any of you feeling a strong earth connection, talk to her after the meeting about helping. This might be the turning point. The piece that shifts everything."

Pearl thought about offering to help but decided to wait. Her affinity was with water magic, not earth. She'd be there, of course. Later, when there were tasks to be done. But planning a ritual revolving around earth magic was just not her forte.

After the meeting, she watched Beryl become surrounded by Jet, Bera, Tau and so many others. She had plenty of help.

Pearl walked outside into the fresh air. It was mid-afternoon and still warmish for this time of year, although gray. The garden had hints of color from the witch hazels, hellebores and cyclamen. Snowdrops popped up at the edges of beds, their white flowers a promise of winter ending soon.

The ancient cedar at the center of the property still stood, despite a blackened tip. Beryl had told her the tree was fine but would grow two leaders now, to heal the wound. Just as if someone had pruned the top off. Which would weaken the tree. When that happened, she'd call an arborist and have the weakest of the tops removed so the tree could direct her energy into one. The cedar top would be stronger then, maybe even be able to withstand the powerful winter gales off the Sound.

It came to Pearl that perhaps part of the Imbolc ritual should concern the cedar. The tree needed a little extra love right now, just a month after being attacked by the Caorthannach.

Pearl walked over to the tree and put her arms around her. She was so old and the trunk so large it took all five sisters hugging the tree to be able to touch fingertips.

She'd always loved this tree.

Pearl pulled up energy from the earth and down from the sky, grounding and centering herself. Then she channeled that power through her hands into the tree.

"Take what you need to help you heal," she said.

And she felt the cedar draw energy from her hands, add it to the power Lucille and Beryl had given the tree. Pearl stood there for half an hour, sending out healing energy.

Finally, it felt right to stop.

"I'll be back," she said, then returned to the house to warm up.

Beryl was sitting at the kitchen table with Jet, Bera and Maria. Willow stood at the sink, filling a teakettle with water.

"Pearl, we were just talking about you," said Willow.

"Oh?" asked Pearl.

Beryl asked, "When do you bleed next?"

"I'm not sure. Maybe a week, maybe two. I haven't been keeping track, really. No reason to."

"Well, we need your blood if it's before the ritual," said Beryl.

Pearl raised an eyebrow at her.

"Yes, we're going to do blood magic. You have to admit, it's powerful," said Beryl.

"But isn't most blood magic about blood from veins?" asked Maria.

"That's the patriarchal strain of the craft talking," said Beryl. "The original blood magic was done with menstrual blood. The ultimate symbol of life and death."

"Sadly, I can't contribute," said Willow. "I'm done bleeding."

"Me neither," said Maria.

"You're not that old," said Jet.

"I had health issues. Had a hysterectomy in my early 30's and they took out everything," said Maria. "Didn't want kids anyway, so it was just fine. Gabe didn't want children either."

They all nodded.

Pearl sat down at the table.

"I've been thinking," she said. "Part of the ritual should involve Grandmother Cedar. She took the brunt of the demon's attack."

"Perfect," said Beryl. "I've been pondering where would be best to do the ritual and that's it. We'll have Grandmother Cedar at the center of the circle. We need the blood of three witches. Hopefully we'll find three women in the household who will be bleeding near that time. So Maria, you're going to write the ritual. I'll lead it. Willow, Bera and Jet are going to do their stuff creating the space. I think we're on our way."

Pearl didn't ask for details. She wanted to wait and see. And be surprised.

CHAPTER 7

LINDA JORDAN

PEARL WALKED OUT OF THE MEDITATION ROOM, RUBBING HER forehead. She felt drained. Kasya just finished a long involved journey and had needed a lot of support. Johanna had been helping Pearl but her energy was off today. It had felt like Pearl was supporting both of them.

Kasya's journey had been all about Ryan. He was planning something big. Putting things into motion that would happen months away. Ugly things.

Pearl crossed the main hallway, heading for her bedroom. Not even aware of her surroundings. A hand grabbed her arm.

Pearl jumped sideways, dropping her water bottle on the floor with a loud crash as metal hit wood.

"Sorry. I didn't mean to scare you," said Beryl. "Why are you so jumpy?"

"I don't want to talk about it," said Pearl. "Not my stuff. Just need to release it."

She picked up the bottle and opened her door. Stepped inside her room.

"Well, get on with it," said Beryl. "We need to talk."

Beryl followed her inside, plopped on the bed and began petting Hema and Beatrice who were curled up, sleeping.

Pearl sighed. There was no getting rid of her sister.

She set the water bottle down then went to her altar and lit a candle. Then she sat cross-legged on her mat on the floor in front of it. Slowing her breathing, Pearl brought up image after image of the journey and released each one. It was clear now that Ryan was deranged. And out for some sort of revenge against her family. But he was also power mad and his plans to gain power went way beyond Everett.

It took nearly twenty minutes to release all that energy. Finally, she blew out the candle and stood. Pearl opened the bottle and drank cool water, emptying it. It tasted refreshing, grounding her back in her body fully.

"That must have been some journey," said Beryl.

"It was. You wanted to talk?"

"Ruby's birthday is 11 days off. Two days after our ritual. What are we going to do for her?"

"No idea," said Pearl.

"Sapphire and Jet have no ideas either. We've got to do something."

"How about a big feast? And a cake?"

"We do that every year. And you know Ruby doesn't even like cake. What else?"

Pearl gazed out the window. The warm sunny winter days they'd had during Ruby's fence painting were gone. Replaced by the usual dark-gray rain.

Imbolc signaled the beginning of spring, even if it wasn't quite here yet. It was about the hope of rebirth. The expectation that life would renew itself.

"We should have a big blowout dance. Ruby didn't get to participate in the last one. Because she was painting."

"Perfect. Absolutely perfect. I'm pretty wrapped up with the ritual planning. Jet and Sapphire are busy plotting about getting someone to listen in on Ryan's meeting. Can you make Ruby's birthday happen? Recruit some folks without her finding out? Tell me what I need to order for food?"

"I can do that. Not doing much else at the moment. At least it doesn't feel like it."

"You are. I can feel you helping juggle the households' up and down emotions. Smoothing the waters. I don't even think you're aware you do it."

Pearl opened her mouth and shut it. Beryl hit on exactly what was draining her.

"I had no idea."

"It's your gift. You've always done it, ever since we were little. Remember when Mom and Auntie Fay used to fight? You stopped them cold. You weren't so subtle back then. I mean, you were only three. I think you levitated a bowl of cold water and dropped it on them. These days, many people don't even notice that you do it because you're so skilled."

"Huh."

Pearl didn't remember the episode with Mom and Auntie Fay.

"Let me know how I can help. Once the Imbolc Ritual is over, I'll be free to do whatever you need. I can definitely do the cooking. Along with the folks who help out in the kitchen," said Beryl.

Her sister stood and walked towards the door.

"Oh, and best step lightly around Jet today and tomorrow. Bera and Jamilla are going to that bar in Lynnwood tomorrow night. Jet's on edge since she can't go," said Beryl.

"Thanks for the warning."

So it was happening. The first steps back into the world. Hopefully, the demon would be busy elsewhere and it would be only Ryan to worry about. And perhaps his security. Who may or may not be human.

Had anyone checked that?

Of course they had. Sapphire didn't miss things that important. Jet or Ruby wouldn't either. Jamilla was skilled at Capoeira. Bera was a demonologist but also knew how to fight. Street fighting if rumor was correct.

Which was probably why they were chosen.

149

Pearl took her water bottle downstairs to wash and refill. Maria was at the sink, washing late lunch dishes.

"Just give it to me," she said.

"I was going to refill it," explained Pearl. "I can wash it."

"Do you have your union card?" asked Maria.

"What?" asked Pearl.

"Your union card. You can't do dishes in this kitchen without one." Maria washed, rinsed and refilled the bottle with cold water. "It was a joke. Just trying to add a little levity around here. We all need to lighten up."

Pearl laughed. "I sure do."

She dried the outside of the bottle with a towel hanging on a drawer pull.

Sapphire, Anya and Raven Blue were at the table having an animated discussion about some complex ritual. It didn't feel like anything Pearl wanted to be part of.

She felt an overwhelming urge to escape the house.

There was no going outside in the garden. Not with the pouring rain.

Pearl went out the back door, slipped her bare feet into Beryl's cold plastic garden clogs and stood beneath the covered walkway to the garage. Rain slid off the peaked roof above her. The trellised sides were still covered with the dead vines of last summer. Clematis, Beryl called them.

Around this time of year, Beryl cut them all to the ground and they grew up with fresh green leaves and big purple flower in early summer, followed by crimson ones later on. There were two different types planted there. The only thing that would have made it better was if they had a scent, but they didn't.

Right now, she could only smell wet soil. That earthy scent Pearl always associated with the garden.

It was cold out again today. She should've put her coat on.

Pearl felt jumpy. She was running a lot of energy lately and it made her itchy and twitchy. And the stuff with Tau wasn't helping. He kept ambushing her with those incredible kisses. Pearl wasn't sure how much more she could take before dragging him off to bed.

That was it. That was it exactly.

He was the problem here.

It wasn't running all that energy. She was used to that. It was her work.

But combined with the sexual energy and desire, she felt close to melting down. Unable to concentrate and focus.

Something had to give. She'd have to talk to him. Get Tau to cool things down a bit. For however long it took for this mess with Ryan and the demons to get solved. Or she was going to completely overload.

And she didn't want to tell him. Didn't want to put her personal life on hold. It just wasn't fair. She hadn't had a lover in far too long.

Pearl clutched the water bottle. She hated feeling conflicted. Just wanted to jump up and down like a toddler and scream her voice out.

Which would solve nothing.

She sat down on the cold wet sidewalk. Trying to get some clarity on what to do. The rain continued, some of it spattered through the trellis. Before long she was soaked through. Her skin grew cold. No clarity came.

She felt a little calmer away from the chaos of the house. That didn't help much.

Basically, she was exhausted. Even though it was the middle of the afternoon, she should just go to bed. Sleep all evening and night. Let the energy work itself out.

So she did.

Pearl woke early the next morning. Lucille had opened the door to let Beatrice and Hema out.

She got up dressed and meditated. Her empty belly grumbled the entire time.

Her dreams had been about Kasya's journey. They had spun out Ryan's plans and the world was destroyed. Meditating hadn't cleared her mind. She couldn't seem to focus this morning.

Finally, Pearl gave up and went downstairs. Willow was already at the kitchen table with two cups of tea and two slices of quiche and scones.

"Sit down and eat," said Willow.

"How did you know I'd be coming down?"

"Beryl told me. She said you skipped dinner. Eat and then tell me what's going on."

Pearl wolfed down the mushroom pepper quiche. She took a couple of sips of the black tea with cream. As she buttered the ginger scone, she told Willow about her conflicting feelings and energy levels.

Willow smiled as if it were completely normal.

"And I don't know what to do. I'm a mess."

"Well first, you go change into gardening clothes. Then go outside and haul all of Beryl's prunings to the compost bin and cut them into small pieces. Then haul some of the finished compost to the garden beds for Beryl to spread. You need to work out some of that surplus energy. Then once you're worn out physically, then and only then, talk to Tau. Ask him to back off some. That things are moving too quickly for your energy right now. Explain how much you're juggling. That won't solve everything but it will help you balance some of it. I think you need a break from doing the journeys with the shamans. I don't think that's the best use of your skill right now."

"If I don't do that, there's nothing left for me to do," said Pearl.

"You're helping Lucille keep the lid on this pressure cooker of a household. That's enough."

"It doesn't keep my mind occupied."

Willow stared at her.

"Then keep your mind busy by planning Ruby's party. And keeping it a secret."

"I can try," said Pearl. "But by backing off the journeys, I feel like a failure."

"You're hardly a failure. Knowing one's limits isn't failing. It's succeeding at life," said Willow.

The older woman gave her a look that Pearl couldn't avoid. She was right, of course. Willow was always right.

"We'll call you if we need you for a journey. There are plenty of us supporting the shamans."

After breakfast, Pearl took herself out to the garden. She worked out there until dinner.

After dinner, she went down to the library and found some paper and began planning Ruby's birthday. It was quiet there and the only person who regularly went there was Beryl. Ruby never came down to the quiet basement room.

———

A WEEK LATER, PEARL WAS ON HER WAY DOWNSTAIRS AFTER breakfast to look at the cookbooks she'd pulled from the shelves. This would be an incredible feast.

Her muscles ached from working in the garden all day yesterday. She should probably do some stretching out. Down in the warm cozy library would be a good place.

She heard raised voices in the small dining room. Ruby and Sapphire.

"These guys are the worst," said Ruby. "They have no ethics and their magic is completely evil. They're so scummy just thinking about them makes me feel like I need a shower."

"I agree but we still need to talk to them," said Sapphire.

Pearl stuck her head in the door.

"No!" yelled Jet.

Bera, Jamilla and Beryl also sat at the table. Beryl's face looked pinched and white.

"Come in and shut the door," said Sapphire.

"What's going on?" asked Pearl.

Jet said, "Ryan met with two members of the Soliece family last night. We think he's probably been meeting with them all along. That's who Max is, Max Soliece. There was another one too. Bera said they could've been twins."

The Soliece family lived in Lynnwood in a large gated compound. They were wealthy, magical and the worst thugs imaginable. They made the drug cartels look tame. And they had never been caught by law enforcement. Pearl always assumed it was because of their dark magic.

"Okay, so we know he's teaming up with them, or using them. What next?" asked Pearl.

"We need more information," said Sapphire. "We need to know what they're planning."

"I think we should see if Connor has anything more to report. If they're planning something, maybe it's on Ryan's computer or phone," said Ruby.

"Bera and Jamilla already risked attack by the demon to get the information they did. It's not worth it to send someone else out again," said Jet.

"I'm okay with the danger," said Bera. "It's what I do. I hunt demons."

"You can't go again. You might be recognized if you go twice," said Sapphire. "Same with Jamilla. It would have to be someone else."

"I agree with Ruby," said Beryl. "Let's contact the hacker first. That way is less exposure. And the potential information we could get that way would be more complete."

Pearl said, "Can we contact the Marssahls? Talk to Sariah and see if she or anyone she knows is up on what the Soliece family is doing with Ryan?"

Sapphire gaped at Pearl.

"I can't believe I didn't think of that. I'll call her this morning. If anyone would know, she would. And if she doesn't know, she'll find out. Thanks Pearl." Sapphire pushed hair back behind her ear. "Okay Ruby, you get hold of Connor and see what he knows. I'll call Sariah. And thanks, Bera and Jamilla. Great job. Ruby, Jet, Beryl, Pearl and I will meet this afternoon after we've got more info."

Pearl nodded and then left. Heading downstairs into the library. She just wanted solitude. Her period started that morning. It had come in fast and heavy with a lot of discomfort. Physical and emotional. Which meant it might be short. Possibly only three or four days. Her intense periods normally were. If there was anything normal about her moon time.

She buried herself in cookbooks, looking for just the right recipes.

She had been downstairs for three hours, perusing old family cookbooks and making lists when the energy in the house felt wrong. It was upstairs somewhere.

Pearl sprinted up the stairs to the main floor. That wasn't it. Then to the second floor. The strangeness was coming from the meditation room. Someone was journeying.

She quietly slipped in through the door, slowing her breathing to quiet it. Tau was journeying. Coal was standing at his head, whining and licking his face. Karl, a witch and shaman was drumming. Sarah was trying to hold the space but failing.

Pearl jumped in to assist Sarah. Caorthannach was there. Tau had gotten caught by her again.

Pearl sent out a plea for help directed at her sisters but was also hoping Anya or Bera could hear.

Karl was beating the drum fast, trying to get Tau to return. Pearl couldn't sense anything from Tau. He was still gone. Just like he had been when she'd assisted with the journey.

How could Pearl sense the demon but not Tau?

Jet and Bera slipped in the door and focused on the problem. Pearl felt the energy in the room shift quickly, boosted by their combined power.

Tau still wasn't returning.

Pearl went and sat by his side, taking a hand in hers. She felt his energy then. It was distant and faint. As if someone were choking his power off.

She pushed her energy through his aura, adding her power to his. Then felt where the drain was.

Caorthannach was sucking his magic away. The demon began to pull on Pearl's energy. Gathering it in to feed her fire.

Pearl held out her hand and felt both Beryl and Ruby take it. Adding their power to her own. Ruby shot a burst of flame through the connection and the demon pulled back as if startled.

Pearl and Beryl yanked on Tau and heaved him out of Caorthannach's grip. As everyone else retreated, Jet, Ruby and Bera threw up a shield of water against the demon.

Pearl tried to focus on Tau to the exclusion of everything else.

She needed to get him grounded back in his body. Coal lay on Tau's other side now. Tau was breathing heavily.

"Tau, you need to pull back into your body now. Completely. Leave nothing behind. Squeeze my hand if you understand," said Pearl.

He slowly squeezed her hand.

"Squeeze it again when you feel like you're fully back."

Pearl could feel chaotic energy roiling around the room. Lucille was trying to balance things out. Pearl couldn't help right now.

She was examining Tau's aura. Trying to be sure he hadn't brought anything back that wasn't his. An attachment of some sort.

Finally, he squeezed her hand.

"Can you sit up?" she asked.

"I think so," he said, hoarsely.

She helped pull him up, which was made difficult by Coal, who immediately sat in Tau's lap, licking his face.

"Hiya buddy. Can someone hand me the water bottle," Tau said, pointing to a bottle on the side table.

Karl handed it to Tau, who opened the bottle and drank deeply.

Finally, Pearl was satisfied that Tau was clean of any entities or attachments.

She looked around the room. Both Karl and Sarah looked exhausted. They shouldn't have been doing this alone. Not with Tau having had this problem before. Why had they been assigned to his journey?

Beryl and Ruby looked furious. Sapphire was whispering to Jet and Bera, who both looked intense.

"What happened Tau?" asked Beryl.

"I don't know. One minute I was talking to my guides in a green meadow, the next I was in the demon's volcano. And she was swallowing my energy. I don't know what triggered it because we weren't even talking about her. I was trying to get information from my guides about Ryan and his plans."

"Maybe they're more closely linked than we thought," said Ruby.

"Maybe," said Tau. "If it's all right with you all, I don't think I'll be doing any more journeys until this is all settled and she's gone."

"I think that's a good idea," said Bera. "You seem to be a magnet for her."

"I don't know why," said Tau.

Bera shrugged. "It happens sometimes with demons. No one knows why for sure."

"Thank you all for rescuing me. Again," said Tau.

He squeezed Pearl's hand and she realized they were still touching. She released his hand and got up, moving behind him and kneeled. With her hands on his shoulders. Pearl did what she could to stabilize and balance his energy.

"Did you get any info about Ryan?" asked Ruby.

"If I did, it's gone now," said Tau.

Pearl felt the door open with a whoosh of cool air. She hadn't realized the room was so hot and that sweat had pooled on her skin.

Finally, Tau felt like he was normal again.

Willow came in the door and took Sarah away to do cleansing and balancing work on her. June had come in and was working on Karl, who looked shaken.

"Thank you," said Tau, touching Pearl's arm.

He stood up and collected his blanket and water bottle. Coal stuck to his leg as if he'd never leave.

"You're welcome," said Pearl.

Bera had left the room along with Jet, Ruby and Sapphire.

Beryl remained. Waiting for Pearl to look at her.

"*Small dining room. Now,*" she mouthed silently.

Pearl waved in acknowledgement and Beryl left.

"Can I talk to you?" asked Tau, as the walked out of the room. "I haven't seen you in days it feels like."

"I can't right now. Apparently there's a meeting downstairs I need to go to."

"Oh, was that why Beryl was waiting."

"My sisters are so subtle," said Pearl, rolling her eyes.

"After dinner? Before I go out on watch."

"Hell no. You're not going out on watch tonight. Not after that journey. I'm talking to Jet because you need to rest."

"I can do it."

"No. I'll talk to you after dinner. You can help me figure out Ruby's party. I'm drafting you."

"Ruby's party?" he asked.

"Yes, her birthday's coming up. You'll just have to wait 'til after dinner for more info. Right now, go for a walk out in the garden. Both of you. Coal just went through hell."

"Will do," he said, heading to his room to drop off the blanket and water bottle.

Pearl went down the stairs to the small dining room. She should have just told him that he needed to back off. Instead she'd just drafted him to help her with the party.

That was a stupid move. She sighed and opened the door.

Her sisters stopped talking when she walked in. Never a good sign.

"How is he?" asked Sapphire.

"Clean. But you're taking him off watch for tonight," Pearl said to Jet.

Jet shrugged in response, not arguing.

"Why the hell were Karl and Sarah assigned to his journey? After the one Tau had where the demon showed up before? Neither of them are strong enough. We needed more strong people, not less," said Pearl, still standing.

"My mistake," said Sapphire. "I was trying to save you for Anya's journeys. Since she was targeting Caorthannach."

"I'm not the only one around," said Pearl.

"I screwed up. It happens to me too, you know," said Sapphire. "I won't make the same mistake again."

"No you won't," said Pearl. "Because he won't be journeying again until we destroy the demon. It's just too dangerous."

"You do have the hots for him," said Jet, her eyes wide.

Pearl opened her mouth to deny it but decided not to. Of course they all knew. How could they not? She dropped into the nearby chair.

"I do. But he's a distraction I can't have right now. I need to focus on too many other things."

"Like what?" asked Ruby.

"Like balancing out all the chaotic energy in this house. Apparently I always do it, at least according to Beryl."

Beryl nodded.

"I knew that," said Jet. "I remember a few years ago, you went away for two weeks to one of those touchy-feely massage-healing conferences. We were a mess the entire time you were gone. Ruby got so mad, she crushed a glass with her bare hands. Sapphire froze a flower bouquet on the kitchen table and I blew up a couch pillow by just looking at it. You keep us all sane. And for the last month or so you've been sort of…crazy."

"I told you all what the problem was," said Ruby.

"Does he know?" asked Sapphire.

"He knows I'm attracted to him. And he's attracted to me. That's as far as it's going for right now. Anything else?" asked Pearl. She stood, ready to leave the room as fast as possible.

"No," said Beryl. "We just were curious about where things stood. Because you're so crucial to the stability of this house."

"And I'm trying to stay stable. I can't juggle a relationship right now on top of everything else," said Pearl.

She left the room and returned to the quiet of the library. Burying herself in recipes and descriptions of Pavlova.

CHAPTER 8

LINDA JORDAN

THE DAY OF THE IMBOLC RITUAL DAWNED FREEZING COLD, CLEAR and crisp. Pearl woke to find her period had begun. She inserted a menstrual cup to catch the blood to give to Beryl later.

Despite having three cups of caffeine tea, she felt lethargic. Groceries arrived, all the supplies for Ruby's birthday feast. For most of the morning, she helped unpack them and put them away.

Thankfully, Ruby was too busy to notice. She'd spoken to the hacker again and was in her room, trying to decipher Ryan's calendar and emails.

In the afternoon down in the seclusion of the library, Tau helped her organize last-minute details about Ruby's party.

Coal and Hema rolled around in front of the fireplace. The dog would lie on his side, pretending to be dead. Hema would pounce on him, growling and hissing. Coal would take the kitten's entire head in his mouth, slobbering all over him. Then Hema would chew on Coal's ears or tail.

Pearl and Tau just laughed.

"Thank you for including me in planning this party," he said. "I feel guilty for not journeying. This makes me feel like I'm helping."

"You always help. You're still on security."

"Not as much as before. And only with Jet or Bera. I know she's afraid I'll attract the demon again."

"Who knows what attracts her. I'm glad you're not journeying. And I really did need help. You're my dose of reality. Keeping this feast from becoming too outlandish."

"Well, I'm delighted to be the one asking 'How much food can 28 people eat'?" Tau laughed.

"You do have a point. You know, when you're not journeying, you eat less."

"Eating keeps me grounded."

"You still need to be grounded, even when you're not journeying."

"I know. But being down here in the library feels so grounding. The smell of the paper. All these books. And being sunk so deep in the earth. I don't even have to do anything. It feels so safe here. I could live in this room."

"Beryl nearly does," said Pearl.

"I can see why. But she hasn't been down here lately."

"She's been out in the garden working. There's so much to do at this time of year. And she's been in the small dining room, planning the ritual with the others. She's normally here late at night or early in the morning."

"Ah. When I'm either on watch or sleeping."

"Yes. Now about the feast, I think we should break out Great Grandma's good china. What do you think?"

Pearl and Tau stayed in the library all afternoon. When they came upstairs it was to find the weather had shifted.

Clouds had rolled in and rain threatened.

The household had a light supper of spicy soup made with black beans, squash, tomatoes and cilantro picked from the garden. Along with freshly baked bread.

It was the last night of January. The evening of Lunar Imbolc.

Everyone bundled up to go outside. Beryl asked that all the animals stay inside. Probably to avoid them getting stepped on by all the humans floundering around in the dark.

Pearl wore wool socks, garden boots, wool pants, a heavy

sweater over another shirt and a long coat. Along with a knitted hat and gloves. She felt like a toddler so bundled up they could barely walk. But she'd be warm.

She followed everyone outside into the biting cold. It was already dark but Jet and Bera had strung golden fairy lights in the garden that afternoon. The lights circled the base of the cedar tree again and again and again. Below her massive branches, the ground and people were alight. It looked magical.

Beryl had everyone spaced around the tree trunk. All 28 people were there. No one was sleeping or on watch tonight. Although at least seven designated people were paying attention to the energy around them. On guard.

Beryl smudged everyone with a cedar bough and asked that they ground and center themselves. Tap into Lucille's energy. It took a long time for her to make it all the way round to everyone.

Pearl closed her eyes. She felt her connection to all of them, to Lucille and to the wards around the property.

They all held hands, chanted and danced in place. She could feel the power moving round the circle even through her gloved hands. The energy traveled through their bodies, sinking deep into the earth.

As they chanted, Pearl could feel the power moving upwards until it connected with Ruby's and Lucille's wards. Forming a cone of power which covered the entire property, the house and all the trees.

Beryl walked around the base of the cedar, her every step loaded with intention.

"Imbolc is one of our most sacred days. One of the fire festivals. This year, the only fire will be in our bellies. It's a time when we're ready to shake off winter and embrace the new growth of spring— who is almost ready to burst forth. It's also a time of recommitment to the goddess, to the earth. If you'd like to embrace that promise— whatever it means to you—then I'd like you to do that. We'll go around the circle and those who want to participate will sing a single note, any note, and keep it going. Those wishing to pass need only turn to the next person and nod. I'll begin."

Beryl took a deep breath and sang a middle-range note. She turned to Jet, who stood nearby. Jet sang a deeper note. Then Bera and Willow. And Kasya and Ben. The singing kept going, each person adding or mirroring another note. No one passed that Pearl could tell. She added her own when it was her turn. This continued until it ended with Sapphire, who stood next to Jet. Finally, they were all singing. The power and intent which moved around the circle felt mind blowing.

The force and intensity of it all made her overheat. She peeled off her gloves and hat, sticking them in pockets. Then unbuttoned her coat.

The heat continued to grow as people breathed and continued singing their one note.

From where she was standing everyone glowed golden from the fairy lights. She could see their individual fires burning as one.

But then it hit her, the entire garden was lit up.

Pearl moved back out from under the tree to see the sky above.

There were flames on the outside of the wards.

Coming from Caorthannach.

The demon was trying to burn through Ruby's wards.

Pearl's heart caught in her throat. She couldn't swallow.

She waved and caught Jet's attention and gestured upwards. Jet stepped back and looked up.

Pearl wanted people to keep singing. To keep the energy and power rising. That might be the only thing keeping the demon outside the wards. Others were beginning to look upwards and glance around the circle for guidance.

Beryl raised her hands to stop the singing. Did she know what was going on? It was hard to miss but she was also running the ritual and might be distracted.

Beryl's voice felt hypnotic. Pearl couldn't look away from her. Couldn't do anything other than watch.

"Tonight we give the earth and Grandmother Cedar an offering. This is not just any offering. It's the blood of what could have been new life, under other circumstances. It's the blood of three women who bleed for all of us, and they gift their blood for all of us tonight."

Beryl held up a crystal pitcher filled with thick brownish-red liquid. She walked around the tree, pouring blood on the roots of the cedar. Then Beryl set the pitcher upside down on the soil, letting the rest drain out slowly.

Pearl's blood. And that of others.

There was silence except for a thrumming sound coming from the wards. A tautness if that feeling could be a sound.

Pearl felt the cedar and the earth accept the offering. The wards strengthened and renewed, making a loud pinging sound.

She looked up and gave a small sigh that the wards held. The demon couldn't get through.

The fire she'd seen lighting up the sky earlier had waned. Caorthannach looked pale and weak. Then she was gone.

For now.

Pearl felt a tinge of relief. She couldn't quite believe the demon was gone.

"I'd like to end with another chant," said Beryl. She began, "Earth, Air, Fire and Water bind us to you."

Everyone else joined in. Some taking it an octave higher or lower depending on their skills. They chanted for several minutes.

Then Beryl stopped and said, "I believe we've annoyed the neighbors enough for one night. Let's continue inside with cake and warm tea. The circle is open and yet unbroken. Merry meet and merry part and merry meet again."

The last section they all said together.

People moved towards the house. Jet and Pearl were the last ones. Pearl turned around to take a final look.

The fairy lights still illuminated everything beneath the cedar tree. But up the trunk of the tree she could see power rising in a way it never had before. But not just the cedar. All the trees in the garden and the neighborhood seemed to glow.

The gift of such elemental energy as blood raced through their root network. Deep beneath pavement and fence lines.

She could feel the earth alive beneath her feet. Much more than normal.

It was as if the offering had woken the entire land surrounding them. Not just an awakening from winter. This felt different.

More like awakening the defenses of the earth.

What had Beryl added to the blood?

"Wow," said Jet.

"Do you see it too?"

"Yeah, I've never seen that kind of energy before."

"We've never done blood magic before. Not like this," said Pearl.

"We'll should do it again," said Jet. "We need to tap into the earth's energy more often."

"I'm so relieved the wards held," said Jet. "I was really scared they wouldn't."

"Me too. Ruby's magic was crucial. We should go around and renew them tomorrow."

"Good idea. I'll put Ruby and several others on it. That'll keep her out of your hair for party preparations," said Jet.

They both stood in the cold silence for several minutes watching all the neighborhood trees glow with magic.

CHAPTER 9

LINDA JORDAN

THE NEXT NIGHT PEARL AND BERYL WAITED UNTIL RUBY WENT TO bed. Beryl cleaned the kitchen until it was spotless—something she rarely did. Pearl paced around the main floor of the house. Tau was outside, pretending to take Coal for another walk but in reality, he was waiting too.

Finally, at 11 p.m. Ruby went to bed. Playing her part and going away an hour earlier than normal.

It took the three of them only an hour to cover the entire main floor with red fairy lights. Vases, mostly canning jars, of sweetly-scented Daphne and Hyacinths from the garden went on nearly every table, windowsill and any other flat surface other than the floor.

Then Pearl looked over the menu one last time. There was a lot still to be done tomorrow.

"Can you do all this?" she asked Beryl.

"Yes. It's all under control. I've got Marcea and Ginny helping with the feast. Others are on breakfast and lunch. And Willow and Gabe are coordinating the dance tomorrow night. You just need to make sure Ruby stays out of the kitchen. Jet's bringing her breakfast in bed. Sapphire's keeping her in meetings all day and we'll deliver food to them. You should pop in to make sure Sapphire doesn't need help."

"I can do that."

"Okay, then we're good. I'm going down to the library to do a little research, then off to bed," said Beryl.

"Good night," said Pearl. "I better get to bed soon too."

"Me as well. I promised to help with breakfast," said Tau.

Pearl turned off the main lights, leaving only the glow of red fairy lights.

Coal raced up the steps ahead of them. They held hands as they walked up the stairs. Then said goodnight with another long lingering kiss that filled Pearl full of tingling energy.

She didn't fall asleep until late.

THE NEXT DAY SEEMED TO DRAG ALONG. PEARL TRIED TO GROUND herself but nothing worked. Her brain felt too full of details she needed to keep track of.

Ruby laughed when she came downstairs in the morning and saw the red lights. Everyone present came over and said, "Happy Birthday."

"The house smells so sweet. All those flowers!" Ruby said. "Thank you."

Then Sapphire steered her into the small dining room. Where they stayed while those in the kitchen bustled around trying to prepare two meals at a time.

After lunch, Willow came downstairs and found Pearl.

"I just wanted to show you how our sweater turned out. Before I wrap it."

Willow held up the bulky wool cardigan. Knitted in a fancy stitch with soft alpaca wool in tones of forest green, pumpkin orange and brown, with wooden buttons. The colors streaked together randomly. Pearl had chosen the sweater pattern and bought the yarn and buttons, Willow had done the hard work of knitting it, but said she didn't mind. It helped keep her calm to have something to work on.

"That's just stunning," said Pearl. "I need to learn how to knit or crochet so I can make my own sweaters!"

"I'll teach you. It really does help with anxiety and you end up with gorgeous clothes or gifts."

Willow went back upstairs to wrap the gift.

Pearl continued writing down the menu on the blackboard.

Aloo Samosa (Savory Pastries with Spicy Potato Filling)

Malai Murgh (Chicken in Creamed Coconut Sauce)

Matar Paneer (Green Peas and Indian Cheese in Fragrant Tomato Sauce)

Kheere ka Raita (Cucumber and Yogurt Salad)

Peele Chawal (Cumin and Turmeric Rice)

Khas Khas ki Poori (Deep-Fried Puffy Bread with Poppy Seeds)

Aam Kulfi (Mango Ice Cream)

Sharbat e Tarbooz (Watermelon Sherbet)

Whew. That was a lot of cooking for 28 people. But Beryl had looked at the recipes and suggested having two main dishes and two desserts. To give some variety for people. The household didn't normally cook Indian food but they both knew Ruby loved it.

She hung the menu on the wall of the large dining room.

Pearl helped set the long table with Great Grandma McMahon's good china and silver. The tablecloth was white lace and the china silver with blue flowers. The good crystal water glasses were brought out, along with blue linen napkins.

She went out to the garden and picked more Daphne stems and Hyacinth flowers, mixing in stems of the red-twig dogwood that Beryl had pointed out. It was another dry crisp day outside. Spring was coming but it sure wasn't here yet.

Pearl closed her eyes and felt the earth beneath her feet and the cold wind swirling around her. The flowers smelled sweet and overpowering in the nearby basket.

"Thank you," she whispered to the garden.

Back inside, she put the flowers in two matching china vases. Then set them along the centerline of the long table.

Back in the kitchen, Beryl handed her two silver baskets lined with white towels wrapped around the bread. They smelled so good Pearl wanted to begin eat them all herself. Had she even had lunch? She didn't think so.

Pearl put the bread in the dining room and went back to the kitchen for the bowls of rice. Then the cooks took in the platters of samosas and bowls of raita and the two main dishes. And pots of tea. There was always tea.

Everyone gathered in the dining room. Sapphire and Jet led Ruby in, who was blindfolded. They removed the scarf from her eyes and Ruby shrieked.

"Oh my god! Indian food! No wonder the house has smelled so wonderful since lunch. Well, dig in. This food's not gonna stay hot. I'm starving."

Ruby sat down and the platters of samosas were passed around, along with the raita. Tea was poured.

Pearl barely tasted the potatoes inside the pasty but she felt the heat and cooled hers with some raita. She felt relieved things were moving along flawlessly. Everything looked and smelled great.

Tau sat beside her, grinning. He ate five samosas, savoring their heat.

Then they moved on to passing the main dishes. The coconut chicken and the peas and paneer. And the rice and bread.

The bread was chewy and the poppy seeds crunched in her mouth. She could eat an entire plate by itself. But the chicken was so creamy. And the zingy tomato sauce on the peas and paneer was just divine. The rice was also wonderful but Pearl preferred the bread.

"I'm in heaven," said Ruby. "Thank you, all of you," she said looking at Pearl and Beryl. "I remember the first time I ever had Indian food. I'd never tasted some of those spices and it was incredible. Like an entire world opening up to me. This feels just like that."

She smiled and returned to eating.

When everyone had finished, the cooks removed the food.

Pearl got up to help and Beryl said, "Sit. We've got this."

They returned with trays of pre-filled bowls of ice cream and sherbet, setting the mango, watermelon and half and half ones in front of specific people. One of the half and half bowls had a candle on it. Beryl lit it with her finger and put it in front of Ruby.

Ruby closed her eyes as everyone sang *Happy Birthday* to her. Then she blew out the candle.

When dinner was finished, Pearl stood and said, "It's time for Ruby to open gifts. Let's go into the living room. Leave your dishes here. They'll be taken care of."

Tau, Anya, Jet and June picked up the trays and began carefully stacking dishes on them. Everyone else went into the living room towards one side where a table laden with wrapped gifts sat.

"This is the best birthday party I've ever had," said Ruby. She began reading the cards and unwrapping things. There was a wonderful wood carving of a fire that Ben had done. Anya gave her a necklace of glass beads, which Ruby put on immediately. Kasya had painted a watercolor of a salamander in a wheel of fire.

Ruby loved the sweater from Willow and Pearl. She put that on too.

"So many gifts," said Ruby, when she finished unwrapping them all. "I feel so blessed."

"Well, let's clear this away and get on with the rest of the night then," said Pearl.

Ruby moved her gifts to a shelf near the window, creating a shrine. A couple of people folded up the table and moved it out.

Then Gabe put the music on.

Finally, her part in all this was done. Pearl went to the middle of the living room and began to dance. Others joined in.

"Oooph, I ate too much," moaned Bera.

Everyone laughed.

Pearl had eaten too much as well. She still danced. Feeling the music move her.

Tau moved close to her. He leaned down and gave her one of those long kisses. She felt the energy move up and down her spine and back up again as she swirled with the music.

This was a good night.

Perhaps the last one they'd have for a while. The wheel was

turning and things were going to shift soon. She could feel things changing.

The battle would begin. They might not survive it. She might not survive it.

But she'd have tonight.

And tonight was the night. It was time to act before she was out of chances.

Pearl wrapped her arms around Tau's neck as a slow dance began. Tonight, tonight would be ecstasy in all its forms.

THE COFFEE FAE

SUSAN OLD

CHAPTER 1 - YOU NEVER KNOW ABOUT WRITERS

SUSAN OLD

DERECHO WINKED AT FRANCES, WHICH MADE HER NERVOUS. "C'mon, you said you wanted to try someplace new, and I know a great little cafe I think you'll like." He was attractive in a young bohemian, sexy rebel kind of way.

"Yeah, but I'm over my budget this month because of car repairs. I'll cook something at my place." Fran's 42-year-old practicality did not dissuade Derecho.

He grinned. "It'll be my treat, Fran. Besides, I owe you for fixing my computer."

"Okay, that's fair." She caved; Derecho was very persuasive and she was a mediocre cook. "But I didn't do much. Honestly, you just need to spend some time learning some computer basics. I'm not sure what you did, but it wasn't that hard to fix."

"Computers aren't my thing. I'm just a great storyteller."

She had to agree. Derecho was the most talented fantasy writer she'd edited for in years. Long dark curls hung over his broad shoulders, and he wore urban pirate attire only he could pull off. Fran knew other women would be delighted to have dinner with him. His social media accounts were full of offers from fans. She decided he was just expressing gratitude for her help.

Frances was self-employed, content being single, living with cats. She tugged at her Levi jacket, and looked down at scuffed Birkenstocks. No time to change. What she was wearing would have to do. They walked a few blocks from her office in downtown Bellingham, then he turned into an alley. Knowing you could sometimes find good little restaurants off the beaten path, she followed.

"Here it is." He stood in front of an emerald-green door with a polished bronze knocker, but no sign that indicated that it was a café. Derecho let the knocker fall three times, then the door opened.

A wonderful aroma enveloped Fran. Freshly brewed coffee with hints of spices she couldn't quite identify. A stern voice called out, "It's about time you got here." Derecho gestured for his editor to go in first. A woman wearing a scarlet caftan, with long silver hair coiled high on her head, stared at her. She looked back at Derecho and remarked, "Seriously?"

Frances stopped, staring past the rude woman at a room filled with small tables lit by tiny sparkling lights and lanterns arrayed around a large live tree. It appeared to be growing inside the building, and the branches were covered with lovely fragrant pink blooms. Fran's eyes went back to the woman's glare.

Derecho stepped in front of Frances. "Grandmama, this is my dear friend Frances. She helps publish my books. I wish to reward her. She has potential."

The women's expression softened. "Derecho, what shall I do with you? You always did bring home stray cats and dogs."

Fran stared at the woman. "I'm not a stray, and strays can be wonderful pets." She thought about leaving, but her curiosity and empty stomach made her stay. "Potential for what?"

Grandmama merely shook her head and gestured to a table.

Derecho said, "I'll explain later." He guided Fran over to a table beneath a mural of a waterfall. When she looked closely, it appeared as if the water was moving. Fran sat with her back to it and wondered if her blood sugar was low.

Derecho gazed at her with a whimsical expression. "I've never considered you a pet."

Fran ignored his comment and stared at Derecho; her oversized glasses emphasized her hazel eyes. After a moment she asked, "Does your family owns this place?"

"Yes, we reside here in the off-season."

Her brows furrowed. He never mentioned coming from money. "Where do you usually 'reside'?" she asked with a touch of sarcasm.

Before he could respond, a waitress interrupted. "What do you desire?"

Fran stared at the platinum-haired, 20 something-year-old, who ignored her and only looked at Derecho. Frances, slightly annoyed, said, "Coffee." The waitress did not look at her.

Derecho's eyes traced every inch of the server, then he said, "The special for both of us."

The waitress leaned forward, kissed him then walked away. He seemed disinterested as his eyes quickly went back to his editor. "We've been engaged for several years." He shrugged and added, "Don't want to rush into anything."

"I'm starting to feel sorry for her." Fran thought they made a perfect pair.

He looked a tad mischievous. "She's probably jealous of you."

"Very funny. My middle-aged ego doesn't need your flattery." She took off her jacket and pushed her shiny straight brown hair back from her face. Fran did not realize how attractive her clean, no-fuss look was to him.

"My people don't think of age the way your culture does. It just makes you more interesting."

"My people?" She never thought about him being from anywhere but the Pacific Northwest. "Where are you from? My dad was born in Cornwall."

He shrugged, "Ah, here's the coffee. Drink first, and then I'll reveal more."

"Why do I feel like you're about to tell one of your stories."

The waitress spilled a little coffee on Fran's hand, but it didn't burn. To her surprise, it tingled a little.

The server muttered an insincere apology, "Sorry."

The coffee was strong and black, just the way she liked it. Fran lifted the caffeinated elixir to her lips and inhaled the scents of an exotic marketplace. She closed her eyes as the rich brew rolled over her tongue and throat; energetic delight filled her brain. She started to drink more when Derecho's hand stopped her. His touch caused the same tingling sensation as the coffee spill had.

"Slow down, Frances, savor your first taste." He sounded older for a moment, surprising her.

She searched his face. "Where did these beans come from? I spent $25 on a cup of Black Ivory coffee once, but that doesn't compare to this."

"Whatever they do with their coffee will never make a difference because the beans in this world come from plants my people discarded centuries ago. The beans we sell to other magickal beings are a lesser grade than we consume."

"There you go again, 'My people.'" She scrutinized him. "You may write about fantasy worlds, but unfortunately, we all live in this one, buddy."

A faint smile came to his lips. Derecho held up one hand, and a small orange flame appeared from it. Without thought, she threw the remainder of her coffee on it. He laughed as the waitress appeared and carefully wiped the stain from his sleeve while giving Fran a dirty look.

He gently pushed her away. "Thank you, Pansy."

"What just happened?"

"Don't you remember how the hero could produce fire with his bare hands in my first novel?"

"The Fae Prince? Yeah, but c'mon, that was fiction."

He just looked at her amused. "I'm not a prince, but my people are fae." Her jaw dropped, and he continued. "We come from a place farther away than Cornwall."

She stared at him. "I must be dreaming, but this seems real."

"Pinch yourself. I think that's what you do, right? Or I could slap you." His eyes twinkled.

"Don't you dare!" She pinched her upper arm hard, and nothing changed. "Screw this. That hurt."

"Well, now we've established, you're not asleep or hallucinating.

We've known each other for a while, and I think it is time I revealed more about myself. What do you want to know?" His deep-set blues eyes held her attention.

Fran sighed. "What kind of freak show is this?"

Pansy and Grandmama arrived with platters of colorful roasted foods, which appeared to be root vegetables and potatoes in a golden sauce. She already knew that Derecho was a vegetarian. Pansy grated cheese on top of her entrée until Fran said stop.

The matriarch placed a small loaf of bread, still warm from the oven, between them. "May the goddess preserve you."

Derecho repeated the phrase and nodded to Frances. She said, "Uh, may the goddess preserve you too."

A tiny smile and nod of approval followed then Grandmama and Pansy left them alone.

Derecho said, "I've wanted to share my life with you, and recent events have made it imperative." He paused, then gestured to her plate. "Please, eat first."

The bread was delicious, and so were the veggies. They ate in silence while he gave Fran time to calm her brain. After finishing only half of the meal, she wiped her lips with a cloth napkin and said, "That was delicious." She sat silently, then continued, "I'm trying hard to believe you haven't suckered me into some grand joke. So, you want me to think that all this time you've been writing non-fiction?"

He gave her a Cheshire grin. "More or less. I had to tone down our reality to make it more believable. Lewis Carrol gave me that advice years ago, and it worked for him."

"Stop it. He died way before your time." She thought she finally had him.

He chuckled. "No, he didn't die. He just went home. Lewis stays in our world now. This reality can be exhausting for fae."

She shook her head and looked around at the beautiful indoor garden. "I'm still not convinced this isn't an elaborate joke, but I couldn't blame Lewis Carrol for leaving if it were true." She paused and asked, "How old are you supposed to be?"

"Our sense of time is different from yours but around three centuries. So, you see, I'm much older than you."

"That's not possible." Sadness started to creep into her mind as she considered that he might be delusional. "Derecho, you always seemed grounded. When did you start thinking you were fae?"

"From birth." He cleared his throat. "One of the reasons I've stayed with you as an editor is your objectivity. Most readers become diehard fans and never question what I write. The magic influences them in my books. But you always have questions and comments. You're difficult to charm."

"That's what my last boyfriend said."

He smirked and said, "Too bad about losing his job and moving away."

"Yeah. I'm not even gonna ask if you had something to do with that." Fran felt like she was being played and kept trying to find a hole in his story. "Is fae a nationality? Where do you all come from?"

He made a graceful gesture with one hand, and the song, " Somewhere Over the Rainbow" started playing. Pansy appeared, cleared away the dishes, and returned with a bowl of candied flower petals and melted chocolate. Derecho dipped a fuchsia into the sauce and handed it to Fran.

There was a slight crunch and then an amazing mix of delicate sweetness with a slight bite of dark chocolate. "That's fantastic!" Her eyes narrowed. "You still didn't answer my question."

"The song is the answer. We are only visitors here. The Fae come here on what you could call a work visa or a vacation permit to challenge their survival skills in a harsh environment." He glanced at Pansy standing several feet away and put one of her namesake flowers on his tongue. She smiled seductively then went back to the kitchen. "That should keep her happy for a bit."

"Magical or not, that was a dick move. You should marry her already."

He swallowed then said, "Yeah, it was. I don't know why she still pursues me. I'm not ready to wed a fae."

"You're hurting my brain. Dude, why did you bring me here and reveal all this craziness to me? Why mess with my orderly boring life? Shouldn't you be hanging out with Tinkerbell in a gumdrop house?"

"Candy houses? We're not witches," he said as though offended and finished his coffee. "I'm writing another book. It's different from the others. I still don't give away fae secrets, just teasing with a little more magick, but it's darker. I loosely based it on a situation confronting me now. I'm telling you all of this because I would like your help dealing with some troublesome fae hiding here." He was afraid to be any more specific until she was onboard.

"Troublesome fae in Bellingham? Gangster fae in Fairhaven?" She rolled her eyes.

"Actually, close to Seattle." He did not smile. "They are a threat to our society."

She frowned. "If this is true, why me? Don't you have cops riding unicorns to deal with your delinquents?" She began to wonder what was in the coffee.

He frowned. "Small dragons, actually, but here they prefer Teslas. Fae security are not involved in this, not yet. This is something beyond my stories, a pressing matter I need your help with before involving them."

"Wow. You're serious." Fran sat staring at the younger man whose books had kept her financially afloat the last few years. She hoped he wasn't nuts. If he weren't, that would mean everything he said was true. Fran couldn't think of any other option and wished there was a logical explanation for the flame that burst from his palm.

His expression became serious. "You can't tell anyone about our reality or our presence in your world. Even in magickal communities, we keep our activities secret to protect our realm. I've taken a risk inviting you here and telling you all this. I hope I it was not a mistake to you." He searched her face for a sign she truly believed him.

"You don't have to worry about me telling anyone. I don't want people to think I've lost it." She stared at him. "I'm normally quite rational, but either I edit your next book or get a second job slinging lattes for entitled suburbanites." She joked, "I guess it's bring on the dragons." Fran looked down at her lap for a minute considering possible weird ramifications. "If you're being straight with me, and that's a big if, I'll help as long as you promise no strange rangers are gonna come after me or mess with my cats."

"Strange rangers?" he scoffed. "You have my word that I'll protect you, and no one will harm Victor and Hugo. My kind worships cats and cherishes dogs but not always people." He picked up the dessert platter and said, "You have so much to learn. Dragons and unicorns rarely venture into this world. Can you blame them?" Derecho smiled, enjoying his knowledge of all things magickal. "Now come help in the kitchen."

"Unicorns are real? I was joking about that." Fran followed him into the back, where his grandmama sat reading next to a window. Derecho walked over to an industrial sink piled with dishes and plates. "You're the dishwasher?"

He nodded. "If you don't cook and serve, then you clean up. We are a communal society so that no one gets taken advantage of."

She looked around. "Is there any more coffee?"

"I'm not sure that's a good idea."

"Trust me." She grabbed a clean cup and held it out.

He filled it, then said, "You've been drinking our version of decaf. You aren't ready for the full magick brew. You have to build up your tolerance for that."

"Decaf?" She almost spit it out.

The matriarch said, "Sit. Derecho do his share. We need to talk."

Fran pulled up a wooden chair covered in brightly painted flowers. Grandmama's eyes were brown with a faint green spiral. Her smile emphasized tiny wrinkles. Fran had to wonder how old she was.

"You have been invited here because my grandson believes you have skills that will aid us in protecting the sanctity of our crop. We are the Coffee Fae. Different branches of our societal tree possess talents in other areas, but we nourish and protect the bean which sustains our powers. In our world, that makes us very important."

"You have a plantation?" She looked to Derecho and he nodded.

"I can't keep a houseplant alive, so I don't think I could be of much help to you."

The matriarch frowned and Fran felt her coffee cup suddenly get cold. Ancient eyes searched the editor's soul. "Your magic resides there." She gestured towards the world outside the window. "You have been a trustworthy friend to Derecho in this dimension. He told me that you're very good with computers. Is this true?"

"Yes, but it's self-serving. Derecho gives me a percentage of his sales which makes me do my best with editing and marketing his writing online and at events. He had an agent, but he turned to me when that relationship fizzled." Fran paused, expecting some comment, but the older woman just stared, waiting for her to continue. "I promote his books on several platforms, do some giveaways. I have found that book blurbs with pics of my cats get a lot of attention. Honestly, his writing, paired with his appearances, is why he's so popular. He can be pretty charming with he turns it on."

Grandmama smiled. "He comes by it supernaturally."

Derecho looked over his shoulder. "Frances got me started at Fantasy Conventions, where my books took off."

Grandmama asked in a serious tone, "I'm glad you helped with his hobby. Which witches do you trust?"

Fran glanced at Derecho's back, hoping he would say something, then back at her. "Witches? None. I don't know any."

He snickered. "Grandmama, you know very well, I'm her only magickal acquaintance."

With a twinkle in her eyes, she said, "Sorry, my dear. We were just teasing. Derecho knows of a coven in Seattle. We shall ask for them help with enemies of our realm, but we require your mortal skills investigating the criminal fae's behavior and sorting it out."

Fran felt a sudden chill, like some dark premonition. "This all sounds out of my league. I fix punctuation and make Instagram posts. You should contact the police to deal with shady individuals. I even failed a self-defense class." She stood up. "Thanks for dinner, but I guess I should go." She finished the coffee. "I'll look over what you've written so far. Just send me the file." She took a step, then stopped. "I won't tell a soul about any of this. See you tomorrow?"

Derecho turned and smiled, drying his hands with a towel. "Sure, Fran. I'll come by in the morning. Everything will be fine, you'll see."

"Yeah, well, I'll just show myself out." As she was leaving, the matriarch mumbled something about giving her a fruit basket, but Frances didn't stick around.

CHAPTER 2 - TROUBLE BREWING

SUSAN OLD

Brazilla was not happy that Emily's Coffee in Everett was out of her favorite bean. As the sorceress in charge of a Seattle coven, she was expected to have high standards and only serve the best. Though most witches were tea drinkers, she and a few others preferred the dark brew. Brazilla stared at the very hospitable kitchen witch and owner of the cafe. Emily appeared her normal, neat bun, tidy apron self, but something felt off.

Brazilla ran a hand through her short purple hair and spoke softly to avoid eavesdroppers. "What is the problem? You usually have my order delivered by the first. Have the McMahon sisters of the Everett Coven suddenly taken to drinking my bean of choice? I would understand if you made their order a priority." Her polite words did not match her rigid demeanor.

Emily sighed. "My dear Brazilla, the local coven remains my best herbal tea customer. I don't have to play favorites. I would like to fulfill your standing order, but there is a problem with...," she paused, looked around, and whispered, "the source has been withholding their beans due to conflicts in their realm."

"How is that possible? Who would...."? She stopped speaking

when Emily handed her an envelope. Brazilla sniffed the air and detected the slight scent of pixie coming from a far corner. When she turned to look, the spot was empty. It had been over a century since she had detected one of those creatures.

Emily's normally happy countenance sported a frown. "I was told to give you this when you came in. I'm sorry, but they requested I not tell you about the problem until I could give you this letter in person. Of course, till this sad affair is resolved, you're welcome to any of the other beans I carry. The Ethiopian blend has a bit of the enchanted bean and is a favorite of some discerning customers. Perhaps it would do for now. Again, I apologize."

Brazilla's dark eyes got big as she felt magick coming through the envelope, tickling her fingers. She read her name in an elaborate glimmering script. "Emily, forgive me for my irritation. I had no idea. Please send a shipment of the Ethiopian at your convenience." She wished to read the message in private as soon as possible and rushed out of the café.

Charles Wang dusted the crystal balls in his shop at the Coventree Hotel near the waterfront in Seattle. His standards as a warlock, running a respected magickal accessories shop, were being tested by his love, the witch Rowena Snap. Her raven, Mathilda, perched on everything in the shop, and Rowena forbade Charles from chastising her familiar. He and the raven had reached an understanding that they would appear to get along to make Rowena content.

Charles' tall frame stretched up so he could grab a feather left on a prized ancient skull that hung on the wall. "Damn it," he muttered. He pushed back his shoulder-length black hair and sighed.

"What's wrong, honey?" Rowena asked as she put some new Tarot card decks on display. Her long thick red hair had turquoise roots, which brought out the color of her eyes.

He didn't want her to know that he was exasperated with the

raven and avoided her gaze "Nothing. Just mumbling about the inventory. We're low on dragon scales, wolfbane, and adder's tongue."

Rowena said, "I'm not surprised that people are stocking up after that episode with the werewolves and the vampires. It's always good to be prepared, but blessed be, the supernaturals appear to be abiding by the peace agreement."

Charles was about to point out Rowena and Brazilla's major roles in that magickal crisis but didn't want to seem critical of his love, much less the head of the coven. He reflected on how their friend Misty, a werewolf princess, had taken well to being transformed into a vampire. Alas, the vampire who had taken her place among the werewolves was reportedly not content. He thought, "It serves Andre right." The new werewolf had asked for a temporary switch, but that had taken place months ago.

He turned to his wife. "My dear, if not for Andre being so self-indulgent and his desire to howl at the moon, we would never have been brought together." Rowena had stayed at the hotel while involved in performing the transformation to avoid unhappy werewolves visiting her house during the crisis. Werewolves hated that one of their own had become undead. "I dislike thinking I owe him, but I do."

She chuckled, "Don't you feel sorry for the pack? Even as a vampire, Andre was always a malcontent." She thought about how he had traded prized vampire blood for a chance to experience the wild existence of a werewolf. "Do you think he will ever forgive Brazilla for tricking him into staying that way?"

"Probably not. The undead certainly got the best of that exchange."

THAT NIGHT A YOUNG VAMPIRE COUPLE ARRIVED IN EVERETT. "So why are we here? I'm not complaining, just curious." Caleb stepped into Emily's Coffee with his fiancé Misty. They had been central to the recent magickal crisis. Misty had gotten involved to save Caleb's life. Before being transformed, he had been a mortal dying of cancer. They were now undead newbies exploring their existence, and frequenting eateries was no longer a normal activity.

She smirked. "Yeah, you never complain." The fondness in her light brown eyes stopped him from responding. "Brazilla said to check out this place, just hang out and let her know if anything seems unusual, out of sync. Because of your old job at Starbucks, she thought you might see something a magickal would miss. I'm here to detect the presence of other kinds of beings."

Caleb ran a hand thru his short red hair and inhaled the aroma of the coffee and tea shop, eliciting memories of his mortal life. "I still love the smell of coffee. Let's sit over there."

They found a table in a corner with a good view of the place. Hardwood floors, uncomfortable plastic chairs, and walls painted in light yellow with green accents added warmth even on rainy days.

Misty said, "It's not as pleasant as it seems. The owner is doing something to make the place happier, like forcing a smile."

"I'll get a double espresso. Do you want anything?"

Misty shook her head. Caleb walked up to the counter, where Emily looked him over as he ordered. He asked about the Congo Espresso, but she recommended Ethiopian. He acquiesced, deciding to trust the barista. Someone bumped into him as he waited. A short young woman with long gray hair and a mischievous grin stared up at Caleb.

"Sorry, honey. I couldn't resist." She paid for a scone and purred, "Nice." Then moved away.

The barista handed him his drink and managed to lightly touch his hand. Even though he was a vampire, the place was giving him the creeps. He hurried back to the table.

"What the hell is happening here?" He took a sip of coffee. "Good beans!"

Misty chuckled. "Unbelievable! A pixie just bumped you. They have a thing for green eyes. They rarely make their presence known, but she had to flirt with you."

"Does this mean we're going steady? I like shorter women."

She laughed. "You want to be turned into a unicorn? Be glad I'm here to protect you. What did you think about the barista?"

Caleb was new to the world of fantastic beings, unlike Misty, who had grown up as a werewolf. "I think I figured her out. She has a Rowena vibe. She made a point of touching my hand, so I think she knows what we are." He finished his espresso and stared at the small cup. "And there's something added to the coffee. Maybe a happy spice. I don't know, but it's more than just caffeine. It's Ethiopian, and I think you'll probably like it."

"You mean my Ethiopian mom would. I'm also half Siberian." Her amber eyes flashed, telling him not to talk about her family. They had yet to forgive her for becoming undead. "The only thing Brazilla mentioned is that she thinks the owner is having trouble and she wants our opinion of what might be going on."

A pale woman wearing a long black coat and a knit cap over green hair wandered in and went up to the counter. The barista's eyes searched the room, landed on Misty then looked back at the new arrival. Without a word, Emily put a large envelope that looked like it could be stuffed with cash on the counter. The young woman placed a tote bag next to the envelope. Emily peeked inside, then nodded.

The mysterious woman glanced around the café, seeming not to find anyone interesting, then shoved the envelope in her coat and took off, leaving the bag on the counter.

"C'mon," Misty was headed out the door. Caleb was used to following her lead. They saw the green-haired woman quietly drive out of the parking lot in an electric car. "Damn those Shadow Fae!"

Caleb chuckled. "She's a fae with green hair and drives a Leaf? Bet she listens to Grateful Dead."

Misty was not amused. "The Shadow Fae are magickal terrorists! I'm sure I saw her on a wanted poster at a wolf bar a couple of years ago. Why mess with a kitchen witch in Everett?"

Caleb said, "Well, this was a fun date night, a flirty pixie and environmentally concerned criminals. I'll try to salvage the evening by buying a bag of those special beans."

"That's it, of course." To his surprise, she kissed him, licked her lips then said, "It's why you liked her coffee so much. Her brew is blended with beans from someplace much more remote than Ethiopia."

CHAPTER 3 - FRAN IN WONDERWORLD

SUSAN OLD

DERECHO'S NEW BOOK WAS A SCARY ACCOUNT OF THE FAE WORLD. Clashes and power grabs between the different types of fae made them seem less superior to people than in his other books. She'd read the hundred pages he sent before falling asleep that night. When he showed up at her office the following day, she was excited.

Fran smiled at him. "This is your best work yet; the characters are complex, and the plot twists are subtle yet engaging. You sell the king of the fae as a charming self-centered prig well."

He grinned. "It wasn't hard. We have to head to Seattle, so grab what you need for a couple of days. Don't worry. Pansy will attend to your cats."

Fran sat back, her good mood rapidly deteriorating. "First of all, no. Secondly, you ask people to go places with you. You don't just tell them." She folded her arms. "Fae social skills suck. I've got a ton of work to do."

"Unfortunately, there is no time to waste. Much is at stake, and there's a sorceress we must meet with. And, as you have suggested, I shall 'ask' for her assistance in a grave matter. See, your human input has already been helpful. Shall we go? That was a question." He stared her down.

Fran sputtered, "But Victor is on a special diet, and Hugo insists on a clean cat box every morning, or my place will be a disaster." She felt her refusal skills waning, so as a last protest, she got personal. "Also, I still consider you human, a really weird, suddenly bossy human."

"Pansy has observed your care of the cats for two weeks and has been giving them treats while you've been at the office. They will be fine."

"She went into my apartment without asking. What the hell, Derecho! No wonder they've been gaining weight."

He put up his hands. "I am what I am. I thought you liked complex fae. I need your help, and we do have to go now."

"Give me a few minutes to pack some clothes."

He handed Fran her backpack and said, "Just grab your computer. I will provide whatever else you need in Seattle."

"You're sure my cats will be okay with Pansy?" He nodded. She packed up her laptop, mumbling, "I'm charging you overtime."

On the way to the airport, he said, "You know that coffee you paid $25 for, well that was all just a stupid joke. People drinking coffee from beans fed to elephants started with a rumor spread by pixies." He paused as Fran just stared. "They told a witch that our coffee was special because we fed the beans to unicorns then sanitized the result."

Fran's mouth was open for a moment before words came out. "Pixies? And they feed unicorns coffee beans?"

"Yes and no. But that wasn't the point. I don't want you ever to trust a pixie."

"Right. Never trust a pixie. So, the beans...."

"Just come from blessed trees."

"I'm really glad you cleared that up. My brain hurts. This is bananas."

He chuckled. "There are some in the fruit basket my grandmama packed for the flight."

"You won't be able to take it on the plane."

"It's not a problem. I have my own jet. Perks of being the Coffee Fae, CEO."

"You have a jet?" Fran crossed her arms. "I want triple overtime."

IN EVERETT, THE GREEN-HAIRED FAE DROPPED THE ENVELOPE ON a desk in an old office building. "Here, I'm tired of this world, and I want to go home." She frowned and settled in a chair.

"Thank you, Calla." The older fae was sitting behind the scared wooden desk. He had long grey hair and was wearing a lavender shirt. He stroked his neat grey beard and said, "I assume it's all there."

"Yes, Stratus, of course, it is. The witch wanted her precious beans though they're hardly worth brewing. The pixie said customers are starting to complain."

"Good, good." He smiled. "Let there be rumors about the failure of the Coffee Fae's crops. We'll soon be welcomed back as saviors of the precious trees. Under my leadership, we'll create a kingdom worthy of us. Now it's full of lazy, lackluster snobs who do not understand what could be achieved with their gifts."

She hated to harsh his buzz, but there was more. "One other thing. Probably nothing, but a couple of vampires followed me out of the café."

He put his fingertips together. "There's only one sorceress in this area who deals with those creatures." Stratus moved to the window and looked out on the street. He looked down at a couple of homeless people with a shopping cart holding all their belongings. "I don't know any fae dealing with her. You were careful?"

"Of course. I took the long way here. I made sure no one followed me. It was probably nothing." She went to the back room where she had created a refuge from this world and closed the door.

Three paintings of their home world hung on the walls of the sacred waterfall, the groves of coffee trees, and a gathering of her family in happier times. She stared at them, sighed wistfully, then lit a green candle that gave the room a warm glow. She knelt and put her palms up, praying to those who had established their kingdom for protection. Sometimes she wondered if her uncle wasn't as bad as the Coffee Fae. She longed for peace. Small pink lilies bloomed in her hand. The scent made her smile.

Stratus flung open the door. "I contacted our pixie. The Seattle Coven is involved with the undead that saw you. Something does not feel right. We must increase security around the trees. Our cousins might be using others to try and find us, which means Derecho is starting to panic."

"They had to catch on sooner or later." Calla stared at her hands as the delicate flowers disappeared. She sighed and pointed to a creature in a large terrarium. "You can take her to the greenhouse tomorrow."

"Excellent."

THE SHORT FLIGHT TO SEATTLE WAS UNDER AN HOUR. JUST AS Fran was settling into the luxury of the jet and nibbling on grapes, they landed. She had never imagined Derecho was wealthy enough for his own private plane. As they got off the jet, he put a hand on Fran's arm to keep her from stumbling. Fran felt the same curious sensation she had experienced when he had touched her hand at the café. Fran hated to admit how much she liked being close to him. She never allowed a personal relationship with a client to develop.

Derecho led her to an electric Jeep, with all the bells and whistles parked at the hanger. She hurried around to the passenger side as the jet steward loaded his luggage, her computer bag, and the fruit basket. Fran reached back for a peach. "Are we going far?" she asked, wiping juice off her chin.

"It's about thirty minutes away. My house is on a hillside overlooking the Puget Sound." He glanced at her. "The staff is preparing refreshments for you and others, whom I hope will be helpful to my family."

"Great. I'm hungry. These others, are they like me?"

"You'll see. That fruit from Grandmama is grown in fae soil; it will help you detect what your mortal eyes ignore."

She stopped eating. "She didn't understand why but she was beginning to believe what he had told her about himself. "You should've told me! Derecho, that is not cool!"

He chuckled. "Info about my realm is on a need-to-know basis."

"Well, from now on, I need to know everything!"

They arrived at a modern, three-story house just North of Seattle with a magnificent view of the water. The back deck curved around overlooking a cliff. He showed Fran to her room furnished with pine furniture. The queen-sized bed was covered with aqua bedding, and there was a bronze sea turtle sculpture on the wall above a small desk. A bouquet of fresh lavender scented the room. She set up her laptop and placed a copy of his manuscript next to it. He always gave her a print copy and a digital file because he didn't trust technology. She rested her hand on the hard copy and thought, "I guess that makes us even. I don't trust magick." She wondered how their relationship would change.

THERE WAS A KNOCK ON THE DOOR; DERECHO ENTERED. "THE others have arrived."

She glared at him. "Usually, people knock, then ask 'Are you decent?' before entering."

He shook his head. "You have too many rules, and I already know you're a decent human being." She decided just to let it go.

As he turned to head downstairs, she demanded, "Before we go down, tell me who or what they are?"

"Witches and vampires. But carefully chosen to help us."

"You know it isn't Halloween yet, right?"

His eyes looked serious. "Don't insult them."

It was getting dark when they entered the large living room with a view of the deck lit up by dangling lanterns. The posh furnishings and enchanted incense made his guests feel comfortable. Derecho first guided Fran to a 30ish tan woman in a tight running suit with short purple hair sitting alone.

"Brazilla is the head of a Seattle Coven. May I introduce Frances, my trusted friend."

The sorceress nodded. "I hope you are skilled."

Fran bristled. "I have my moments."

Derecho turned to face the others. A couple dressed entirely in black sat on the couch looking perfectly goth. The woman had dark brown curls, and a slight smile warmed her sculpted features. Her companion had short auburn hair and striking green eyes.

Fran said, "Hi." And looking gob smacked, blurted, "You're vampires." Grandmama's fruit was working.

Caleb said, "And you're not."

"Sorry, I didn't mean any offense." Fran considered making a run for it.

Caleb grinned, "It's all right. For what it's worth, this is the first time I've spoken to any fae."

"You'll have to excuse him. I'm Misty, and he's Caleb. I know it must be strange to meet our kind, but know we mean you no harm."

"Phew, that's a relief," she said, wiping her brow.

Rowena walked over with Charles and took Fran's hands. "You're safe here. We only use our magic for good." Fran felt comfort from her touch. "I'm Rowena, a witch, and this is my husband, Charles."

Charles smiled and said, "You can call me a witch or a warlock. It's all the same to me."

"Yeah, sure. Everyone assuring me they aren't going to hurt me makes me a bit nervous." Fran sat in a chair and looked at Derecho. "Can I have some coffee?"

He said, "And that brings us to why we are all here." He made a gesture with his wrist, and his staff came in with refreshments.

The witch couple had tea and cookies. The vamps drank something red in crystal shot glasses that made Fran cringe. Brazilla sipped from a coffee mug while Derecho bit into an apple. Fran was handed a shot of espresso, which she downed in one gulp. She noticed that there was something sexy about how Derecho was consuming his apple. All the women in the room were locked on him for a minute.

To break the tension, Fran bit into a cookie and said, "The ginger snaps are good."

Charles frowned, feeling the weight of the moment. "I think we should get down to business. Derecho, why have you gathered such an eclectic group to come to your aid? What could the fae possibly need from us?" He always resented the way the fae held themselves above the other supernaturals.

Derecho put down what was left of his apple, and the room became a bit cooler. "A crisis looms that will have an effect across all of our worlds." Always a storyteller, he made a dramatic pause. "Some of our rare coffee trees were stolen, and the rest of our crop was attacked by an insect never before seen in our world."

Caleb sat up straight. "Could a Fae with green hair have something to do with this?"

Derecho's eyes lit up. "A female?"

"Yes," Misty answered. "Brazilla asked us to do some reconnaissance at Emily's Coffee in Everett. I sensed a darkness about her. We were able to catch her license plate when she drove out of the parking lot. Also, there was a pixie who might be involved."

"Shadow Fae," Brazilla said. "Derecho, it's sad to believe any of your kind would be so ruthless and irresponsible, but I sent Misty and Caleb to verify my suspicions. The witch at the café is paying them for fae beans, though they appear to be of a lesser quality than your harvest. The pixie shows up every time the Shadow Fae are around."

"I feared they were trying to grow them here." Derecho hung his head. "This is terrible. It means they are already being distributed. May the goddess help us."

Fran looked confused. "Why is it such a tragedy? I mean, it's a free market. When your trees recover, you can compete against them. Your beans are better, so they will lose."

Speaking in a serious tone, Derecho looked around the room, "What I share with you must stay among us. Brazilla has assured me you could all be trusted. Our trees will take a hundred of your years to recover. Our only hope is to find the stolen trees and return them to our enchanted groves. The beans are the source of our magick. We have enough in the warehouse to last fae society for four hundred days. Then our world will begin to crumble. For us, it would be as if all food suddenly disappeared."

"Without their source for magick," Brazilla said, "they will die, and their kind will cease to exist."

Rowena asked, "Wouldn't it make sense for your security to take on Fae criminals instead of us?"

Fran elbowed Derecho, but he ignored her.

Misty replied before Derecho could. "They can't kill another fae. They could fight but not take a life without being excommunicated from the magick realm."

Caleb stared at the fae leader. "That's why you suddenly want to interact with us? I'm sorry your world is messed up, but that doesn't make it right to demand we do your dirty work. I haven't sipped a live source yet, so forget using me to be an assassin."

Misty walked over to Derecho and touched his arm. "I know what it is like to be shunned by your kind. I don't want that for you or anyone." She glanced back at Caleb. "If we don't help, he will have to commit the ultimate fae sin to protect magick." She turned back to Derecho. "I'll help you."

Rowena said, "If the Fae world is destroyed, it will weaken all of us and take much of the beauty out of the world. I do not wish to live in a society where Shadow Fae might control us by putting a stranglehold on magick. I will do what I can to help."

Charles put a hand on Derecho's shoulder. "I've always been suspicious of the Fae, but if Rowena trusts you, I will trust what you say to be true and support your efforts to defeat these thieves."

Caleb stood up and announced, "I'm out of here." He left quickly, slamming a door behind him.

Misty did not follow him, which surprised Brazilla. It was probably better to give him time to cool off. No other vampires or witches would be called on to help Derecho. The fae feared if more knew about the conflict, some of the nocturnal maniacs might side with the Shadow Fae, not understanding the impact on all of them. Brazilla finished her mug of coffee, hoping it would not be her last taste of the magick beans. The energy of the coffee warmed her being and galvanized her resolve to help Derecho.

Brazilla stood and said, "I will help but not entirely out of my desire for justice or survival of your family, the Coffee Fae nobility. We must safeguard the balance between our worlds. I shall do whatever is needed to return the trees to your realm." She didn't add that having the Coffee Fae beholden to her coven could be an asset in the future.

Fran's eyes got big. "Nobility? You said you weren't a prince."

Brazilla chuckled. "He didn't lie. Derecho is their Emperor."

He bowed slightly and said, "But you don't have to call me your highness."

"Yeah, I'll leave that to Pansy."

CHAPTER 4 - JUST FRAN

SUSAN OLD

AFTER THE OTHERS HAD GONE, FRAN MOVED TO THE SOFA FACING
the picture windows that looked out on the deck. Derecho was
standing in front of the windows staring out at the deck. Twinkling
lights seemed to guard the house against the darkness of the coast.
Neither of them had spoken for a few tense minutes.

Fran caved. "So, you just forgot to tell me who you were and that
there might be bloodshed involved in this fae conflict?"

He sat beside her with the expression of a guilty puppy. "I'm
sorry about that, but it couldn't be helped. I had to prepare you to
accept my reality and the crisis my people face. The coffee I've
shared with you and the fruit from Grandmama were meant to help
you recognize the supernatural folk to help you believe.
Unfortunately, the timing of the crisis didn't allow time for me to
explain everything to you before our meeting."

"I think their matching black attire might've tipped me off about
them being vamps. Derecho, you can't have them murder for you."
Her expression was stern.

He gently took one of her hands. "I have no choice. To save my
people, I must have their help."

She felt his power start to affect her. She pulled her hand back and moved a foot away. "But you're an emperor and surely you have other resources at your command."

"Fran, I will do everything possible to bring the Shadow Fae back to my world to face a tribunal. If they threaten my existence, more extreme actions must be taken. I am the last of my line, and if I fall to the Shadow Fae, it will mean chaos for all magickal beings. I never wanted to be an emperor, but I am an only child. Much of the time I've spent in this world was to escape my duties. My parents destroyed themselves trying to build wards to keep out the Shadow Fae."

Sadness began to seep from him, infecting Fran. "I'm sorry about your parents, but why do you need the help of all the others?"

"We thought their sacrifice had secured our safety, but we were wrong. I'll oversee our efforts, but I won't be hiding from my responsibilities anymore. I will fight them but not to the death. I cannot, and they know it."

A shiver rand down her spine. Despite not being a touchy-feely person, she moved over and hugged him. "I wasn't saying you were a coward."

His arms circled her in a gentle embrace. His scent was intoxicating. He looked down at her and his gaze made her feel aroused.

Fran quickly moved away to put some space between them. "Against my better judgment, I'll do whatever I can to help. What do you need me to do? Obviously, I'm no assassin."

"If any of the vamps or witches came near the Shadow Fae headquarters, they would be detected but not you." He called out, "Rain."

She glanced up at the windows. "It's raining?"

A blonde man entered with a silver goblet containing a turquoise liquid. "Fran, this is Rain, my trusted companion. We are named after creations of nature like weather phenomena, plants, bodies of water, etc."

The tall Fae had tied his long hair back, showing off his slightly pointed ears. He moved gracefully in a silk shirt and dress pants. "A pleasure, my lady." He bowed and placed the goblet on the table.

Derecho rolled his eyes. "Update yourself."

Rain blinked. "Of course, sorry, English is my twenty-ninth language. Hi Fran. Derecho says you are cool." He paused, looked at Derecho, and asked, "Is that better?" Derecho ignored the comment.

"Thanks." Fran chuckled. She looked at Rain then back at the emperor. "Pull back your hair."

The ruler sighed. "Very well." He ran his fingers through his thick curls in an upward motion exposing elegant points on his ears.

She blurted out, "Spock!"

Rain began laughing, "Even I get that." He excused himself and quietly left the room.

Derecho asked, "Satisfied?"

Fran stared then said, "Absolutely. Now I believe you." She fought back her inclination to ask to touch his ears. "So, what's the story with Rain?"

Derecho said, "He doesn't get out much. I can't blame him for preferring to stay in our realm, only visiting here when necessary. Now drink this. It will erase every trace of magick from the coffee and the fruit so that by tomorrow your connection to me won't be detected."

"I wish it were that easy to get the whole magickal world out of my life." She knew it was harsh, but he had just exposed her to vampires. Vampires!

He ignored the comment as he handed her the goblet. Fran inspected the blue liquid questioning her life choices. It smelled like licorice and cough medicine. "I hope I'm not going to regret this," she sighed. "Bottoms up." Fran took a large drink, almost gagged, but finally got most of it down. "That was god awful."

Her throat started to burn and then she felt stomach cramps. Derecho crossed the room and opened the door to a small bathroom. She clutched her stomach, bolted to the bathroom, and slammed the door. She was miserably aware that he could heard her vomiting, and after a few minutes, she yelled angrily, "Couldn't you have just waved a magic wand?"

Derecho began laughing so hard he bent over. This laughter was such an extraordinary feeling countering the dark forebodings that had been filling his thoughts. This was the priceless gift Fran gave him, and she had no clue how much he cherished her.

CALEB WAS ALONE IN THE CLUB, THE FUNERAL PYRE. THE OWNER had left him and Misty in charge while attending a vampire ball in New York. He sat on a bar stool, staring into his cup of espresso when Misty joined him.

He looked up and glared at her. "You can't be serious. I've accepted having been transformed to save me from cancer. It wasn't my idea, but I've come to appreciate it. Now attacking fae? Killing them? You must know, I've never wanted to hurt any living being. I wouldn't even hunt ducks with my dad." Caleb was a different kind of vampire.

Misty kissed his cheek. "It's one of the reasons I love you, but we're not the same. I grew up hunting and killing during the full moon." He sensed her passion rising. "We must help. If I get a chance to take out a Shadow Fae who threatens the magickal balance, I won't hesitate."

While not entirely understanding why Her passion and bloodlust aroused him. Caleb leaned over towards her for a kiss. Moments later, he was on top of her on the band stage. They affectionately tumbled a few times while kissing and trying to disrobe.

Slow clapping interrupted their romantic moment. "Don't let me stop you." They looked up to see Andre standing at the back of the club watching them. He held up a key and grinned.

Caleb jumped to his feet and snarled, "What do you want?"

Andre still had the light blue eyes and blond hair he had had as a vampire, but his complexion had more color, and he looked more robust. "The pack sent me to inquire about the increased presence of fae and why you would be meeting with them." He paused and sat in a chair at a small table by the stage. "I still like the scent of the undead, but the others find it ghastly, so you're stuck with me as a go-between." He took off his leather jacket, revealing a dress shirt and tight black jeans.

Misty smiled. "You're a wolf now, yet you've still got that undead pompous shit going on. Amazing." She and Caleb straightened their clothes and sat on the edge of the stage facing him. Misty and Andre were old friends.

"I've ingratiated myself with the mutts, but I refuse to wear flannel. I still have a sense of style. Now, please enlighten me about the Fae visitors so I can get back to the pack. Tomorrow will be a full moon, so we're celebrating tonight."

Misty remembered the drinking, fights, and one-night stands before the monthly hunt fondly. She said, "Ah, yes, good times. I'd like to tell you why a member of the Fae is here, but it is confidential."

"Not as confidential as you think. From what I've picked up from the pack leaders, it has something to do with a magic crop."

"They know?" Caleb's brow raised.

Misty sighed. "Can we trust you not to share details with the pack and count on you revealing all you know to us?" He nodded. "The Shadow Fae destroyed most of the realm's coffee crop. They stole some of the trees and hid them here. The realm is seeking leads."

"You left out that you met with the Emperor." He glanced at Caleb. "Is he looking for a barista?"

Caleb crossed his arms. "Don't you need to relieve yourself on a fire hydrant or something?"

Misty shook her head and asked, "What have you heard? Are the thieves working with the pack?"

"Only to provide security. Several left for a secret location to guard a building. The Shadow Fae pay well. You can't let anyone know I told you this." He frowned and said, "They don't understand how bad things could get if those maniacs get into power. The emperor may be boring, but he understands balance and respect for others. Sadly, neither the Shadow Fae nor the pack do."

Misty said, "The wolves are short-sighted. Our..., I mean, their culture lives from moon to moon."

Caleb added, "You took a risk telling us what they're up to, almost like you care about someone besides yourself."

A slight smile came to Andre's face. "Seriously, good deeds make me queasy. I hope you can convince Brazilla to change me back before I start liking the scent of wet dog. I'll just tell them the Fae have no clue about what has transpired and are grasping at straws." He looked about the club. "I miss this den of debauchery. Ah, well, time to frolic in the forest. Good night."

CHAPTER 5 - BITTER BEANS

THE NEXT DAY STRATUS LEFT THE OFFICE, GIVING CALLA THE barest of nods before heading to the garage, where his chauffeur driven Mercedes waited. She watched him leave with a sigh of relief. Her uncle's crusader intensity was hard to be around. Stratus would spend the day setting up another level of protection for the greenhouse, giving her a break.

Calla longed for her younger carefree years in the shadow of Mount Calypso. Her hometown had been known for growing rare flowers, and the most amazing butterflies. The markets around the realm welcomed their exotic plants and insects before Mount Calypso suffered a volcanic eruption. If she and her uncle had not been away visiting merchants, they might have perished with the rest of her family and friends. The survivors became known as the Shadow Fae and were shunned by those who thought they had angered the goddess Calypso.

She filled her mug and looked out the window at a woman entering their building. Although it was raining she did not have an umbrella so was probably a local. The clerk at the front desk spoke with the woman for a moment then walked to the back where Calla was sitting at her desk.

"Ms. Lily, there's a blogger here doing something about cannabis farm start-ups and wants to know more about our operation. Do you want to speak with her?" The clerk was semi-retired and could not care less about the company as long as he got paid.

Calla, looked over at Fran, who was checking out the office and got an uneasy feeling. Calla reached out with her fae senses but could not detect any magick. "No, I don't want to talk to her. Politely tell her to get lost."

The clerk returned to the front and delivered the message. Fran stared at Calla for a moment looking disappointed before leaving. Calla went back to the window and watched as Fran left the building and hurried away. Something about the woman that bothered her. How could anyone know about their fake cannabis business? The only indication of their business was a small sign above their door, Calypso Farms Incorporated with a pot plant painted underneath.

Calla quickly headed out of the building and turned in the direction she has seen Fran go. The sidewalk was empty, and the only traffic on the street was a yellow Porsche and a few delivery trucks. As she was about to return to the office she felt a hint of familiar magic. She paused as a sweet memory teased her for a moment. Calla knew she should tell her uncle right away, but something kept her from calling him. Nostalgia for a happier time kept her searching the area, but she lost the trail.

IN THE CAR FRAN SAID, "SHE SEEMED ANNOYED I WAS THERE, BUT she didn't act particularly weird. She was just like a normal person who didn't want to be bothered. But I saw some printouts about fertilizer shipments to a farm in Mt. Vernon, but I couldn't read the address."

"Excellent! Her tresses were green?" Rain sounded excited.

"Yeah, green hair but her ears were covered. The only person there was the clerk and he seemed normal."

Rain smiled, "I waited till her paranoid uncle was gone to send you in. The others are just paid lackeys without a clue."

"Thanks for the heads up." Fran replied sarcastically sank down in the seat.

"No problem."

"Shouldn't we have followed him?"

"No need. A pixie put a tracker on his car."

Her voice got higher. "So why did you send me in there?"

"To confirm the intel from the Pixie. They're untrustworthy."

"So how can you trust the Pixie to put a tracker on his car?"

"We pay better than the Shadow Fae."

"Well, that makes me feel better. Can I go home now?"

STRATUS ARRIVED AT THE HUGE GREEN HOUSE, AND THE ,SECURITY guard, one of the werewolf pack that Stratus had hired opened the door. The shifter stayed outside as the Shadow Fae entered. A large black widow spider crept down the wall and jumped onto his shoulder.

"Ah, Hercules. I brought you a friend." He opened a cardboard box and a giant silver praying mantis with red claws jumped out and ran into the trees.

The spider crawled up closer, staring up at him. "She won't hurt your children. She's a present for the Fae Emperor."

With one finger Stratus gently stroked the back of the poisonous creature, who scrambled down his arm to launch itself onto a coffee tree. Stratus went to a small desk in a corner and opened the laptop which controlled the irrigation, temperature and additional growing lights that provided a suitable environment for his crop. Everything seemed to be running fine, but the air never felt quite right.

Stratus walked through the grove, checking the leaves, and looking at the delicate white flowers with a touch of gold. "It's not good enough!" His temper flared. Spiders came out of nearby trees and scurried away. He could tell the harvest would be smaller than last year. He could not understand why these plants did not flourish in the perfect environment he had created.

The Shadow Fae uttered a spell for growth. The sweet scent from the flowers increased a little, soothing him. He would ask Calla to research new incantations. His stern features relaxed as he thought of one day returning victorious to their homeland with the precious beans. Stratus would arrive just in time to stop the crisis he was fomenting.

Stratus, disdainfully muttered "Derecho!" then spit on the ground. He vowed to be the ruler his people truly needed.

THE EMPEROR ARRIVED ALONE AT BRAZILLA'S HOME IN THE Queen Anne neighborhood of Seattle. He walked through her complex wards as easily as stepping through the spray of a lawn sprinkler. He didn't even bother to take them down. Brazilla watched in awe. Those wards would have fried a lesser magickal being.

She stood in her doorway, smiling. "Welcome your majesty." She could not wait till word got around the covens about her visitor.

Derecho nodded and followed her into the living room overlooking a beautiful garden. He asked, "May we sit outside?"

"Of course." They went out on the patio and settled in wrought iron chairs. She knew he would feel revitalized by the selection of plants used for spells that thrived there. The late afternoon sun broke through the clouds and warmed them. She liked looking at this fine specimen of the realm and wondered about his relationship with the woman he had brought to Seattle. The sorceress had sensed the woman had a brilliant mind and independent spirit.

A butler presented a bowl of pomegranate seeds, a plate of honey cakes and tea. Derecho popped some dark red seeds into his mouth savoring their tart sweetness. He spoke without looking at her. "Since we met fifty years ago, you seem to have evolved." Then he turned towards Brazilla. "Is it true that you've acquired the ability to shift to vampire or werewolf at will?"

Brazilla took a breath, tucked in her chin and crossed her arms. When she relaxed Derecho was amazed. He sensed her temperature diminishing. Her brown eyes darkened, and her facial features sharpened. He gasped as she revealed fangs.

Brazilla said, "I didn't think you'd just take my word for it."

"Even in sunlight?" He stared trying to grasp her abilities.

"Yes. It's the same for my werewolf form. I don't need a full moon. I'm everyone's nightmare, and very hard to kill."

"Nightmare or savior," he said. "You must call me Derecho, no more your majesty. I have never been in the presence of a more talented sorceress."

She changed back to her normal appearance. "It is taxing to transform, so I won't do show and tell with my wolf nature just now. Your respect is appreciated. I'm still learning how to find a balance between my three incarnations."

"I can only imagine how difficult that must be." He took a sip of tea from a delicate cup.

She watched him knowing her attraction to his handsome features and thick curly mane were partly due to his unnatural charm and reined in her desires. It was never easy to work with the Fae. Without much effort they were more seductive than vampires.

"The time for recognition of witch magic is long overdue." She bit into a honey cake.

"I agree. When this affair is over my realm will know of your assistance." He looked back out on the garden. "We have learned that Stratus has engaged several pack members to guard his greenhouse. You can see how your abilities could be crucial to retaking possession of our crop."

Her eyes widened. "Tonight is the full moon. The shifters won't be any good to the Shadow Fae."

"And we shall strike with the help of our nocturnal allies. Can I count on Caleb? I worry that he won't take a stand against our enemies. I cannot risk him faltering during our attack."

"He is still growing into his fangs, but Caleb is honorable and once he makes a commitment he will follow through. I don't believe he'll let Misty fight without him, and she is waiting for directions from us." She stared at him. "How did you find out about the werewolf involvement?"

"Misty called me last night." He smiled, realizing Misty had acted like a member of the pack showing loyalty to the highest-ranking leader by telling him first. "A trusted confidential informant had contacted her."

Brazilla chuckled. "Andre! I helped transform him. He wants to get back in my good graces. If the pack knew of this betrayal, his existence would be in jeopardy. I must consult with Rowena and Charles to try and protect his devious little heart."

Derecho stood and leaned down to kiss her cheek. He lingered long enough to allow her to be smitten by his spicy scent. Before walking away, he said, "We shall attack at midnight. I'll be in touch with details."

Brazilla shook her head. He had just tried to insure her loyalty with that magickal kiss. "Damn fine fae, but what a dick," she uttered and smiled. Brazilla knew his heart belonged to another and wished whoever it was good luck.

The sorceress pulled out her phone and left a message for Misty to call her when she woke. Then she decided to visit her favorite coven members at their shop in the Coventree Hotel. At the last minute she packed a bag. If Derecho could just stroll thru her wards, the Shadow Fae could too. She'd spend the night at the hotel until this was crisis was resolved.

CHAPTER 6 - MAGICKAL HEARTS

SUSAN OLD

RAIN SENSED CALLA BEFORE HE SAW HER. HE LOOKED AROUND Emily's café until his eyes fell on a green haired beauty alone at a table in the back corner. She had removed her knit cap and coat allowing her long wavy hair to be visible, eliciting quite a few stares. Rain knew she was trying to entice him.

He slid a chair close to Calla, and said, "Hi love!"

She stared at him with a look of longing. They were beyond games, or casual flirtation. "I'm sorry you are with Derecho."

"I'm not sorry. After all these years are we going to spend these precious moments arguing?"

"There is no place for me in your world, and my uncle would behead you." She looked down at the table, then took a sip of coffee. "The Pumpkin Spice isn't horrible."

He smirked. "I'm glad the chance of my being decapitated that doesn't get in the way of enjoying an inferior brew."

"What are we going to do? When I picked up your presence, I felt shaken and relieved at the same time. How could you and I have a chance?" She rested her hand on top of his, and a wonderful sensation of comfort filled them both.

Behind the counter, Emily detected the glow from Rain and

Calla, but not from any of the other customers. She wiped the counter, hoping they wouldn't make a scene.

"Things have changed. The tribunal ruled that the eruption was a supernatural event. It was not because of a curse on your family. If Stratus would only turn himself in for destroying the crop, I could ask Derecho for mercy, and we could end this." His eyes held hers as he stroked Calla's hand.

She pulled her hand away. "It's too late for that. He will never surrender. I helped place the voracious caterpillars in the groves that attacked the crop. Will you bring me flowers in prison? This world is bad enough, but at least it has sunlight." She looked out the window at the gray overcast sky. "Some of the time."

Rain leaned over and gave her a kiss which ended in a mutual sigh. "We must find a way to end this madness." They both knew he was speaking about her uncle's behavior.

Calla sadly shook her head. "He is the only family I have left." A single tear rolled down her cheek.

"You have me, and I'm grateful we aren't related." He gently wiped away her tear.

"You still believe we can ignore the hatred and discord between our families and find happiness?" She got up, laid her hand on his shoulder and said softly, "Wishes cannot make it so my love." She left quickly.

ROWENA'S EYES WERE BIG AS SAUCERS AS BRAZILLA STOOD IN the shop detailing Derecho's visit, and the news about Andre betraying the pack. When the sorceress had finished her update, Rowena said, "I get this feeling you want to do more than protect Andre."

The raven landed on Brazilla's shoulder. "Good evening, Mathilda." The bird rubbed her cheek with its beak. "Yes. I think the king of self-centeredness deserves to be brought back to his original identity. Andre seems to have matured."

Charles said, "Let's not thwart the progress he has made by

changing him back." He thought back about what a demanding ass Andre had been.

"That wasn't very nice," Rowena chuckled. "Is it even possible to change him back without another willing to change places with him?"

Brazilla walked over to the cabinet filled with herbs and enchanted ingredients. Mathilda fluttered down to the counter as though helping her look at their stock. The sorceress opened the glass door and checked several containers. "We'll need more dragon scales and a phoenix feather. You seem to be well stocked with everything else."

Rowena said, "I can get them from Amazon Magickal within the hour, but it will be pricey."

Charles raised his brows. "You can't be serious. Those feathers with the scales are only combined for..."

"The Resurrection spell, I know. It's only used on the dead, but never tried on the undead or shifters. There's always a first time. The fae are aware of Andre providing assistance and have requested that we have it available and besides Derecho is paying for it. Try to get some rest. May the goddess protect us. We'll go after the Fae coffee trees at midnight. Now please excuse me, I'll be in the penthouse suite."

WHEN DERECHO RETURNED TO HIS HOME IN SEATTLE HE WAS IN high spirits. His crew was coming together nicely for tonight. With any luck, only Stratus and his niece would still be at the greenhouse. He had had no idea Brazilla had become so powerful. The witches were often considered useful but not terribly important by his people. Brazilla and the others would change that perception tonight. Despite his confidence there was a nagging feeling he was overlooking something. Stratus was undoubtedly planning a nasty surprise at the greenhouse, but Derecho wondered what weapon Stratus could use against him that would not risk harming the trees.

The emperor walked into the kitchen and found Fran sitting at a small table, eating a sandwich. "There is a dining room," he joked and sat beside her. The Fae cook quickly bowed and left the kitchen.

"Now you've upset the chef. Terrific!" She continued to eat.

"What's wrong? Rain reported all went well at the warehouse." His closeness and concerned stare were getting under her skin. She was used to talking to him in her office with a desk between them.

"I want to go home. Victor and Hugo need me." She scooted her chair back.

"And?" He patiently waited for her to say what was really on her mind.

She gestured angrily. "You used me like a pawn in your squabble. Who knows what might have happened if Rain had been wrong and the other Shadow Fae had been there. Would you even care if they turned me into a toad? I'm done!" She pushed her glasses up and took a deep breath to compose herself.

Derecho bit his lip and covered his mouth with his hand to hide his grin. It didn't work. She could see the spark of amusement in his eyes. He gave up and burst out laughing. "Toad?"

She went over to him and before he could stand, tried to push him over by the shoulders. He grabbed her tightly as he fell backwards causing Fran to land on top of him and the chair. Derecho quickly rolled them over pinning her hands to the ground. "Forget editing my books, you can be my physical trainer."

Her face became red. "Derecho, I quit!"

He climbed off Fran and tried to help her up, but she pushed his hand away. She stood and gave him the finger, then started to leave.

"Wait!" He held out his phone. He had pictures of Pansy with the cats asleep on her lap. "See, they are well cared for."

"Fickle little furballs," Fran said and started laughing. "Derecho what am I going to do with you?"

Rain standing in the doorway smiling said, "I could make some interesting suggestions, but I think we should prepare for tonight instead."

Fran blushed and tugged at her shirt. Derecho headed out of the kitchen, looked over his shoulder and said, "Follow me."

They all went into the library ,which Fran had not seen before. It had rows of books with little brass plaques designating the genre. A section, off by itself caught her eye. She took a first edition of Alice in Wonderland from the shelf, opened it to the flyleaf and quickly returned it to the shelf. Stunned she turned to Derecho. "He wrote a dedication to you!"

Derecho sat in the middle of a large leather sofa and gestured for Rain and Fran to sit on either side of him as he opened a laptop. "I have some photos of the greenhouse."

Fran was impressed by the size of the building. "That's huge."

Rain looked at Derecho. "That's what they all say."

Fran said, "Zip it, fae frat boy. I liked you better before you updated your vocabulary."

Derecho shook his head. "Stratus bought the warehouse at a premium from a cannabis grower. Our pixie spy has never been allowed inside but said it has a simulated realm environment." Derecho scoffed. "That's not possible. Our world is unique. The quality of the air and soil could not be replicated here."

"Let's hope the trees are not dying off." Rain asked, "What do we know about the security besides the shifters?"

The emperor said, "That's what bothers me. The only ones that go in are Stratus and Calla. Our team can take down any wards, but Stratus must be quite confident about the protection inside."

Rain frowned. "I have a confession."

Derecho stared at him. "You secretly met with Calla. The Pixie told me all about it. If you hadn't brought it up, I would have sent you back to the realm tonight."

Fran gasped. "You met secretly with the enemy?"

"Forgive me." Rain looked at his hands resting on the table. "I just wanted to give her a chance to break away from her uncle. I called their warehouse, and she agreed to see me. Her family loyalty prevents her from joining us. Calla didn't give me any information, but I believe she'll do the right thing if the opportunity arises."

Derecho sighed. "I don't agree. Calla could have asked for mercy many times, but instead she helped kill our trees. She has been poisoned by her uncle. I'm sorry Rain."

"You know I will do what is best for our people. Even if it means taking her prisoner, I will support you." He held his hand out, palm up.

Derecho made a magickal sign in the air and a blue flame shot up from Rain's palm. "You speak the truth."

Fran said, "I'm sorry Rain. You must really care about her." She looked back at the screen and pointed to a small house behind the warehouse. "Do you think they stay there?"

"Yes." Derecho said. "The werewolves guard it as well. I shall send the vampires to stall anyone that comes out once we enter the greenhouse."

She was afraid to ask but had to know. "Can the Shadow Fae kill Misty and Caleb?"

Rain answered, "No, but they can injure them. Fortunately, the undead heal quickly. If they can slow Stratus down it will give us time to secure the trees."

Fran sighed. "Caleb is really gonna hate you after this. So, it sounds like you don't need me." She stood. "Well good luck storming the greenhouse. I'll just find something to read and see you in the morning."

Derecho lightly touched Fran's hand. "We need you to act as a witness in case it comes down to negotiations. Though I fear that won't be possible. I must be able to tell the Fae world we had a non-magickal third party standing by in case the Shadow Fae would allow arbitration instead of violence."

"Now I'm a freaking witness?" She pushed his hand away. "I'm going to head back to Bellingham when this is over." She left the room in a huff.

"That went well," Derecho quipped.

Rain grinned. "She's not like Pansy."

"Not at all." His features became serious. "Why do I not feel confident? Two Shadow Fae should be easily overcome by us. My gut tells me I'm missing something."

Rain frowned and rubbed his forehead. "We must expect the dark side of their magick and enhance our spells accordingly."

"Agreed. Please prepare my most powerful wand." They heard

the front door open and Derecho scowled. "Grandmama is here. I asked her to let me handle this."

Rain grimaced. "Didn't she have…"

"Rain!" A fae woman's voice stopped him in mid-sentence.

"Your Highness!" Rain stood and bowed.

She glared at them. "Our realm is threatened, and you two sit about gossiping? Tell me of the plans for tonight."

She settled into a chair.

Derecho knew she would accompany them. "Forgive us. Of course."

CHAPTER 7 - MADNESS

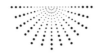

SUSAN OLD

BRAZILLA HAD BEEN ON THE PHONE FOR 30 MINUTES WITH A respected green witch in New York. Meredith had an impeccable magickal heritage and a doctorate in biochemistry.

"Meredith, thank you for your help. You've given me some very sound advice about ways to protect and nourish the rare trees."

"I wish I could do more but I'm occupied preventing some unlawful spirits from rising in the graveyard. You'd think living in an old church would offer some protection, but it seems to attract mischievous souls. You know how tricky those portals to the underworld can be."

Brazilla said, "I've never had much experience with that, but I take your word for it."

"I couldn't believe how difficult it was to remove a hell spawn's blight from my roses."

"News about vanquishing those powerful restless ghosts even made it to my coven." Brazilla had wanted to discuss her fears about what the Shadow Fae were up to but knew the Coffee Fae would feel betrayed if their scandal was revealed, so she politely said, "Thanks again. I must be going."

After Brazilla hung up, she stood alone on the tiny hotel balcony. She noticed a potted dwarf cherry tree losing leaves as it was past fruit bearing season and getting ready for the cold. She touched a delicate branch and let the resiliency of the plant flow into her being. Brazilla was grateful for the green spells and horticulture cures that Meredith suggested. She raised her hands to the horizon as the rising moon pulled at her werewolf nature.

There was a knock at the door. She sensed it was Rowena and Charles. "Come in."

They noticed a slight glow about her that gave them pause. Rowena asked, "Brazilla are you about to shift?"

The Sorceress took a deep breath and shook herself. She came in from the balcony and gave them a comforting smile. "I was teetering but your presence pulled me back. Thanks. I will develop more control in time. I just had the most enlightening conversation with a witch in New York about trees. You must help me gather some items before we meet with the others."

Charles eyes widened. "Is her name Meredith?" Brazilla nodded. "I met her at a green witch symposium on the east coast years ago. She's brilliant but many scoff at her university education."

Rowena elbowed him. "Brilliant? Really?"

Brazilla noticed Rowena's reaction. "No time for petty jealousy now."

Rowena said, "Sorry." Charles raised his eyebrows in amusement.

The sorceress ignored them. "I shall combine Meredith's research with my knowledge of sacred plants. We must forage in a hidden corner of an enchanted forest on our way to the rendezvous."

Rowena's eyes lit up. "Near Granite Falls? That's a lovely spot, too bad we can't linger there."

Charles kissed her cheek. "We'll go up there another time my love."

Brazilla's eyes flashed. "Tonight, we must protect magick!"

At ten o'clock, Calla arrived at the warehouse. She saw the security detail and nodded at the two shifters leaning against an old oak tree. She let her senses explore the environment. Everything seemed the same as the other nights that she had stayed here. Calla looked across the field to the huge greenhouse. There was a glow of the grow lights in the upper windows. She felt as if a piece of her old life was being held captive in that building. She had sympathy for the trees, but believed it was only right they share her fate in this world until the fae realm submitted to her uncle and allowed them all to go home.

Inside, at a small desk, Stratus was pouring over journals. He obsessively recorded every detail of the precious trees. Without looking up he said, "Something is awry. For the last two quarters they have been decreasing in quality. It makes no sense."

Calla collapsed on an old leather couch. She ignored his ramblings. "Rain contacted me."

His head jerked up. "What did you tell him?"

She frowned. "Not a thing, then I took the long way here using back roads."

"And?"

She sighed, "They're worried about the grove disaster and are sure we were responsible."

He smiled which was unnerving to Calla. "Excellent. Soon they will lose power and favor with the other fae."

She stared at the wooden floor wishing she could be somewhere else.

Stratus regarded her. "Calla, how can you still desire his company? He is not worthy of you."

She stood. "I have no life besides this crusade."

His eyes gleamed. "One day you shall have all of the fae bowing before you, seeking to be honored by your attention."

"Rain would be enough. He makes me smile, even in this harsh world. Goodnight uncle."

MISTY AND CALEB WATCHED THE WEREWOLVES GUARDING THE house. About eleven o'clock the shifters began pacing then drifting farther out away from each other before running off into the night.

"You were right," Caleb said. "Those faeries should've picked more reliable security."

Misty handed him a flannel shirt, down vest and a Seahawks knit hat. "Take these, we gotta look the part." He kissed her passionately and Misty pushed him away. "Time and place dude!"

After they both changed clothes, they looked like members of the pack. She pulled a small axe from her backpack, a memento from her former life. Caleb managed a little growl sound to Misty's delight. At times she missed the werewolf world but sharing this new existence with her soul mate was worth it. They made their way to the oak tree the pack members had abandoned.

Stratus glanced out his window before retiring. Seeing the guards in place gave the Shadow Fae a sense of relief. The shifters would alert them to any intruders and be the first line of defense. The werewolves lived to fight. He congratulated himself on winning over the pack to help him. The fae tended to be even more narcissistic than vampires, and Stratus was no exception.

RAIN DROVE THE JEEP WITH GRANDMAMA IN THE FRONT SEAT. Fran sat up against the door in the back glaring at Derecho who managed a polite smile.

The Empress glanced back at the mortal. "You may call me Orchid."

Derecho and Rain were surprised by her gesture. It seemed she had taken a liking to Fran friend.

Fran unaware of the honor said, "Sure." Then asked, "Now that you've figured everything out, isn't it time to call in your police, or military or somebody?"

The emperor cringed. "It's complicated. We can't get the authorities from this world involved."

Orchid added, "We must not appear to have been unable to defeat the Shadow Fae."

Fran sensed that Derecho was trying to soothe her with a light enchantment. "Don't even go there!." She crossed her arms. He looked out the window.

Rain parked a half-mile from the greenhouse, alongside fields that would be full of daffodils and tulips next summer. Skagit might have been a fitting place for faeries if not for the foul magick of the Shadow Fae.

Rain turned to the others. "Calla would never have done this if not for her uncle's madness. I beg you to spare her."

Orchid touched his sleeve with a jeweled hand. "Dear Rain, she chose to stay on this path, let us hope she is not wedded to it. We shall see."

Fran frowned. "This has a Romeo and Juliet vibe. I hope I'm wrong."

Derecho asked, "What kind of vibe do we have?"

Rain answered first. "Taming of the Shrew."

Right on time a vehicle slowly approached them. The van parked behind them, and the witches got out. Orchid pointed at Brazilla. "Not her! What were you thinking?"

Brazilla approached the fae matriarch with a slight smile. "For tonight at least let it go."

Derecho moved between them. "Grandmama, this is why I didn't want you to come. We need the Seattle coven to help us. Please put your grudges aside."

Orchid turned away. "As you wish."

Charles and Rowena looked confused. Brazilla whispered to them, "Don't concern yourselves, it's nothing."

Fran shook her head and spoke like a true editor. "The plot twists are killing me. Isn't anyone happy and well-adjusted on this team?"

Rain said, "The vampires."

She replied, "We're all screwed."

Derecho took a deep breath and pulled an oak wand from his pocket.

Fran stared. "You do have a wand!"

Rain glanced at the Empress and decided not to comment.

Derecho walked around the vehicles chanting in a language Fran did nor recognize. He finished his task and said, "The cloaking spell will last about an hour we must go now."

CHAPTER 8 - BITES IN THE NIGHT

SUSAN OLD

ROWENA ALWAYS TRIED TO FIND BALANCE IN HER ENVIRONMENT, actions and life events. It put her mind more at ease. There were three witches and three fae but only two vampires and a mortal. The last group bothered her; they needed another vampire. It felt like the mortal was a weak link but there was no time to rectify that.

They grabbed their supplies from the van and Charles sensing her anxiety said, "Honey, it will be okay. Someday we'll have a great story to share with our children."

Rowena looked at him and thought. "If we survive this to reproduce." But she stayed silent and gave him a tight-lipped smile. She clutched the selenite wand in her pocket to help her focus on the task at hand.

The group quietly made it to a clump of large bushes close to the greenhouse undetected. Rowena pulled out a bundle of sage and smudged each member of the team.

Fran coughed. "That smells like pot."

Everyone ignored her. Brazilla held up her arms whispering an incantation that was carried away by the breeze. Orchid moved beside her and spread out her hands uttering an additional spell of protection. The two women nodded to each other.

Orchid said, "There is a barrier pushing back against our magick."

Fran was growing impatient. "Derecho if you're so high and mighty do something."

Derecho grimaced, "I sense forbidden fae magick. Poisonous to our kind."

Rowena stepped forward. "Wait!" She and Charles raised their hands up high while whispering a reveal spell together. Suddenly a grid made up of pale green lights appeared like a great net covering the building.

Brazilla said, "I can break through!" She fell forward onto the ground as her body shook and her clothing tore. The painful change was shocking to witness. The sorceress tried to mute her groans. Brazilla lifted her wolf head as fur quickly covered her body.

Charles looked at the others. "It's okay. She's in control." Rowena nodded though she had no idea if that was true.

Shocked, Fran moved behind Derecho. "What the hell?"

Brazilla took a big leap then ran through the wards tearing a whole in the barrier. The green lights flickered, then went out just as an upstairs light came on in the house. The toxic barrier dissipated.

Derecho moved quickly. "Now!" They all followed Brazilla into the greenhouse.

Stratus yelled for Calla as he ran down the porch steps. Caleb jumped on him flashing fangs, only to be thrown against a tree so hard he fell to the ground unconscious. Misty stood in Stratus' path holding her axe. The axe handle was covered in glowing runes. The Shadow Fae stopped sensing the power in the ancient weapon.

Without removing his gaze from Misty, he yelled to Calla, "Protect the greenhouse." She took off running, out of Misty's reach. A creepy smile came upon Stratus' face. "I heard about the pack leaders' errant offspring. Perhaps I'll return you to them when I'm done with these fools!" He had used the time he stared at Misty to identify the runes. With a wave of his hand the markings went dark.

Misty cried out as the axe suddenly burned her hands before it rose up in the air. Stratus aimed it at Caleb. With vampire speed she flew to her lover's side deflecting the blade as it stuck in the tree close to his head.

Seeing Misty distracted, Stratus raced to the greenhouse. The team was scattered about inspecting the condition of the foliage. Orchid's eyes were tearful. Unseen, Calla moved quietly to a corner, put out her hands and yelled, "I will set fire to this building before I let you take our trees!"

They all watched as Rain approached her with his hands down. "Calla, our precious trees are dying. Can't you see that? They are not meant for this world."

Stratus entered, pulling out an ash wand he ordered, "On your knees!"

Brazilla was somewhere amongst the plants growling.

Fran felt her balance faltering and started to go down, but Derecho grabbed her. He cried out a curse in fae that was followed by loud rumbling thunder. The greenhouse began to shake, and the wind howled. The roof of the building cracked andFran cringed putting her hands over her head. The sudden storm tore off the roof sending it crashing into a field. More thunder and lightning crackled overhead.

Fran peered at Derecho. "What was that?"

"I'm named after a powerful storm."

They moved to the doorway where Stratus stared daggers at them. He began to raise his arms but the Empress pointed an ebony wand and he was frozen in place.

Stratus grimly smiled. "My lovely Orchid, so you've come to hunt me with the witch I left you for. Where is the delightful Brazilla? I was sure I caught her scent."

BRAZILLA HAD CHANGED BACK AND CAME FORWARD IN SOME discarded overalls she'd found. "Your magick has not evolved Stratus. Shoddy wards. Easily destroyed by witch magic."

Fran looked around at the chaos, shaking her head. "Are you kidding me?"

Stratus did not dignify Brazilla's insult with a response. He quietly intoned a spell and black widow spiders began began to fall from the trees. They began going after the team. Rowena screamed as she stomped on the spiders as they raced towards her.

Charles yelled, "Everyone, close your eyes!" He rolled his hands then pushed them forward sending a blinding flash of light causing the spiders to scurry away. Rowena looked at him with relief and pride.

"You depend on these lesser beings?" Stratus stared coldly at his rival the emperor. "And you stupidly bring a mortal here. Coffee Fae!" He spit on the ground. "You heart was always your weakness." He nodded to Calla.

His niece called out. "My beauty!" The large silver praying mantis flew at Orchid's face. It's claws cut her cheeks but she refused to drop the wand which was keeping Stratus frozen in place. Derecho ran to her, pulling the mantis off Orchid before burning the creature between his hands.

Rain attended to the empress wiping the blood from her face. She said, "It's but a scratch." And kept the wand steady, staring at Stratus. "You've failed! Surrender Shadow Fae if you value your miserable existence."

Stratus shook his head then yelled, "Mars!"

A giant black widow came out of nowhere and landed on Fran's wrist biting deeply as she screamed, "Get it off me!"

Derecho realized the mantis had been a distraction. The fae could survive these poisonous creatures but not a mortal. He leapt to Fran's side grabbing the spider which he threw on the ground where Rain stabbed it with a dagger. He was too late to prevent the spider from injecting its venom. Fran tried to speak but foam appeared on her lips as she passed out.

Rowena cried, "You monster!" She touched Fran's neck and felt the toxin taking Fran's life force. She looked at the emperor and shook her head.

"The antidote now!" Derecho demanded looking to both of the Shadow Fae.

Calla said, "My uncle has it."

Stratus smiled as Orchid lowered her wand. "Make me emperor and I shall spare her and return the trees to our realm. I shall make the fae more powerful than you can imagine. The humans will serve us as it was meant to be. Hand over your power."

"No!" Derecho cried as his heart broke, sensing Fran's life slipping away and knowing he could not give into Stratus.

A loud growl came from the tress. Suddenly a ferocious wolf ran out, leaping onto a surprised Stratus tearing his throat open sending blood everywhere. They all stared as the beast continued to rip into his flesh until a dark green mist rose up from his mangled remains and dissipated into the night.

Rain grabbed a shocked sobbing Calla. "Where is the antidote?"

"In a pouch around his neck!" Calla fell to the ground.

Brazilla touched the wolf. "Andre, move away. You've earned what you seek."

He snarled and ran into the darkness past Misty as she was helping Caleb towards the greenhouse. "Andre?" she called after him.

Caleb said, "Hurry!"

As they entered the battered building, Brazilla moved a hand across Stratus' remains and a bloody pouch rose up into her palm. She ignored the gore and quickly removed a glass vial with a red cork. She carefully gave it to Derecho. His hands trembled as Fran lay in his lap while he tried to open the vial. Orchid took it and Derecho held Fran's blue lips open while his grandmother carefully poured the precious fluid into her mouth. The emperor hung his head and held her gently.

Brazilla said, "Now we must wait." She went outside and made a small altar with the stones, leaves and branches. The sorceress bowed before the moon with hands over her heart.

Inside Rain put a hand on his friend's shoulder while silent tears spilled down Derecho's cheeks. Orchid chanted softly begging the ancients to preserve the life of this mortal. Rowena and Charles began chanting healing spells for the growing environment They hoped as the magick level in the building increased it might help Fran recover. Their sadness pushed them to try anything they could think of. Calla watched these powerful beings showing such distress over a nobody and her moral outrage towards them crumbled.

Misty was kneeling besides Derecho. She called out, "Her eyes fluttered!"

They all swarmed around Fran as she looked up at Derecho. She lifted her shaking hands and grabbed his shirt. "I had a nightmare that I was attacked by a giant spider. Am I okay?"

"Better than okay. You are seriously fine!" He chuckled, then kissed her forehead.

Every muscle and every joint in Fran's body was sore from the toxin. "I feel like crap. What did I miss? Did we win?" Her eyes took in the bloody remains of the Shadow Fae. "Gross!" She leaned over and started losing her dinner.

When her stomach was empty, she fell back into Derecho's lap. Rain handed her his handkerchief to wipe her face. "We'll explain it all later. The good guys won."

Derecho helped Fran stand and kept his arm around her waist. She started to push him way. "Don't get so handsy."

Derecho smiled at her. "Never!"

Rowena looked up and frowned. "We placed mushrooms and rainbow worms around the trees to imitate your world but unless you repair the building, I don't think it will be enough to save them."

"You are right, of course." Derecho called out a reverse spell as the roof rose from the field. He gestured with his hands, guiding it back into place. Then to everyone's amazement, except the fae, the battered beams began repairing themselves as though alive. His gaze touched each member of the team. "You have our gratitude. The Coffee Fae are in your debt. An unusual occurrence for my kind"

Brazilla pointed to Calla, standing alone staring at the ground. "What about her?"

Rain moved to her side. "Spare Calla. I beg you. You have my word that I will be responsible for this rebel. She told you where to find the antidote."

Derecho said coldly, "She attacked the Empress."

The once proud Shadow Fae raised her head. "I expect no mercy."

Orchid stared at her, as she considered an appropriate punishment for the failed usurper. "I understand the suffering you have experienced. Even so your decision to give blind loyalty and support to your mad uncle's dangerous destructive schemes gives me no choice but to banish you to this world. If you returned to our realm the Tribunal would not be so kind. I only do this because of Lord Rain's entreaties on your behalf. He sees some good in you, though I do not."

Calla's eyes met Orchid's and in a trembling voice said, "I'm not worthy of your mercy. My uncle told me you were all the same, like those who judged us as cursed. I see now that he was wrong. I don't care for this world, but it is preferable to imprisonment without sunlight."

Rain bowed his head. "Thank you, Empress Orchid."

Derecho pursed his lips. "Calla will need an occupation that is helpful to us." He glanced at Fran. "My editor could use an assistant."

Fran mumbled, "More fae with attitude, great." She tried to walk out but fell back against him as her balance was unsteady. "Maybe just help me to the Jeep."

Charles tugged on Rowena. "Let's go get the cars." Rain threw him the keys.

Outside they looked up at the stars now visible in the clear sky. "I don't get it." Rowena took a deep breath. "Nothing happened as I had expected. My crystal ball showed images of a fight to the death between Derecho and Stratus. Thank the goddess it wasn't right."

Charles put an arm around her as they walked. "Rowena Snap, don't you see it was a battle to the death between their spirits and Derecho was able to win with the help of those he attracted."

"Like Andre? I never knew he was even there."

"I saw Brazilla sneak him into the back of the building when we first arrived, but I didn't say anything. Thank the stars that that conflicted soul is on our side."

Charles nodded. "Yes, and he will expect something in return."

They reached the vehicles and he asked, "Do you think Fran will recover fully?"

Rowena grinned. "From the poison? Yes, but not from Derecho."

CHAPTER 9 - ICING ON THE CAKE

SUSAN OLD

THREE NIGHTS LATER THE MAGICKAL BEAN TEAM GATHERED ONCE more, this time at Emily's Coffee which closed for their private party. Calla was included which was awkward as they celebrated her uncle's demise, but Rain would not attend without her.

The kitchen witch was in her glory. Emily set out special delicacies she normally would not offer in her café. The centerpiece was a cake sculpted into a coffee tree with lovely sugar butterflies circling around its blossoms. Winking unicorn cookies with rainbow manes startled Fran. The chocolate mushrooms were delicious. She was gingerly taking small bites to be sure her tummy could handle the exotic treats. Though the editor had recovered, she had a lingering fear of spiders.

Derecho kept an eye on her but did not smother as he drifted between the beings who had helped save his realm. Fran tried not to stare at stare at how handsome he looked in a pale blue ruffled shirt and silver vest unbuttoned enough to show off his ripped chest. At the request of the Empress Orchid, she wore a long black dress with silver embroidery that matched Derecho's vest. A bit too cute for Fran but after all they had been through, she acquiesced.

Brazilla and Orchid put aside their past rivalry and stood in the corner talking like old friends. It made Derecho wonder if Emily had uttered an incantation for peace when she created the cake. Orchid whispered to the sorceress, "Stratus was a good lay if you ignored his personality."

Brazilla chuckled. "When he would shut up."

Caleb and Misty sat in the spot where they had positioned themselves several nights ago. He sipped the enhanced espresso with an expression of delight. "We should serve this at the club." Caleb took another sip savoring the spicy dark roast and its effect. "This is close to the high from blood. We should ask for a bag of the good stuff."

Misty shook her head. Caleb playfully pulled on one of her spiral curls. "They owe us but the fae are never giving their beans away to be consumed at the Funeral Pyre. Besides, what you're drinking is the watered-down version of what they have in their mugs. I've heard the pure stuff causes the non-fae to hallucinate. You don't realize what a big deal it is to socialize with the fae, especially the Emperor and Empress. They invented snobbery."

"Yeah," he grinned, "But what about Brazilla. Rowena told me that she had an affair with Stratus. I mean sometimes they get up close and personal with us earthlings, and there's Derecho's obsession with Fran…"

"All right, but I'm telling you this is rare, and fortunate we are considered their allies."

A sugar butterfly landed in his cup dissolving into the espresso. "Wow. What's it like in their world?"

"I don't know anyone who has been invited to their realm, but I think Fran stands a chance."

Movement at the entrance caught Misty's attention. "Look at the door! Should we let him in?"

Caleb saw the figure in black leather and shook his head. "Let the fae handle it."

Rain went to the entrance ready to unleash a repel spell when Derecho said, "No! He helped us." The emperor walked over and unlocked the door himself. "Welcome."

"Good evening." A self-satisfied grin came over Andre's face as he moved past Rain. Calla sniffed the air and said, "The assassin."

Andre made a gesture in her direction. "AKA the silver wolf."

The Shadow Fae started to raise her hand, but Rain touched her arm. "He stopped me from having to battle your uncle. I owe him a debt."

She sighed. "It's true I could never have forgiven you."

Andre made a beeline for Brazilla. He stopped in front of the empress and the sorceress and bowed. "Thanks for inviting me. May I know when you will fulfill your promise?"

Orchid's eyebrows raised. "Promise?"

Brazilla said, "This is the shifter, Andre, without the fur."

"Oh, I see."

Misty, Caleb, Rowena and Charles joined them. Andre was glad to have an audience as he pressured Brazilla. "I don't want to spend another day as a werewolf. I should never have asked to be more than a vampire. I have never been more miserable. The scent of wet fur makes me want to gag." Andre glanced at Misty. "Though your mother is quite engaging."

Misty added, "But my father is quite enraging."

"Exactly." He turned his attention back to Brazilla. "So?"

Caleb whispered to Misty, "Now?"

She softly said, "Having all the magickal folk here for the ceremony would be helpful in case something goes wrong."

He whispered back, "Or for body disposal."

"I heard that!" Andre stared at Caleb.

Brazilla gestured to Rowena and Charles to join her and Orchid off to the side. They discussed Andre's request with hushed voices. Derecho looked on with an amused expression. Finally, Orchid's gaze fell upon her grandson, and she nodded.

Derecho touched Andre's shoulder and guided him to a chair. He called out to Emily, "Blessed be."

The kitchen witch rolled a little cart out from the back with a goblet and potion ingredients including a phoenix feather. The bitter scent of dragon scales along with rare ingredients from the realm filled the air. Brazilla assisted Derecho in preparing the potion.

Orchid approached Andre. "It is prohibited to use the switch potion outside of our territory. It is more powerful than the one you took before, and the effects are permanent. If you tried to change again you would perish. Are you certain this is what you wish?"

"I'm desperate to regain my nocturnal nature."

She looked about. "The use of this potion must be kept a secret. Despite our feelings of trust, if you start to speak or write of this to anyone beyond this unique group of allies, you'll lose all memory."

Brazilla said, "Of course."

Derecho looked around as everyone nodded their understanding and agreement. Except Fran who uttered, "Cross my heart and hope to die."

Orchid stared at Fran, while Derecho tried to suppress a chuckle. He said, "She accepts."

Brazilla turned and handed a small dagger to Caleb. "You have the purest vampire blood as Misty was once a werewolf. You must bleed several drops into the goblet."

For a moment Caleb hesitated as Andre stared incredulous. Then he grimaced while fulfilling his part in the ceremony. "You owe me dude."

Derecho stirred the potion with the Phoenix feather then handed the goblet to Andre. "Because of your service to the Coffee Fae we shall restore you."

Orchid demanded, "Drink now!"

Rowena added, "All of it. Don't you dare waste my dragon scales."

As Andre gulped the bitter fluid down Rain came up behind him and rested his hands on Andre's shoulders so he wouldn't fall over. Brazilla grabbed the goblet as he started to drop it. Andre's skin emanated a faint lavender glow, as his eyes rolled into in his head. He trembled and clasped his thighs. Everyone stared as his color returned to normal. He lifted his head and cried out, "My fangs!" displaying his pride and joy to the room. Rain let him go as the worst of the transformation had passed.

Misty embraced him as the others went back to their conversations as though nothing remarkable had occurred. Emily returned her cart to the kitchen.

Caleb said, "I don't know why but I'm glad your back asshat."

Andre replied, "I just want a bergamot scented bath to wash away the fido scent before I slip between silk sheets then rest until the sun has left the sky. I'll never complain about my exquisite existence again."

Misty smirked. "Until next week."

Caleb ran a hand through his hair. "And things were going so well at the Funeral Pyre."

Andre stared at him. "It pains me to say this, but you have my gratitude."

Caleb beamed. "Well, if it causes you pain, it was worth it."

Misty said, "C'mon. Let's get back to the club. Your old apartment is waiting."

They said a quick goodbye to Derecho and headed out with a nod to Brazilla and Orchid.

Rowena smiled at Charles. "I knew it! The third vampire. We had three of each and just didn't see it.

"Yes, the balance was achieved."

Fran pulled Derecho away to a corner of the room. "I have no idea what just happened. I'm so out of my league." She felt lost in his intense gaze which didn't help. "Can't I just go back to being your editor? I'll pinky swear to not tell anyone, anything, ever." She held up her hand displaying her little finger.

That was a mistake. Derecho curled a finger about hers before leaning closer with passionate intent. That little contact caused a tingling sensation to run through her body. He eased forward giving her every chance to pull away. His lips lightly brushed hers, sending promises of passion to come. He smelled like the delicious spices in his coffee. She moved into the kiss despite her best intentions. Derecho did not hesitate or disappoint.

She came up for air. "Damn it! You and your fae charm. It wasn't supposed to go like this. We are not supposed to happen."

He gently held her face in his hands. "Oh, but it was, and it is. By the way, Pansy will relinquish any claim on me if you give her your cats."

She pushed his hands away sputtering. "Victor and Hugo? Never! How could you even ask?"

He laughed, and his eyes twinkled. "Pansy said if you took the offer, you wouldn't be worthy of my love." He waved a hand in the air. "It was a test which you passed easily."

Pansy appeared carrying Fran's beloved felines in a velvet lined basket. Fran took her fur babies, kissed their heads and marveled at how nice they smelled. She was surprised the cats were being so mellow in this new environment with strangers as though they liked the fae. She had to ask, "They let you bathe them?"

"Of course." Pansy looked a tad indignant. "They also demanded you provide more treats and Hugo said you're rather stingy with the catnip."

"You had a conversation with my cats?"

Brazilla spoke up. "My dear, you could develop the ability to communicate more fully with your familiars. You have hidden magic that I would be delighted to help you tap into if Derecho has no objections."

"Me a witch?" She pursed her lips. "Well, I've been called worse. Anyway, it's not Mr. Coffee Fae's decision." She looked at him. "If I can't go back to my normal ignorance, then I want to learn about magick. So there!"

"I would never stand in the way of your pursuit of knowledge." He moved beside her and petted the cats.

They purred loudly which made Fran huff. "Traitors."

Brazilla exclaimed, "Welcome Frania. Some of our coven members add an "A" to the end of their names. I think it suits you."

Rowena and Charles hugged her. Rowena said, "It's been ages since I mentored a new witch, how fun!"

Derecho said, "First Frania has to edit my new manuscript."

She shook her head. "It's not bad enough that my client is a Fae Emperor, and I have a Shadow Fae clerk, but I told myself I would never date a writer!"

The room erupted with laughter, except for Fran who was totally serious.

Emily pulled Brazilla aside and whispered, "After tonight no more Fae beans. I don't like the drama that seems to come with their world. I prefer to use my own magic to customize my beverages for my customer's needs."

Brazilla smiled. "I may try to work out something with Derecho, but I agree that a witch with your abilities does not require help from other magickal beings. For me, however Frania is another matter."

Emily nodded. "I'm glad that you are taking her on. Blessed be she has no idea of her potential."

"Yes, but Derecho does."

THE NEXT EVENING MISTY YAWNED AS SHE ROSE FROM THE BED she shared with Caleb. They had both slept past sunset after staying up with Andre till sunrise chatting about everything. She grabbed her phone and her eyes lit up.

"Caleb, listen to this!"

He sat up rubbing his eyes. "What?"

She read to him. "Dear Misty, thank you for taking Andre back. Your mother is upset but you have the pack's gratitude. Dad."

She became tearful though she was smiling. Caleb pulled Misty back down on the bed and held her in a gentle embrace. "Wow, the pack and Andre owe us now. I bet your mom will come around too. She might even like me."

Misty shook her head, "When did you become such an optimist?"

He chuckled. "I think I drank too much of that damned fae coffee."

A WEEK LATER IN NEW YORK MEREDITH RECEIVED A SMALL package via raven mail. Inside she found a small silver box that tingled the tips of her fingers. Once sure it bore no evil intent, Meredith opened it to find a single green coffee bean on a bed of lavender silk. She opened the note card. "A gift for your rare plant collection. Brazilla."

ABOUT SUSAN BROWN

What happens when the extraordinary erupts into an ordinary life?
Award-winning author, Susan Brown, fuels her books with
adventure, mystery, and magic.

Susan's books ripple with strong characters and thrilling action
in genres like urban fantasy, young adult adventure, and romance
(written with Anne Stephenson as Stephanie Browning). Witches,
dragons, falling in love, unicorns, and the ins and outs of
contemporary life can all be found in Susan Brown's novels. Dive
into her books for an extraordinary reading adventure!

Susan lives with her border collie rescue dogs amid wild woods and exuberant gardens in Snohomish, Washington. From there she supervises her three grown daughters, assorted sons-in-law, and two grandsons.

Find free stories, contact information, and news about upcoming books at:

www.susanbrownwrites.com

Find her on Amazon at:

amazon.com/Susan-Brown

ABOUT LINDA JORDAN

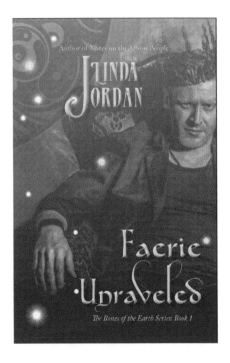

Linda Jordan writes fascinating characters, visionary worlds, and imaginative fiction. She creates both long and short fiction, serious and silly. She believes in the power of healing and transformation, and many of her stories follow those themes.

In a previous lifetime, Linda coordinated the Clarion West Writers' Workshop as well as the Reading Series. She spent four years as Chair of the Board of Directors during Clarion West's formative period. She's also worked as a travel agent, a baker, and a pond plant/fish sales person, you know, the sort of things one does as a writer.

Currently, she's the Programming Director for the Writers Cooperative of the Pacific Northwest.

Linda now lives in the rainy wilds of Washington state with her husband, daughter, a glaring of cats, a cluster of Koi and an infinite number of slugs and snails.

Visit her website: www.LindaJordan.net

ABOUT SUSAN OLD

Many years ago, in a suburb far away, a teenager finished reading
Lord of the Rings and thought, "I want to write about a kick-ass
heroine who overcomes and vanquishes evil." Then life happened!
College, the Peace Corps, marriage, children, cancer, young
widowhood, remarriage, and twenty-five years as an addiction
therapist. Through everything, Susan kept writing. Even a power
surge that destroyed her first manuscript couldn't deter her. She
reconstructed it from memory and handwritten notes. When Susan
retired, she published her first book and continues to write novels,

short stories, and novellas. She lives on a river north of Seattle with two rescue cats and her editor/hubby. When she is not writing about vampires, witches, and werewolves, she volunteers at an animal shelter, gardens and drinks a lot of coffee.

Amazon: www.amazon.com/Susan-Old

Visit her website: susanold.com

Made in the USA
Columbia, SC
18 September 2022

67465783R00141